NEW FAMILY REQUIRED

CARMEN REID

Boldwood

First published in Great Britain in 2022 by Boldwood Books Ltd.

Copyright © Carmen Reid, 2022

Cover Design by Debbie Clement Design

Cover Photography: Shutterstock

A CIP catalogue record for this book is available from the British Library.

Paperback ISBN 978-1-80162-799-3

Large Print ISBN 978-1-80162-800-6

Hardback ISBN 978-1-80162-798-6

Ebook ISBN 978-1-80162-801-3

Kindle ISBN 978-1-80162-802-0

Audio CD ISBN 978-1-80162-793-1

MP3 CD ISBN 978-1-80162-794-8

Digital audio download ISBN 978-1-80162-795-5

Boldwood Books Ltd
23 Bowerdean Street
London SW6 3TN
www.boldwoodbooks.com

For my family – such laughs, such tears, such fun, such fights, such drama, such dogs and so much love.

PROLOGUE

Mama: WE HAVE BOOKED THE MARQUEE!

Sasha read the brand-new message on the GriffonFamWhatsApp, and before she could reply, in whizzed a response from her big sister.

Adele: A marquee – how amazing!

Sasha wondered if Adele really did think it was amazing, or if she was just being polite. And now her baby brother was jumping in, Mr Biz... Mr Entertainment.

Beaubro: Are they including tables and chairs? Do you need any recommendations for anything? I can get my contacts on it.

Sasha thought she should maybe step away from the phone and let this happy family-chat play out without her. She was totally harassed and not in the mood to hear about this wedding anniversary party fun and frolics.

But, no, she couldn't help herself from typing...

Sasha: A marquee??? Can I just point out that you live in a 12-bedroomed mansion with four enormous public rooms?

Mama: But it's such an upheaval... this way we can keep the party contained, plus, a marquee is so romantic. There was no romance to our wedding at all. Just me, your father and a passing witness at the registry office in Paris.

Good grief, let me get out my tiny violin, Sasha thought, but instead typed back:

Sasha: Paris though... must have been a bit romantic.

Mama: C'est vrai... Paris mon amour. So the important question, mes enfants, is can everyone come? Saturday, September 9th. I know school will be on for Sylvie; and Beau, your new baby will only be a few weeks old if he arrives in time.

Sasha: He? I didn't know the baby was a he. Why does no one tell me nothing?

Mama: Surely it should be 'anything'?

Sasha: Sigh. Congrats Beau... the first boy grandson... I expect he'll be spoiled to death...

Adele: Just like his father, you mean?

Ooooh, Sasha thought... *that was brave.*
There was that pause for a moment when no one typed. Mama

always, always denied having a favourite, even though it was plain as the nose on her face that she had always loved Beau the best.

Mama: Now, now... you are all fully grown up with your own children. No more time for these petty squabbles surely?

Petty squabbles... is that what she was calling it now? Beau had been the only one of the three of them to get a freaking *pony* one Christmas... and what about those trips to Paris with Mama for the sake of his *Art GCSE*... oh, and let's not forget *the car* he got for his twenty-first.

Beaubro: As long as Sura and the baby are fine to travel, we can all come. It will be completely awesome. So glad you and Dad are celebrating. So are you both all set for this weekend?

What were her parents and Beau doing together this weekend? Sasha wondered, feeling the jealous tug that Beau and his family seemed to get far more attention than her family did, right along with the thought that having her parents to stay right now would actually tip her over the edge.

Adele: Sylvie will be working hard for her exams from September onwards. But I want to come and I know she'll want to come too. So we'll make it work. Sadly, I think Henry has a work trip that weekend. I'll check.

That seemed odd... considering Henry was a freelance editor, who rarely went anywhere at all. But then, Adele and Henry were only just getting started with a divorce after twenty-two years together. So maybe they didn't know how to negotiate family events yet... or even divorced life. Henry was currently living in a lovely basement flat in Adele's beautiful new modern mansion on the outskirts of Zurich. Yup, you know you're the failure when every other member of your family has a house with at least three times as many bedrooms as your *flat*. *We're much more eco-friendly*, Sasha reminded herself. *And think of their heating bills.* Certainly, her mum and dad started complaining mid-August about the prospect of having to put the heating on and then didn't stop going on about it until the following April.

So, her parents' fortieth wedding anniversary party... Sasha turned it over in her mind for a few moments. Like most family commitments, she sort of wanted to go but she also sort of didn't. Right now, a big, swanky family event was about the last thing she needed, but equally, she knew she would regret not going. And both her parents and her siblings would go on at her, probably forever, if she missed it.

Sasha: That weekend in September won't be a problem for us. Really looking forward to it.

Mama: I am already so excited, thinking about food, menus... I might have to make a special trip to London to get some of the things that are harder to find up here.

Sasha: Let me know nearer the time. Happy to do some gourmet shopping for you. It can be our anniversary gift to you both.

Adele: Must dash... have a Zoom in two. Lovely to hear the party is shaping up. Looking forward to buying a new dress... and the bag... and the shoes. I blame having a French Mama.

Mama sent a heart emoji in response to this.

Sasha: How is Dad? Looking forward to the party?

Mama: Tiens... husbands! They never think they want anything like this and then they always enjoy every minute.

Sasha: Ha ha... big hugs to you all, speak soon xx

She decided to leave it there, put her phone down and turned to her husband, Ben, who was busy with the post-supper dishwasher loading.

'And how is the Addams family?' he asked, after one glance at her face.

'How can you tell?' she asked.

'You just have that look... what have they asked you to do now? Join them for their "let's rent a cute little chateau in France" summer holiday?'

'No, nothing like that,' she said, rounding up the last of the dishes on the small kitchen table. 'Mum and Dad are planning to have a big fortieth anniversary party in September... Saturday 9th September, I think she said.'

Ben immediately groaned and rolled his eyes. 'Oh no!' he exclaimed. 'We'll have to get all dressed up... drink horrible champagne – why does no one ever, ever offer me a beer up there? – listen to the chat about summer in St Bart's, or is that where you go in the winter? I can never remember... and the cost of school fees and how you just can't get anyone decent to lay reclaimed parquet flooring these days. Sounds totally ah-mazing. Meanwhile... here in the real world...'

'Well, they are my family,' Sasha reminded him.

'And they are such hard work,' Ben complained, as they took up their positions, side by side, at the sink to get the last of the washing-up done – Ben on washing, Sasha drying and putting away, as usual.

'I do love them, you know,' Sasha said, but she already knew what Ben was going to say to this.

'Do you, though?' he asked, smiling with his eyebrows raised. 'Really?'

'You know I do,' she said.

'Are you sure it's not just an unhealthy dependency based on shared past memories?'

'Isn't that what all families are?'

This made them both laugh.

'My family is so much nicer than yours,' he said.

'Shut up!'

'I think the problem is, you just don't really suit your family...' he said, taking in Sasha's short, white-blonde hair, thick eyeliner and general London-cool look. 'Maybe we could do a family swap? Or take out an ad for you: *New Family Required*,' he began. '*Must live in north London, in nice, manageable family house... warm, caring, loving mother with no interest in Paris, Chanel, make-up or fashion, who just wants to spend time with her grandchildren, doing arts and crafts and reading...*'

This made Sasha laugh again, because her mother was nothing like this, which was the point, of course.

'Dad must be amazing at DIY and staunchly left-of-centre,' Ben said, again prompting a big laugh from his wife, 'happiest taking granddaughter to track and field events. Big sister must be regularly available for girlie nights out to drink cocktails and watch Henry Golding movies...'

'You know me oh-so well,' Sasha smiled.

'And little brother... do you even want a new little brother?' Ben asked.

'Could he be an ace mechanic... and cook... who is also happy to take me on spa weekends?'

'That's perfect,' Ben replied. 'Right, let me get this written up and I'll post it on the *Ham & High* website.'

'Very funny... and surely a bit old-school. You'd probably have to make a TikTok to get anyone to pay attention, do a little dance...' She put her arms around him and looked at him closely. It was good to see him laughing and looking more relaxed.

'Are you feeling a bit more optimistic about everything?' she asked.

'I have no idea,' was his honest answer, 'but I do know we can't worry all the time. Hopefully, the worst won't happen. Who knows? It might all be so much better by September,' he added.

Sasha, who had been feeling really quite cheery and hopeful for a few moments there, went back to feeling anxious. 'Or so much worse,' she said.

1

FRIDAY, 8 SEPTEMBER

'Sasha, I don't want you to worry—'

Good grief! As soon as Sasha heard her husband say these words, she immediately panicked and suspected that the news she had been dreading, the news that she'd so hoped for months now would somehow not arrive, was about to come crashing down on their world with this phone call.

'But...?' she asked.

'The absolutely shameless tossers aren't going to pay,' Ben said, sounding calmly furious. And so here it was – the disaster they had been trying to avoid for week after incredibly stressful week.

'Not going to pay?' she heard herself repeat, as she tried to take this in. 'Not anything at all? No goodwill gesture, or monthly instalments, or promise of something further down the line?'

'No,' he said, 'and you know how much I've tried, and the accountant has tried, but they have basically made the company that owes us the money bankrupt.'

For several moments, Sasha couldn't think of anything to say, she just squeezed her eyes shut and tried to carry on breathing.

'Oh my god...' she managed finally, 'so we're not going to get a single penny of the £75,000 they owe us for the work?'

'No,' Ben confirmed, and he sounded completely deflated.

Seventy-five thousand! It was an enormous sum for their little business to bear.

They'd been waiting for this money for months. The work – extensive garden design, landscaping, planting and gardening – had been done back in the early spring at a brand-new housing development. It had been the biggest contract they had landed in five years of trading. They'd had to bring in extra people to help and buy new equipment, not to mention all the plants, trees and materials. In short, they'd borrowed serious money on the back of this contract and after months of worry, to hear that they weren't going to get any of what was owed to them was devastating.

Yes, they did have some other work on the go, but it was very small-scale and now it was September. There was already the hint of a chill in the air, and autumn and winter lay ahead – always a very quiet time for the business.

'So... so...' Sasha sensed her rising panic, 'what are we going to do? You're absolutely sure there's nothing more we can do to get the money we're owed?'

'Not right now,' Ben confirmed. 'Maybe further down the line when they tender for this kind of work again, but not right now.'

'You're absolutely sure?' she had to ask once again because it was far too big a sum of money to just walk away from if there was still any hope at all.

'I'm going to go and see Jason tonight to sound him out,' Ben added, mentioning a friend who was an experienced corporate lawyer. 'And then... I'll come home and we'll talk it through. We'll brainstorm and we'll start to get over this. I have lots of ideas and I'm sure you do too.'

'Oh yes,' she agreed bitterly, 'my best idea right now is to drive round to their headquarters and throw bricks through their windows. No, even better, smash up their Range Rovers, carefully and thoroughly with a set of golf clubs, using different clubs for different parts of the car, then slash all the tyres.'

'I know, Sash, I know,' Ben said, 'and that would work off a lot of tension, but I don't see how a criminal conviction would be a massive help to us at the moment.'

'If anyone deserves a criminal conviction, it's them! This is just so unfair!' she protested. 'Those houses are still for sale! Their companies are still going to make millions. How can they get out of paying our bill?'

'Clever accounting, apparently,' Ben said, and she heard the bitterness in his voice. 'Development companies do it all the time... apparently.'

'I see,' said Sasha, 'and that's why they've picked some little, small-fry company like ours to completely stitch up, is it?'

'Maybe,' he admitted.

'Ben, we've got no money left,' she reminded him. 'What are we supposed to do about the bills that we need to pay? We've had the mortgage on hold for three months; there's the VAT bill; those final instalments for the rotivator... and... so many other things! What do we do about all that? And there's hardly any money left in our personal account.'

'We'll talk it through when I get home,' he assured her. And she wondered how he could even be trying to sound so calm, when she felt like running round the room and screaming at the top of her voice.

'We are so close to our overdraft limits on the business and the personal accounts,' she reminded him.

'I know,' he said.

'We'll have to arrange bigger loans... I don't even know if we can... they'll want to charge us a lot of interest. And... we're not the crooks... we're not even bad at business!' she complained, really not willing to accept yet what had happened. 'We've been defrauded, Ben! There should be a way to get this money back! We're just two ordinary people with a small business that will now very likely go...' Sasha paused. She didn't want to use the word. She wasn't ready to accept it. They had done everything, every single thing they could think of to get this money: they had made a beautiful job of the contracted work; they had opened up endless conversations with the development company; they had talked to their accountant at length and at further expense; even filed a claim through legal channels.

They'd borrowed a lot of money to do this work. They'd cut their own personal costs to the bone and still this was now happening. They were not going to get paid. They were very likely going to go *bust... broke... bankrupt...* all those terrible words. All the words she'd never, ever wanted to apply to them.

'Sash, I know,' Ben repeated, 'but we will sort this out. We will handle it and we will get through it.'

Ben was by nature a charming and delightful optimist. He always wanted to believe that everything could be okay again, that it could still be sorted out and they would get to a better place. He didn't ever want to join Sasha in the doom spiral. But for weeks now, she had been gripped by the doom spiral. She had been sure they were not going to get the money and she was exhausted with trying to cope with this eventuality and trying to work out a clear and sensible way forward.

They had a cosy little ground-floor flat in a London suburb, which they'd been slowly making their own over the years they'd owned it, and now she regularly woke up in the middle of the night, panicked that they would have to sell it. Meanwhile, Ben remained calmly confident that life could still be breathed back into their mortally wounded company.

'We're going to have to borrow some money pretty quickly to keep everything going,' he told her now, 'and preferably not from a bank.'

'I know what you're going to suggest, and the answer is *no*,' she said sharply.

'Sasha...' Ben sighed.

'I'm sure you remember how the conversation went when we were starting up.'

'But this is different.'

'How is it different?'

'We've been in business for five years – we've had really steady income and we were good enough to win a major contract.'

'From a bunch of crooks!' she reminded him.

'We've done the work. It's in our portfolio and on our website. We'll win more contracts like that and start to make good money. But we need to keep ourselves going through the winter, so we need a fast and cheap loan, from the people who care about us and can help us.'

'Ben,' Sasha began, 'we are not telling my family about any of this, and we are not going to ask them for money.'

'We've been very unfairly treated,' Ben said. 'Why don't you think you can tell your parents? They will understand... or *we* can tell your parents... I'm happy to take the lead. I'm happy to take the blame, Sasha, for all of it.'

'Please, Ben, don't say that,' she told him. 'There is no blame to take. We have a signed contract that they have broken. We made all the important decisions about taking that work on together; we signed for the loans together. We did a great job,' she added, 'and... we've had some very bad luck.'

Saying it was bad luck didn't make her feel any better about it. There was a hard, painful knot building in the back of Sasha's throat. She felt stupid. These people had taken them for a complete ride. She should have known better; she should have researched the company harder; she couldn't help feeling that she should have done much more to avoid this. But they had been so thrilled to get the contract. It was four times more than any work they'd won before and instead of looking very carefully, they'd jumped in, rolled up their sleeves and concentrated on doing their best work.

'Sasha, your family will understand,' Ben insisted, 'just like mine will. I promise, they will understand, and they will sympathise with what's happened.'

At this, she'd had to shake her head, even though he couldn't see her, because wasn't it totally obvious from everything he knew about her family that they would definitely not understand?

Sasha's family was all about success. Her father was a success, his father had been a huge success, Sasha's older sister was a roaring success, her younger brother was a big success too, and they'd all been so proud of her when she and Ben had started their own business and had begun to look as if they were all set to join the family of successes as well. And although their business had been slow and small-scale at the start, the big contract had given her hope that, finally, she and Ben were going to begin earning some decent money too.

'I don't want my family to know anything about the situation we're in,' she repeated.

'But it's going to come out,' Ben told her, 'one way or another. And I won't exactly enjoy telling my family about how things have turned out, but I know they will be really supportive and will want to help in any way they can.'

Of course they will, Sasha couldn't help thinking, because they're all really nice and really normal – just like Ben – but not one of them could write the kind of big cheque currently needed to bail Greenhope Gardening out of the hole it was in.

'Ben, you've known my family for twelve years,' Sasha reminded him. 'You *know* them, you *know* they will be weird and ashamed and awkward about everything, and can't you just leave this? I don't want them to know and that is final.'

'You're not really close as a family, are you?' he said, sounding exasperated now.

Sasha didn't want to hear this. She really didn't want to do the 'my family/your family' discussion, so she told her husband defensively, 'All families have *their* stuff, and *their* issues. We *are* still quite close...' But even as she said it, she couldn't help thinking that surely your family was *close* or *not close* – *quite close* sounded completely unconvincing.

'Yeah, right,' Ben almost laughed, 'as close as the Borgias, maybe, or the Medicis, where family get-togethers are all about power games and stabbing each other in the back.'

'That's a complete exaggeration and not true at all!'

'I think it's a class thing,' Ben said. 'The posher the family, the less they get on.'

'Oh, for goodness' sake, let's not get started with this,' Sasha warned him.

'I have a theory about it—'

'Ben... *really*?' Wasn't there quite enough to be harassed about without Ben having a go at her family?

'For a start, there's more money at stake – who's been given what and who'll inherit this or that. And then there's the fact that your homes are so much bigger.'

'I really don't think this is very helpful right now,' she said.

'Well, if you live in a big, draughty place like Chadwell Hall, and you've had a row, you can go and storm off to the library or... I dunno... the east wing. But if you're growing up in a little two-up, two-down, everyone's on top of one another, sharing rooms, crammed into the space, and you have to button your lip, patch things up and generally learn a lot more social skills… and I'm not talking about the correct way to hold a dessert fork, *darling*.'

This pithy home truth and Ben's comical mock-posh accent stopped her in her tracks and suddenly she wanted to laugh, in spite of herself, in spite of her family, and in spite of everything she and Ben were going through.

'Ha ha, very clever,' she admitted, 'maybe you have a point.'

'Of course I have a point!' he said. 'In fact, I don't just have a point, I'm right!'

'My family is awful and snobbish and literally obsessed with money,' she said, 'but they're still my family and you married into us without having a clue—'

'Yeah… but I got the best one,' he chipped in.

'Very nice… but that doesn't mean I'm discussing any of this with any of them. I will not ask a single one of them for money, because that would be playing their game and admitting defeat and needing their help. I won't do it ever again and that is final!'

Ben actually began to laugh at this. And the sound of his laughter did lighten some of the awful tension pressing down on her.

'I'm glad I got the rebel,' he said, 'and it may not be making our life any easier, but I admire your stand and your independence, okay, Sash? See you very soon.'

* * *

Then the call was over, and Sasha was left alone in their sitting room. She looked at the banking app on her phone, saw the small amount of money left before they reached their overdraft extension and thought about what she really needed to buy today. The fridge was almost empty, so she had to go to the supermarket to get something for dinner tonight and tomorrow's breakfast. She remembered that she'd just put through a payment for a school trip for LouLou... and unless some new funds came in very soon, that payment was likely to bounce back. And... oh, good grief... she was supposed to go to Waitrose to pick up the elaborate order of cheeses, port and brandy that she and Ben were bringing to her parents' wedding anniversary party tomorrow. It was part of the menu and also their present to her parents: a whole stilton, a whole camembert, other special cheeses, quince jelly, bottles of vintage port and good brandy – the works.

Sasha sat on the floor and stared into space, mind whirling. At Greenhope Gardening, Ben was the head gardener, along with two freelance guys he used regularly. Sasha's role was marketing, admin, plant ordering and collection and person who made all the calls, appointments and follow-ups. Occasionally, she helped with planting schemes and even lawn mowing if Ben was snowed under. She knew that several hundred pounds would come in from this month's work in ten days' time. Next month, there were only a few minor bookings.

Really, she knew she should be on the phone, on social media, marketing their little company to the moon. But right now, she was completely winded by the crushing disappointment of the news from Ben, and she had to get out of the house and somehow do her errands.

How the bloody hell was she going to buy the groceries they needed *and* pay for that cheese and wine order? There was absolutely no question of turning up at her parents' without it. She tried to imagine her mother's face if Sasha announced, 'Oh, I'm sorry... I just forgot to pick those up.' Not that there was any danger of the guests going hungry if she didn't bring these luxury add-ons, oh no, this was going to be a full-on, three or even four-coursed event, in a glamorous marquee, with all the trimmings. This was a full fortieth anniversary, pull-out-all-the-stops, blowout extravaganza.

If she was honest, for weeks now, her heart had been sinking at the thought of this big family party. It wasn't just the cheese, or not being able to pay for the cheese; it was nothing less than out-and-out dread of the whole event. She and Ben were almost completely broke; their business was teetering on the brink because their major customer wasn't going to pay and there was no prospect of things looking up any time soon, but nevertheless, tomorrow morning, they were going to have to travel up to Norfolk, glam up, put on their best faces, their best possible shiny, sociable sides and endure a full-on family event. She would have to admire her mother's latest designer outfit, listen to her dad's complaints about his tax bill, hear about her little brother's latest property deal and ask how the new high-powered finance job in Switzerland was working out for her big sister. All the while, not admitting to any of the stress and problems raining down on her and Ben's heads.

Oh dear god.

There was no question of telling her family that she didn't want to come to the party, and absolutely no question of telling them what was really going on with her. She knew that would just cause an endless amount of disapproval, not to mention torrents of unwanted advice. No, she really could not bear it. She had her pride. And the less her family knew about Greenhope's disaster, the more she and Ben could keep their dignity intact.

For as long as Sasha could remember, she'd had the feeling that she could never do things the way her family wanted her to do them. She held a different attitude and different opinions from 'them'. And she could somehow never 'fit in' with them. So, at some point in her teens, she'd given up trying. She'd decided that, within reason, she would do things the way she wanted to, rather than trying to live up to the impossible demands and expectations of her family. The result of this was that they always considered her a bit of a rebel – the black sheep. Her parents liked to make out that she'd been 'impossible' and a total 'wild child' in her teens and twenties, when she knew that, compared to many of her friends, that just wasn't true. However, she quite enjoyed the 'rebel' badge and sometimes had to play up to it.

For a moment, her thoughts turned to her wardrobe, and she mentally ran through possible outfits for tomorrow. One thing she knew was that there was still a sizeable amount of bleach left in the box in her bathroom, so she would make sure that her funky, unruly short bob would have a fresh platinum shine for tomorrow.

Yes, sometimes she just had to play up to her assigned role as the family misfit. Surely that would distract her family's attention away from the business disaster? At least for a while.

2

'Hi, Sasha! Hi, LouLou – how are you both doing?'

Sasha turned to see raven-haired Deepa, one of the mummies from LouLou's friend group that she really liked, just as the Waitrose customer collection desk came into sight.

'How are you, Sasha?' Deepa asked with a big smile. 'I've caught glimpses of you now and then on the school run, but you've obviously been really busy and not had time to stop and talk to us for weeks.'

Sasha and her daughter both said their hellos, and Sasha apologised for the lack of contact.

'Just been so busy with work...' she added and then wasn't sure what to say next. One day, she probably would have to tell friends just what they were going through. But today was not going to be that day. It was still too soon, too raw. Maybe when she and Ben had solutions in sight, it would be much easier to have these conversations. But for now, that left her telling vague half-truths.

'Well... yes, I suppose it's autumn, everyone is getting one last garden tidy in and you've no doubt been rushed off your feet,' Deepa sympathised.

'Oh, absolutely...' Sasha said.

'You're so lucky, I envy you so much. Having your own company, being able to work on your own terms and in such a growing business. And you probably keep really fit doing the work too.'

Sasha managed an enthusiastic smile. 'Yes, it's hard work, but we really enjoy it,' she said. 'I'm mainly on the admin and marketing side, but it's great to be able to fit around school hours. You love me being around, don't you, LouLou?'

At this, both Sasha and her daughter pulled silly faces at one another.

'Anyway, how are you, Deepa?' Sasha asked, 'How's everything going?'

And then Sasha listened for a few moments to an update on this busy lawyer's life. She tried to imagine the wonderful comfort of a generous monthly salary, a predictable job... *paid* holidays!

'Are you heading for customer collection?' Deepa asked.

'Oh yes,' Sasha said. 'I'm picking up some things for my parents' big wedding anniversary party this weekend.'

'Oh, that sounds lovely!' Deepa said. 'Are you driving up to Norfolk?'

'Yes... tomorrow morning.'

'Well, we'll catch up soon, okay?' Deepa asked. 'I'm going to dash. My car's on a meter outside and I only ever come in here for my face cream and a particular brand of wine. Usually, I'm strictly Lidl.'

'Yes!' Sasha agreed. 'So pricey here.'

'Absolutely! See you soon,' and with a swish of red raincoat, Deepa and her daughter were gone.

So then Sasha, with LouLou by her side, was explaining her mission to the man behind the counter.

'Hi, I'm here to pick up an order that I phoned in earlier in the week.'

He took her name and the details and went off to the storeroom to get the order. When he returned, he was carrying a large sealed cool bag and a substantial cardboard wine box, packed with bottles of different types and sizes.

'Have you got a trolley there?' he asked. 'To get this to the car park?'

'Yes, all set,' she told him.

He took the receipt that was stuck to the side of the box and ran it through the till.

'That will be £457,' he said briskly.

'*What*?' she asked, absolutely incredulous, knowing there was no way she could cover that with the little bit of overdraft leeway in the joint current account.

'How much?!' LouLou asked her mother.

The assistant looked at the receipt again and informed Sasha, 'Well... that's what it says here.'

'For cheese... and wine?' But as she said the words, she remembered the request for a vintage brandy and several elaborate dessert wines that her mother, the indefatigable gourmet, had made.

'Can I take a look at the receipt, please?'

'Of course.'

Aware there were one or two people behind her in the queue, Sasha nevertheless cast her eyes over the list, noting the bottles of £55 wine and £135 brandy listed. *Would it be better to take out the three dessert wines or the brandy? Or maybe subtract the brandy and a lesser bottle of wine?* She did the maths in her head and considered the use of the ultra-emergency credit card in her purse. It had a hideous rate of interest and was there for last-resort, extreme emergencies only, as all the more reasonable cards were already up to the max... that's how tight things had been over the past months.

'Okay, let's lose the brandy and the bottle of Bordeaux,' she said quietly, hating that people in the queue might be listening in.

The assistant obliged and removed the bottles from the box. Now when he ran the total through the till, it came to £278.

She took out the ruinous card, put it into the machine and tapped in the number. After a moment or two, up popped the horrendous, heart-stopping 'card declined' message. Sasha could feel her stomach clench.

'Oh dear,' she said. 'Can I try that again? Maybe I've put in the wrong number.'

'That's usually a different message,' the man behind the till told her, 'but give it another go if you want.'

Same result – card declined.

She couldn't understand it. This card was off-limits. *Verboten.* Do not use. And she hadn't used it. The interest rate was 25 per cent or something totally unreasonable. But there was a £20,000 limit on it, back from the pre-LouLou days when they were buying the flat and both had full-time, well-paid jobs. She had seen this card as a sort of emergency parachute if things got really rough. So what had happened? Had the account closed down? Had the limit been changed? What was going on? And how was she going to pay for these overpriced groceries?

'Do you have another card you can use?' the assistant was asking her now.

'Well... erm... let me take a look...' She cast about her purse hopelessly. There was nothing else that would work.

'Your phone, maybe?' the assistant suggested.

She had no idea what to do. Part of her wanted to just turn on her heel and run out of here and away from this and never set foot in public again. She could feel her cheeks starting to warm up with embarrassment.

There was a tug on her arm.

'Mummy!' her daughter LouLou said with a giggle. 'What's the matter?'

'Oh... for goodness' sake,' Sasha managed in an audition-worthy performance, mainly for the sake of the shop assistant. 'I don't know what the problem is today... it's bound to be something techie at the bank.'

This was ridiculous, she couldn't help thinking to herself, she could not spend her last bit of available money on luxury groceries that party guests wouldn't even notice were there or not.

'I'm so sorry,' Sasha said, holding LouLou's hand tightly. 'I'm going to have to leave this for now.'

'Okay,' the assistant said, 'that's no problem,' although the sigh that followed suggested that it probably was.

Sasha walked with LouLou quickly out of the upmarket supermarket.

'What are we going to do now?' LouLou wondered.

'We're going to go to our usual supermarket, and we'll get every-thing that we need there,' Sasha assured her daughter.

LouLou looked up at her with round, surprised eyes. For ten years old, Sasha's daughter was very perceptive.

'You're going to buy a present for Grandma at *Lidl*?' LouLou asked.

'Yes... it will be fine... they have brandy, they have nice wine, they have cheese.'

'For *Grandma*?' LouLou repeated.

'Yes...'

There was a good word for women like Sasha's mother, Delphine; it was 'precious'. Delphine was originally from Mauri-tius, but she'd moved to Paris aged seventeen, lived there until she was twenty-five and had declared herself a Parisian for the rest of her life. She dressed like a Parisian, ate, spoke and lived like a Parisian, or at least as much as a Parisian who lived in rural Norfolk could. All her children spoke French, *naturellement*, and to their toe-curling teenage embarrassment, had to call their mother 'Mama' even in public. So, *naturellement*, they all called her either Mum or even Delphine as soon as she was out of earshot.

'Has Grandma ever shopped in Lidl?' LouLou wondered.

'Well, probably not,' Sasha said. Delphine shopped in delis and *boulangeries* and had requested very special and particular items from Waitrose because she'd not been able to 'source' them in Norfolk.

'Do you think she'll mind?' LouLou asked next.

'Honeybun,' Sasha paused, holding tightly to LouLou's hand. It was time to be honest, but not alarming: 'Mummy and Daddy don't have a lot of money right now. So we can't waste it on fancy things that Grandma has decided she might like. We have to use it sensibly, until some more money comes in... which it *will*,' she added quickly. 'I don't want you to worry about that. So let's go to our supermarket and choose nice things and we'll buy greaseproof paper and wrap the cheese like a deli does... and we'll buy some flowers for Grandma, too, and maybe she won't mind... too much.'

3

The turn of the key in the front door let Sasha know that Ben was home. It wasn't long after 9 p.m., so LouLou was already in bed and Sasha had done the prep she needed to for their weekend trip tomorrow. For the past half an hour or so, she'd been sitting in the dimly lit sitting room, doing what she had actually wanted to do all day long – she'd had a little cry about everything.

'Hi, Sasha,' Ben put his head around the sitting room door. 'How are you doing?'

'Oh... hello... not amazing,' she admitted, wiping at her face. 'I don't think this will go down as the best day ever.'

'Come on,' he said gently and walked over to her. Sitting down beside her on the sofa, he put his arms around her, his biking anorak crunching as he hugged her.

And it did feel better. It always felt better when Ben was holding her. He was strong, broad-shouldered and physically fit, and he had an inner confidence that she'd always admired. Plus, and maybe most importantly of all, he believed in her. Unlike her family, Ben made her feel clever and capable. She loved being taken seriously by him. And usually, maybe even tonight, he could make her believe that they would work it out together and everything would, eventually, be okay.

'It's just so unfair,' she told him once again.

'I know... I know...'

'And you're sure there is absolutely nothing we can do? No lawyer's letters... or further action we can take?'

'I've been out buying more legal advice from Jason with beer, just to make completely sure. And no, they've made the company that we did the work for bankrupt, so we're in a long line of creditors that aren't going to get anything. I did also mention your idea about the golf clubs and the Range Rover,' Ben smiled as he said this, 'and he couldn't recommend that either.'

'Shame.'

'Can I suggest that we try to take some time off from even thinking about it, and enjoy this weekend, then get fully back into problem-solving mode on Monday?'

'I can try,' Sasha told him, 'but it's pretty hard to stop thinking about it. I had to go to Waitrose to pick up the fancy cheese and wine for the party, Ben, and my credit card wouldn't work.'

Ben sighed. 'Well, I think we know the reason for that... they're all at the complete limit.'

'But no,' she protested, 'not that one. That was my total-emergency parachute card and I didn't think it had been used at all... and now I can't find out because I don't have the online details and phoning gets me in a twenty-five-minute-long queue and—'

'Sash...' Ben said, putting his arms around her once again. 'Please, I'm sure we can sort it out. I'm sure it's nothing mysterious. But could we just try and take some time off from all this? We're both thinking about it all the time, stewing it over, and I definitely need a break.'

It was true. He did look really tired. He'd been working hard and he'd been out a lot, too, meeting people he thought might be able to help, pitching for new work, going to events to network. She knew she looked worn out as well. There were rings under her eyes because she wasn't sleeping, and life didn't feel like much fun. There was no time or money or mood for them to go out, have a good time and really enjoy each other's company. Their happiness, their spark was fading away under all this pressure, she thought with a lurch. This was how it happened... this was how people grew older and wearier and bitter. It had all been so very different in those early days when she'd thought he was the most gorgeous man she'd ever met, when she'd believed they were the most wonderful couple ever, ready to do anything... ready to take on the world.

One snowy February in Switzerland, twelve years ago now, that was when they had first met. Sasha had said yes to the offer of accompanying a friend on a skiing holiday. She couldn't ski, had only had a few lessons on an artificial slope as a gangly kid and had pretty much spent that time falling down, grazing her hands and face and deciding skiing was definitely not for her. But her friend, Lottie, had convinced her to come along, assuring her that it wouldn't just be about the skiing; it would also be about being on holiday in February, enjoying snow, sunshine, mulled wine and fun. They were both single at the time. Lottie had just been through a horrible breakup and Sasha, who'd been single for almost a year, had helped her to get through it.

'Take some skiing lessons when we're out there,' Lottie had urged her. 'Honestly, you'll enjoy it.'

And in a last-minute whim of a decision, Sasha had booked four beginner's lessons. As she'd snapped her ski boots into place, attached them to skis and clumped gingerly along to the line-up of absolute beginners, she'd totally regretted it and almost decided to bottle out. But then this lithe blonde athlete on skis had swooped gracefully up to the group, skis and poles so perfectly under his control they almost looked part of him, bright-blue anorak, thick goggles and dazzling sunshine behind him, so she couldn't even take in his features properly, but Sasha had registered immediate interest in him.

'Hello, newbies,' he'd grinned at the little group of six or seven people, 'well done for getting here and hands up if you've never ever been on skis before.'

This was a down-to-earth London accent, when she'd expected him to be Swiss or Austrian with that kind of skiing ability.

Everyone else had put up their hands.

'Hands up if you had a few lessons as a kid?'

Sasha had put her hand up.

'On an artificial slope?' he'd asked.

'Yes,' she'd replied, already nervous about this session.

Ben had pushed his goggles up into his hair and given her a very cute grin. 'I'd just like to apologise in advance for that experience – this won't be anything like that, I promise. For a start, I'm not expecting you to dislocate a thumb or lose even one layer of skin.'

She'd not been able to stop herself from grinning more than she probably should at this really handsome guy.

'It's so brave of you to come back,' he'd said, smiling straight at her.

It was too cheesy to say that she'd 'known' at that moment that he was *the one* for her. She couldn't have known that right then. But she had realised straightaway that she was totally interested in getting to know him and what made her almost a little breathless with excitement from that very first smile was that she could tell he was interested too. There was a tension in those very first glances they were making at one another, a feeling that something was going to happen.

And there had been those little moments when he'd shown her how to grip her poles, when he'd caught her before she'd snow-ploughed right into another member of the group, when the expectation of something more had grown.

By the end of lesson three on day three, Ben had invited her and Lottie to a party at a chalet in the glamorous little skiing town. That had gone a little like this:

'So are you on holiday with anyone else?'

'Yes.'

Cue his crushed: 'oh'.

'A friend,' she'd added quickly. 'We didn't know what to do with ourselves on Valentine's Day, so we decided to go skiing.' Then he had looked delighted and invited them both to a party.

And about one hour and several glasses of *glühwein* into the event, Ben had led her out to the chalet's balcony and in the crisp, cold, dark-blue air, which had actually twinkled with ice crystals, he'd bent his head over hers and asked if he could kiss her.

'Yes, please,' Sasha had told him. And it was a stunning kiss that pulled them tightly together, attracted them first of all towards one another's bodies and then, over the next weeks and months, lured them right into one another's lives. At first, it felt like an extended holiday romance; there was lots of exciting flying between Switzerland and London, airport reunions, snatched weekends spent almost entirely in each other's bedrooms. But it had quickly started to get more serious, with tearful airport farewells and intense discussions about whether Sasha could move to Switzerland and work there, or if Ben should find something in London.

'Just not the artificial ski slopes,' he'd warned.

It had proved to be a difficult decision. Sasha had then looked into moving but could not find the right kind of job without learning fluent German, plus she'd realised she loved her life in London and didn't want to give it up. Ben, on the other hand, was totally at home in the freedom and adventure of the mountains – a ski instructor for eight months of the year and a hiking guide in the summer. Sasha didn't want to take that away from him. Plus Ben had grown up in London and didn't want to come back to city life.

So over a year of indecisive to-ing and fro-ing between Switzerland and London followed and then the decision – after one fraught weekend and a flight that was five hours late – to try splitting up for a while. Those heart-breaking weeks were the tipping point.

Sasha had been sitting alone in her flat on a Friday night, searching for jobs in Zurich, while listening to a German lesson on headphones, when she'd realised that the doorbell was ringing.

'Who is it?' she'd asked.

'Delivery,' had come the reply.

But when she'd opened the door, there was Ben, rucksack on his back, bags all around him, including one great long bag that must have contained all his skis and poles.

'I'm moving to London,' he'd said. And even though she couldn't believe it, and didn't know if it was the right thing for a man who loved the mountains to do, she'd fallen straight into his arms and known that, no matter where, this was the person she wanted to be with.

'What on earth are you going to do in London?' she'd had to ask him.

'I'll bring my bags in and I'll tell you all about it,' he'd said.

It turned out that he was going to start work with an outdoor adventure company that took children on trips away from school, but he'd already arranged that in November, December and January, he would go back to Switzerland for the skiing season.

'Do you think that could work for you?' Ben had asked her.

Sasha thought it was the most amazing solution she could ever have imagined. And here was Ben, right here in her home, and he was going to stay.

'And what about this?' was his next question, as he'd taken a small box from his pocket and opened it to reveal an adorable emerald ring, dainty, but definitely serious. 'Do you think this could work for you too?' he'd asked, his eyes on hers, no doubt about what he was asking her.

'Yes!' She'd not hesitated. 'Yes! Yes, this could definitely work for me!'

Then came a wonderful blur of happiness when it felt as if everyone was happy: Sasha and Ben, of course; Ben's lovely family, delighted that Sasha had brought him back to London; Sasha's friends... but Sasha's family, just not quite. There had been some awkward phone calls and a formal lunch meeting in a London restaurant, which had not gone as well as she'd hoped.

Both her parents and her siblings had been a little too focused on what Ben did for a living and his 'prospects'. Her father and mother had even made a special trip down to London and taken Sasha out for tea at Fortnum's to suggest that her father introduce Ben to some friends who could put him forward for 'something in the city'.

'He's very personable,' her father had said, 'he could be a financial adviser, or work in financial sales.'

'He doesn't want to work in the city,' Sasha had insisted.

'But he would earn much more money than he will for this adventure company,' her father had told her.

'Ben is an athlete, Dad; he doesn't want to wear a suit and sit in an office, he wants to be outside and active, doing the work he loves.'

'Oh dear,' her father had actually laughed a little at this. 'That's all very well... but is it going to give you the life you want?'

'A happy, healthy life, full of love?' Sasha had replied angrily. 'Yes! I think that's exactly the kind of life *we* want.'

And at this point, Sasha's mother, Delphine, had leaned forward to intervene. 'Oh, Saaaaasha,' she'd begun in her best 'lady-of-the-manor' voice, 'one has an affair with one's skiing instructor, one doesn't marry him.'

It had been unforgettable and unforgiveable. It had also served to bond Sasha even more closely to Ben.

4

Just like Ben and Sasha's beloved daughter, LouLou, the first inklings of Greenhope Gardening had begun as a slightly wild idea on a tipsy night out. A few short years after getting married, Ben and Sasha had become parents, and this had changed *everything*. Ben had stopped spending the skiing season in Switzerland because he didn't want to be away from home for such a long time, and life at the outdoor adventure company had become disappointing. It only ever seemed to involve dragging reluctant teenagers to places they didn't want to be, then listening to them moan about the lack of Wi-Fi and hair straighteners. Sasha was exhausted with the toddler-parent juggle of three days a week working for a marketing company and four days a week of full-time, full-on parenting. At the time, four-year-old LouLou still didn't sleep well, still raged in protest when she was taken to nursery, still caught every kind of illness cooked up in that toddler viral laboratory and Sasha could find no sympathy or allies for her problems because her work colleagues were all child-free girls-about-town who still cared way too much about eyebrow styling, lip plumping and where to find the most Instagram-worthy holiday destinations.

Having just pulled out all the financial stops to buy their flat, Sasha and Ben did not have one spare penny to spend on anything. But that was when Ben mentioned that two old skiing friends of his were now running a gardening business in Manchester and it was going really well.

'Gardening?' Sasha had asked, a little tipsy on her third glass of wine.

'Yeah,'

'What kind of gardening?'

'The hard work kind,' he'd replied, 'mowing lawns, digging, cutting hedges and trees, building pergolas and trellises. Apparently the guys bring in someone else when they need to mess about with plants.'

'So... what are you thinking?'

'They've asked me to come and work with them for a month or two and learn enough for us to set up our own gardening business down here... well... if we thought it was a good idea... obviously.'

'*Really*?' The idea had taken Sasha by surprise, but her thoughts had moved quickly. Ben loved being outdoors; he was fit and strong; he was practical, great at DIY and would learn how to trim trees and look after a garden very quickly. She could be part of this business, too, she'd realised. She could do the admin, the marketing, be the contact point with the clients and maybe she could even start learning enough to become the plant person.

So her first response had been enthusiastic. 'Wow, so you're thinking about leaving your job and starting a gardening business?'

'Yes... I suppose I am. I'm even thinking that if it goes well, you could leave your job and join me. Think about all the things you'd be good at...' and then he'd listed everything that she'd just thought of.

'I'm even thinking, there must be online courses where you can learn about plants, planting schemes and all that kind of thing,' she'd said.

'We could make up pots with seasonal bulbs and plants... sell those as extras to clients and online even...' Ben had thought out loud.

'It sounds like you really like the idea...'

'Well,' her husband had admitted. 'I am only at the "I wonder what this could be like?" stage, and that is all... but I want to go to Manchester and work with them. If I like it, then yes, let's have a hard think about it. I know it will come with a lot of challenges, but I really like the idea of being my own boss... of *us* being our own bosses,' he'd added, putting his hand over hers.

The more Sasha had thought about it, the more she'd loved the idea. She saw herself designing the logo, the flyers, the website and social. Yes, she would have to learn about plants and Ben, always at pains to do an excellent job, would no doubt have to learn how to mow lawns, trim hedges, build summerhouses and all the other jobs required, to perfection.

'You should be the one who starts it, Ben. I can keep my job as a bit of security until we know how this could all go.'

'Exactly what I was thinking.'

Working for themselves had been such an enticing prospect. She could work around LouLou – no more dragging her to nursery against her will at 8 a.m. And they could spend chunks of the year outside, doing manual labour, free from the chains of the office desk. Surely this could be a win-win, all round completely amazing idea!

'How much money do you think we would need to start up?' Sasha had asked. 'Could your friends give you an idea?'

'Whoaaaa... steady on,' Ben had warned, 'let's not race ahead... I need to spend that month with them first and see if I like it.'

But she'd seen the glint of hope in his eyes. It was a *great* idea. They could make a terrific go of this.

'I know what we need to do... you go and spend the month with them, and we'll get as much info as we possibly can, then we'll go and talk it over with my dad,' Sasha had suggested.

Her father had run his own successful business for many years and Sasha was sure he would be able to give them good advice, talk them through all the pros and cons. He would know how much money they would need to start the business up, get it going... and keep it going. He would be able to advise them about tax and all that kind of thing and he would know how much the business would need to make to really work for them. And she had liked the idea of having this important, grown-up conversation with him. Also in her mind had been the thought that maybe her dad would loan them the start-up money to make this all work.

She had seen from the excited expression on Ben's face that this was even more encouragement from her than he had even hoped to hear.

So, once Ben had spent the month working alongside his friends in Manchester, and come back completely enthused about the new business idea, they had bundled into the car, along with LouLou, and headed up to Norfolk for a weekend with Sasha's parents so they could brainstorm with Sasha's dad, Tony.

Carefully and thoroughly, Tony had listened to them, looked through their business plan and the projected numbers Ben had been able to put together with the help of his friends; then he'd asked them both lots of questions about their finances and what money they wanted to make and how much could they possibly scrape together to put in and get started. He'd given them a rough guide to tax and quizzed them about how hard they wanted to work and what their best skills were.

Finally, he'd leaned back in his leather desk chair, taken off his reading glasses and told them, 'You're both young, you're keen, you want to run your own show, so why don't you just go for it? If it doesn't work out, what's the worst that can happen? I'm sure you can go back to other jobs. So why not give it a try?'

Then they'd swallowed their pride and spoken to him about the possibility of a small start-up loan, but on that point, he'd been very clear.

'Well... look,' he'd begun. 'I absolutely don't blame you for asking... but my policy is not to lend money in the family, for very good reasons – people can be upset by that kind of thing and feel they've been treated unfairly. Plus, I do believe it's much easier to spend other people's money than your own. So you need to scrape that money together somehow, and you're homeowners, so the bank will lend you something. But, be very careful of debt, almost all businesses fold because there's far too much enthusiastic borrowing in the early days.'

While Sasha had heard the grown-up business sense in her father's words, she'd also felt the sting of rejection. Her parents lived in a vast, sprawling house. They were wealthy and enjoying a very comfortable retirement. Before, they'd offered to help Ben get a better job, so could they really not spare the few thousand she and her husband were asking for, not as a gift, but as a loan?

'We'll pay you back, Dad,' Sasha had added, 'in monthly instalments, from day one.'

But Tony had shaken his head. And once again, Sasha had had to experience her father's version of tough love. He did love her, she knew that, but he was allergic to any kind of 'spoiling' or 'indulging' of his children. He believed his most important job as a parent was making sure his children could stand on their own two feet. That was how his father had treated him and, as he loved to say, 'It didn't do me any harm now, did it?'

* * *

So Ben had quit his job and Greenhope Gardening had been born with a very modest start-up loan from the bank that had allowed them to buy a decent second-hand lawnmower and an elderly, but reliable, pickup truck.

And for the past five impossibly busy, steep learning-curve years, the business had been a success. Ben had built up the work and his experience slowly at first, but then new work had started to flood in, and he'd had to add on regular help from two other guys. Two years in, there had been enough work and income for Sasha to leave her job and work at Greenhope full time.

Much of her work could be done from home, but she often went out on site visits to speak to clients, take photographs of the work they'd done and to make the planting suggestions. Working together had been good for them as a couple, too, giving them new challenges and ideas. They had relished their early success. When they'd broken the target they'd set themselves, they'd bought new furniture for the flat and gone on a lovely late-autumn family holiday.

And then talk had begun about a second baby. Ben was very keen, as he'd grown up in a family with four children and he'd loved the company of his two sisters and one brother, as a child and still as an adult. Sasha was not so sure. She had an older sister and a younger brother and her relationship with them back then and now was... *complicated*.

'I love the three of us,' she told Ben regularly, 'and we're so happy together... imagine if we spoiled it? What if LouLou doesn't like her new brother or sister? There's going to be such a big age gap...'

And now LouLou was ten... and they were still discussing that second baby, and the question was still unresolved.

All the success the business had achieved over the past five years had led to the contract with the housing development company. In fact, it was Sasha's brother, Beau, who had several properties himself, as well as two bars, who suggested Sasha contact developers and offer Greenhope's services.

'Grass, trees, some low-maintenance planting.... developers are looking for ways to do it efficiently, cost-effectively and you guys would be great at it,' were his words of advice.

So, they'd carefully costed out a bid, submitted it to several developers not too far away from their home and had been completely elated to win the £75,000 contract.

It had involved investment in new equipment, in paying some extra staff to help out, in buying all the trees and plants. But it had never occurred to Sasha and Ben, who were straightforward people who always played fair, that the company they were doing the work for might not share the same values.

They'd worked really hard; they'd accepted the condition that no money could be paid upfront; they'd taken out the loans and scrimped, excited about the big payoff at the end.

And now they were in this horrible situation with no obvious solution.

5

'Hello, Mummy!'

Sasha woke to see LouLou at the bedroom door.

'Did you say we had to get up and get ready to go to Norfolk at 7 o'clock? Or 8 o'clock?' LouLou asked in a whisper, as if waking her parents up by whispering didn't count as waking them up.

'Eight,' Sasha whispered back.

'Oh... sorry,' LouLou said.

'So what time is it?' Sasha asked.

'Not 8,' LouLou replied.

Glancing at her bedside clock, Sasha saw it was 6.39 a.m., definitely not yet time to wake up for the party. LouLou had always been an early bird, and this didn't look like it was going to change any time soon.

'I don't want to get up yet,' Sasha protested. 'Why don't you make some toast and go and read for a bit?'

LouLou rolled her eyes, clearly keen to get this party day started. Sasha wished she could feel as enthusiastic about the day and evening ahead as her daughter did. But a Griffon family event was usually quite enough to have to deal with... a Griffon family event plus impending bankruptcy... *oh god*, it made Sasha want to bury her head under the duvet and not emerge again until next year.

'Can I try my dress on?' was LouLou's next question.

'Yes, of course,' Sasha said. If it would make LouLou go away for a bit and let her at least try and get back to sleep beside Ben, who hadn't even stirred from deepest slumber, she was willing to give it a go.

'Can I wear my dress in the car?'

'Maybe...' was all Sasha would commit to here.

'Mummy... can I wear eyeliner to the party?'

'No.'

'Lip gloss?'

'Ye...ess.'

'Blusher?'

'A hint,' Sasha conceded.

'Perfume?'

'A waft.'

'Do you think Grandma will like my dress?' was LouLou's next question. She was obviously determined to wake her mother up.

'Well... we all know Grandma,' Sasha said. 'She's hard to please.' And to be honest, Sasha didn't absolutely love LouLou's dress... it was a bit frothy and a dark-purple shade that didn't quite suit pale LouLou with her dad's blue eyes and the mousy brown hair that Sasha used to have, until she'd discovered bleach. But LouLou had set eyes on it and fallen in love.

'Oh, *ma petite*, I think this is a touch *déclassé*,' LouLou said in the unique mix of English and French that her grandmother liked to use.

Sasha couldn't help giving a laugh, because for a ten-year-old, that was a killer impersonation.

'Oh, *ma petite, ma cherie... oh la la*,' LouLou went on in her excellent French accent.

'LouLou, I love you,' Sasha said, 'but please can I go to sleep for just a little longer?'

* * *

A week ago, when Sasha had gone dress shopping for the party with LouLou, it had been a lovely afternoon of trying on and fun decisions. The only tension had come at the till, when Sasha had to calculate how much overdraft would be left for the week's groceries.

Of dress shopping with her own mother, Delphine – much as Sasha had wanted to conjure up some good memories – she could only remember two very fraught occasions. The first was way back, she must have been about the same age as LouLou, maybe even younger, when she had emerged from the dressing room in her favourite, a red and purple floral number with a flower print and added flounce around the cuffs and hems.

'Oh no, this one I do not like,' Delphine had pronounced firmly. 'This is too... *fussy*.' Fussy was the death knell for Delphine. She never, ever wanted anything that was fussy, not clothes, not food, not curtains, not sandwiches – she had that classic French eye for the non-fussy and the *tout simple*.

So Delphine had made her try on another dress that had a plain navy-blue top with a little collar and buttons. This one Delphine had declared was *perfect*. Sasha remembered protesting hard in favour of the red and purple flounces. Delphine never usually 'gave in' to her children. She was confident in the belief that parents knew best for children and giving in to childish whims was 'spoiling' and no good would come of it.

Sasha couldn't remember the details, maybe there had been some sort of special offer on, but on this occasion, Delphine had relented and said that they would take both dresses. Sasha had been utterly delighted, but the happiness had been short-lived because what had happened next was that every time there was an opportunity to wear a dress, they had the very same argument all over again – Sasha wanted to wear her flouncy one and Delphine insisted on the plainer collared dress. In the end, Sasha wore Delphine's dress to every kind of public event and wore the flouncy dress around the house, at the weekends and after school, even when it was short, a little too tight and outgrown.

There had been another horrible dress-buying incident when she was a teenager. There was a school dance planned – not the big, final hurrah, but a Christmas dance. Sasha must have been about fourteen or fifteen, the truly awkward age. She'd felt absolutely hideous, with spots, her unmanageable frizzy brown hair that seemed to corkscrew straight out of her head, new womanly thighs and buttocks, not to mention breasts that she felt as if someone had stuck onto her front. She'd wanted that classic English, princessy dance frock: one with a tight bodice and a full skirt. She'd thought maybe pink or blue with sequins and netting, tulle and frou-frou. In her mind's eye, lashings of party flounce would detract from the boobs, the chubby thighs and the horrible rash of pimples on her face.

But in changing rooms across Norwich, the attempt to find *the dress* had grown more and more fraught. Sasha had hated herself in just about everything. When she'd put different dresses and looked at herself in the mirror, she could see only flaws. Maybe no mother in the world would have been able to talk Sasha round that after-noon, but Delphine failed more than miserably.

'Yes, you do have spots, but so does everyone your age,' had been one memorable comment.

'Oh no, not that one,' when Sasha felt a glimmer of hope at

fuchsia-pink sparkles, '*mon dieu*, you look like something from the circus.'

'What about a chic little black dress?' Delphine kept asking, showing that she had not the slightest inkling of what was required for a posh school dance.

'No!' Sasha had hissed as her mother had brought yet another classical black column dress to the fitting room.

'Just try one... you'll look so grown-up, so *soignee*.' Another one of Delphine's favourite Parisian phrases. Finally, it had all become too much, and Sasha had burst into dramatic tears and actually run out of the shop. Instead of rushing after her, Delphine had actually stayed in the shop to apologise.

'Oh, it's that awkward age,' Sasha had heard her mother saying to the shop assistant, as she tried to slam the door, which had an infuriating slow-pull arm. 'What can you do? What can you do? Wait for her to grow out of it, I suppose.'

At crisis point, the day before the dance, some random dress from her big sister, Adele's, wardrobe had been taken out and a zip had been hastily replaced with ribbon lacing so that Sasha and her boobs could fit into it. Adele, of course, had that rail-thin, flat-pack look which exuded the kind of French chic Delphine adored.

Adele had helped a little to make things better – curling Sasha's hair, lending her some glamorous silver sandals and applying make-up so the offending zits were toned down a little. But Sasha had not been able to rid herself of the ugly duckling feeling for years. It was a special, if slightly wild, third boyfriend who'd finally made her see that chopping off her hair and dying it blonde, dark eyeliner and wearing clothes with defined waists, were the way to make her feel so much better about herself. Maybe even more so especially *because* of all the eye-rolling she now caused her mum and dad.

* * *

The funny thing was that Sasha hadn't thought about any of this for years, until she had been in the shop watching LouLou try on several dresses and allowing her to make the decision for herself with just a little guidance. Sasha didn't blame her mother for her strictness and her rigid ideas; she knew that was how Delphine had been brought up and Delphine continued to think it was the right way, even if sensitive Sasha sometimes found it hard to live with.

'French mothers know best. French *grandmothers* know best. This has always been the way,' Delphine would say firmly. And, oh, the irony, she wasn't even properly French! She'd grown up on the island of Mauritius, in a family with several French ancestors, but she'd moved to Paris to study and completely fallen in love with the city. In fact, she had only returned to Mauritius once, for the funeral of her mother. When her father had died several years later, she had sent extravagant flowers and a card, but didn't make the journey.

'We weren't that close,' she'd said simply when her own children had asked about it many years later.

Delphine had been so captivated by Paris, that she'd decided her Mauritian relatives didn't have any importance for her any more, so Sasha and her siblings had never been there. They knew Delphine had older brothers, so they had uncles, aunts, cousins and now the children of cousins there, but aside from Christmas cards – becoming much more infrequent now – they didn't know anything about these relatives.

So, in Delphine's mind, she was French, *absolument*.

Unfortunately, and much to her ongoing chagrin, this Parisian had married an Englishman and spent the rest of her life living not in the 6th *arrondisement* of Paris, but in what she continued to refer to as 'the depths' of Norfolk.

6

Despite growing up in central London, Ben had enjoyed an outdoorsy, sporty childhood packed with football, tennis, climbing clubs, adventure playgrounds and, of course, a teenage obsession with skiing. He was determined that his daughter would have the same healthy, happy childhood experiences and took a dim view of kids obsessed with their devices.

This meant that LouLou, in the back of the car as they set off for Norfolk, was plugged into an audio book – she loved ones with detectives or a mystery theme. She listened intently and looked out of the window, as her parents' discussion in the front seat grew more stressed.

Ben, despite already knowing how Sasha felt about this, was once again suggesting that she should tell her family what was going on with the gardening business.

'Please, Ben, you're going to have to stop talking about this or I am going to get really, really annoyed,' she warned.

'But don't you think they might want to help us?' he asked. 'I know that my mum and dad and the rest of my family would all want to help us if they could, but they can't.'

'If you mean lend us money, just forget it,' Sasha declared. 'I am not going to tell them, Ben, and I am not going to ask them for money and that is absolutely final. Don't you remember when we were first starting up?' she asked. Surely he couldn't have forgotten that conversation.

'Yes, I remember,' he said flatly.

At the time, she had found it harsh. She had turned her eyes away from her father and run them over the paintings, the bookcases and all the little treasures that lined the walls of his study, any one of them probably worth enough to help start their company.

But hard though it was, he had sort of been right. They had absolutely scrimped to get the last of the money together, downgrading their car, selling Ben's skis and even a lovely brooch Sasha had inherited from her aunt to get the money together. Then they'd only needed a small top-up from the bank.

Maybe she should have turned to her dad for business advice more often than she had, she thought regretfully now. Maybe they wouldn't have got into the contract with the now-bankrupt company if he'd been there to help. Maybe they would have had the confidence to ask for the money upfront and not taken all the additional loans that were causing them such enormous grief.

'Why is it always so hard with your family?' Ben asked gently. 'I know that you find them difficult,' he added, 'I know that you don't like to engage, you prefer to just get the heck out of there after a visit.'

'Who wouldn't?' she asked him.

'Yes... but when a family isn't working very well... everyone tends to get stuck in a role and then feels they have to step back into that role whenever they go back. But apparently, as an adult, it just takes one person in the family to behave differently and the whole family has to change.'

'Really?' This sounded unlikely to Sasha. She couldn't imagine that her doing anything different would make any of the others pay even the slightest bit of attention.

'Well... I'm no expert,' Ben said quickly, 'but maybe when you think there's a moment when you would usually do one thing, maybe try and react differently. And see what happens.'

'World War Three, probably,' Sasha muttered.

Sasha turned her head to look out of the side window at the motorway traffic and felt a lump build up in her throat. She could not tell them about the business because... well, it was to do with how she felt about her siblings and her parents and how she wanted them to feel about her. She had her pride. She didn't want them to feel sorry for her. She wanted them to be proud of her.

Growing up, she'd always had a sense of being second best. She'd felt outshone by her clever older sister, who'd dazzled at school and gone to Cambridge, of course. And then there was her funny, cute baby brother, Beau, who was the absolute apple of his mama's eye. It wasn't that her parents didn't love her, but Sasha had always felt overlooked and sort of left out. And now that Adele and Beau were such high achievers, she did not want to be seen as the adult failure – the one whose business had failed, who was struggling. *No! Absolutely not.* Her family was not going to be told about any of this. Sasha and Ben would just pretend that everything was fine, and they would get through it and somehow come out on the other side and her parents would not be any the wiser.

But then, was that realistic? How are we going to just breeze through to the other side of this? Their debts were now way beyond what she was comfortable with; there was currently only a trickle of cash coming in and it was quite possible they would have to sell their flat. And how would she explain that to her parents?

Not many couples with a young child were downsizing. What would Tony and Delphine make of them moving into a rented flat? Having no cars? Not to mention her and Ben going back to their old jobs. But even if they did all of those things, she didn't think that it would be enough. It would still take many years before those debts were paid off.

Sasha had grown up in a beautiful, stable family home. A wonderful, big country house that had always been there from the day she was born. All her childhood memories were wrapped up in the house and it was still there, still the home where her parents lived. Her dad's study... the kitchen table... the glamorous dining room... the broom cupboard... the improvised height charts, her and her sibling's bedrooms – not the same as they used to be, gradually redecorated over the years – the familiar sofas and nooks and corners. The feeling when she walked up and down the broad staircase that their tread and curve were woven into her muscle memory.

The thought that LouLou wouldn't have any of this stability and familiarity in her life made Sasha really, properly sad.

'We've messed everything up,' she whispered to her husband, 'we've made a mess of everything and now we're going to pay for it. And LouLou's going to have to pay for it too. That's what's the worst. That's what's really, really bad.'

'Sash,' Ben sighed and put his hand on hers. 'I don't exactly know how yet... but we will get over this, and without the help of the Medici family, if that's what you prefer.'

She couldn't help giving a laugh at this.

'You know, I do understand why you don't want to talk to them about all this,' he told her now.

'So can we stick to that?' she asked him. 'Please? You won't let anything slip?'

'If that's what you want,' Ben replied. 'I mean let's face it, if we told Tony, he'd probably go into full Tory MP mode.'

'Tory MP' was Ben's nickname for Tony, which was hardly surprising. Tony was exactly that character, a corduroy-trouser-wearing, *Telegraph*-reading, old-school gent, wearied with the world.

Sasha's mother was occasionally *La Reine* to Ben. And that suited her too. Delphine was queenly, not to mention drama queen-ish. She was the queen of Chadwell Hall, and it was her way or the highway there.

Very unfortunately, the nicknames cut both ways. And her entire family still thought it was quite okay to keep on calling her by the stupid, stupid nickname she'd hated ever since the day it was first coined when she was eleven.

Ben turned the car off the main road, first of all onto a short stretch of dual-carriageway, then to a two-laned B-road, and finally onto the narrow, twisty country road that felt so familiar to Sasha, she thought she could probably drive it with her eyes shut. There was a final left turn onto the long, curving road with steep sides of banked red Norfolk soil that led only to the house and nowhere else.

'Do you think Adele and Sylvie are there yet?' LouLou asked, unplugging herself and referring to her auntie and excitingly much older cousin.

'I don't know,' Sasha told her. 'I think they're supposed to be arriving just a little bit later than us.'

Brusque and business-like Adele, who worked in finance, gave advice to millionaires and even billionaires on where to invest their wealth, now lived in Switzerland. In a blast of 'I want to change my life, shake things up and do it all differently', Adele had moved with her husband and daughter out to Zurich two years ago, landing herself an extremely fancy new job in the process. Then she had divorced Henry, who was utterly heartbroken and refused to move back to the UK without his family. So now he lived in a little flat in the basement of Adele's beautiful lakeside home, which sounded complicated.

Sasha felt very sad for Henry, who had been part of the extended family for close to twenty years but was now missing out on the big get-together.

'Is there any word of a new boyfriend... and if so, is he coming to the party?' Ben asked.

'I don't know,' Sasha replied, 'she's being very secretive. And we're not supposed to mention anything to Mum and Dad.'

'In the usual open and loving Griffon tradition,' Ben couldn't resist.

They were on the very last part of the drive, when the high earth banking at the side of the road smoothed out, and rounding a final corner, there was a full view of calm, flat fields, solid oak trees, a driveway lined with pristinely neat hedges and there, at the heart of it all, Chadwell Hall, a properly grand three-storey country house with twelve windows on the front façade alone and a portico around the double front doors.

As they turned into the driveway, the gravel crunched under the tyres and Sasha felt a heady mix of emotions. She was very fond, proud even, of her beautiful family home. It was part of her, her memories all interwoven with the house and its extensive grounds. But she always felt some uneasiness about family reunions, especially now when everything was so all over the place for her and Ben. Her family was complicated; their relationships were tricky and often prickly. But, as always, she loved them. She wanted this weekend to go well, and she hoped that maybe, despite everything, it could.

* * *

'Hello!' her father, Tony, was already out of the front door and waving a welcome. 'Here come the London contingent. Must be a relief to get out of that bloody awful place.'

See... that was the Griffon way, say whatever was right at the forefront of their minds and never mind how anyone else might feel about it. At least they were honest, she thought, you certainly always knew where you stood.

'Hello!' he enthused again, coming down the front steps to meet them in his usual checked shirt tucked into comfy cord trousers, belted low to accommodate the solid paunch that a career as a wine merchant had given him. He was still a handsome man, though, with a dense thatch of steely grey hair, clear blue eyes and the kind of strong jawline that was staving off the double chin.

Part of the tradition of arriving at Chadwell was that you unloaded the car at the front of the house and then Tony told you where to park it round the back beside the outbuildings. Sasha and Ben jumped out and as Ben opened the back door for LouLou Tony went to hug and kiss his daughter.

'Pump!' he greeted her with the loathed nickname. 'Lovely to see you. And Ben...' he shook Ben's hand, 'and how is my LouLou?' Tony gave his granddaughter a warm hug.

'Hello, Grandpa, do you like my dress?' was LouLou's first question.

'Oh yes, I love your dress. You look fabulous,' her grandpa told her with the kind of absolute conviction that Sasha could never remember receiving.

'So, Ben, once the bags are out if you wouldn't mind putting the car...' Then came the elaborate 'second shed on the left' type of instructions that seemed so unnecessary when there was so much space round there. But never mind, there wasn't much point in railing against this particular bee in Tony's bonnet.

So she and LouLou picked up their bags and followed her dad into the beautiful wood-panelled hallway that always smelled of the beeswax furniture polish used on the wood, as well as the lime, eucalyptus and bergamot candles that Delphine would arrange on the antique sideboard.

'Your mother's upstairs getting ready,' Tony said with something of an eye-roll.

'Getting ready for the party?' Sasha asked.

'No... this is phase one, getting ready to greet you all. Anyway, come in, sit down and let me get you something to drink.'

It was 12.45 p. m., not a time when Sasha would usually be on the alcohol. But her dad definitely had pre-lunch drinks on his mind and to be honest, maybe drinks were what was needed to take the sharp edges off the family reunion.

'What are you having, Dad?' she asked, as he led them into the stunning drawing room, all shades of pale-blue and pale-beige with velvety rugs, lavish curtains and glossy polished wood. As children, they were only ever allowed to come in here on special occasions and it still felt out of the ordinary to be sitting on the plush sofa.

'I'll have a fully leaded G&T and I recommend you do the same,' Tony said. 'There's still some prep and heavy lifting to be done this afternoon, and you'll want to be a little merry to get through that.'

'Possibly...'

'Definitely! Now, LouLou, my darling, if you go the kitchen,' Tony instructed, 'you'll find Marla there and she will get you a juice.'

'Okay!' And LouLou, in a swish of purple, went out of the sitting room and off to find lovely Marla, the part-time housekeeper and helper, who'd started work a few years ago when Delphine's long-suffering cleaning lady had finally had enough. Just one of the problems of maintaining a twelve-bedroomed, three-reception-roomed home was that there was always something tricky to clean, fix or replace.

Tony came back into the room with two large crystal tumblers fizzing and clinking with ice cubes and lime wedges. He handed his daughter a glass, clinked his against hers and took a long appreciative sip, while she did the same.

'So how are things?' he asked, settling into his armchair.

'Fine... pretty good, considering,' she replied. 'Can't complain.'

'I guess that's the busiest season behind you now. You can wind down a little over the winter, maybe?' he asked.

'Yes... we're trying to think of lots of ways to keep busy over the coming months,' she said, and that certainly wasn't a lie.

In fact, it didn't feel so odd to be glossing over their failure like this with her father, because for the past five years, she had also glossed over their success. 'Yes, things are fine... going well... better than we had expected,' was all she'd said when thousands of pounds beyond their expectations had come rolling in, because it was her dad who had given her that first harsh lesson in never being too 'full of herself'.

* * *

It was in her final year of primary school, although Tony and Delphine had sent them to the area's exclusive little private school, so it was 'prep', not primary school. The convention was to stay there one year longer than primary school, until the very beginning of self-conscious, gawky adolescence, with most people turning thirteen in that final year. She'd been 'a plodder' at the school, always near the bottom of the class – you gauged these things, even when you were just nine or ten, by comparing your marks to others. Plus it was the kind of competitive school where they gave prizes at the 'Speech Day' at the end of the summer term. That was when she would sit for what seemed like hours, watching what felt like everyone else in the entire building getting a prize. There were prizes for every kind of sport, prizes for every school subject, prizes for the best marks, prizes for 'character' and leadership and music and drama and art. But there never seemed to be any prizes for being Sasha and for having to watch your mother fuss endlessly over your little brother, and your big sister, Adele, go up on stage over and over again, all big grins and happiness, to collect trophy after trophy.

But in that final year at the school, everything sort of came together for Sasha. A growth spurt dramatically improved her tennis game, and she was made captain of the team. Lovely weather meant she'd done a lot of swimming in the small lake near Chadwell Hall, and she won a regional medal in a front crawl race. Her school fundraising team had made the most money at their charity bake stall. And on top of all this, she had tied in first place in Maths and come top in French. French was a cheat, obviously, according to everyone in her class. 'Her mum is French, is that even allowed?' had been the complaint.

So the night before Speech Day, she'd excitedly told her parents at dinner that she was going to get a lot of prizes.

'The tennis captain's cup... and they're going to give me my swimming medal too. And I came joint top of Maths and top of French. Oh, and the best fundraising team too. That's four prizes! No, five!' She'd been almost breathless with excitement. She'd never been up on the stage at the event before and now she would have to go up five times.

'You need to come early and get a good seat, so you can take some pictures,' she'd instructed her mum and dad.

She remembered Delphine smiling at her and saying something about making sure her shoes were polished and putting her hair in plaits, which Sasha already knew she did not want and there was going to be a fuss about that in the morning.

But her dad carried on chewing his mouthful of food. Then,

when he'd swallowed, he'd said something that Sasha had never forgotten.

'In this family, Sasha,' he'd said solemnly, 'we don't boast about the things we've achieved.'

He didn't elaborate, just went on eating.

And she was absolutely crushed. That dreadful word *boast* – we don't *boast*. He was saying that she was boasting. A boaster. Had he ever accused Adele of boasting? She didn't think so.

She didn't remember if she made any kind of reply other than a mumbled 'oh' perhaps. But it spoiled the whole of Speech Day for her. Everything was ruined. Every time she went up on stage to collect a prize, she blushed with shame and couldn't smile. Boaster. Boasting.

When her parents had tried to make her pose with her prizes afterwards for a photo, she'd burst into tears.

'What on earth is the matter with you?' Tony had asked, as if he'd blanked out the whole of the previous night's conversation, as if it meant absolutely nothing to him – which made everything worse.

'She's sad to be leaving, Tony,' Delphine had explained, 'she's been here for nine years. Of course you're sad, darling. Now smile for the camera. And aren't those plaits adorable?'

She wasn't allowed to be proud of herself. She couldn't be proud of herself. And the shame of it all had burned for years. It had even taken her years to tell Ben about the incident.

'I am so sorry,' he'd told her, hugging her tightly. 'That's so unkind. I am so proud of you, my love. You are so brave and hard-working and adventurous and positive. I saw all of that the moment I met you. And you're so almost painfully humble. I'd love you to boast. You boast away, you extraordinary, wonderful human being.' And he'd held her and kissed her better. And that is how life partners can heal those family wounds.

Now, looking back as a grown-up, she still didn't really know why her father had said what he'd did, but she tried to be understanding and give him the benefit of the doubt. Maybe he'd had a shitty day. Maybe Delphine and Beau had been on his nerves all evening. Maybe he'd encountered some friend's obnoxious child and been determined his own child wouldn't turn out like that... who knew? When she thought back on it now, it didn't stab her in the heart nearly as much as it had at the time. She had recovered from it and, maybe even more importantly, she had forgiven her father. Maybe one day in the future, they would even have a conversation about it. Although she suspected he would never remember what he'd said or why. That tended to be the way: you held onto some insult or upset for years and years after the person who'd made it had forgotten all about it.

7

Sasha tapped on the door of her mother's bedroom.

'Hello, Mama,' she called out, 'it's Sasha.'

'Come in, *ma petite*,' Delphine replied, and Sasha stepped into the pretty light-blue room, where her mother was seated in front of her dressing table.

Delphine gave her daughter a hug and a peck on each cheek, then turned back towards the mirror. She took a heavy antique comb from the top of her dressing table and ran it carefully over her short dark bob. Fresh from the hairdresser, the bob was sharp and the exact shade of ebony that Delphine loved.

'Your hair looks really soft and shiny,' Sasha said kindly.

'Thank you, some kind of new mask Julie wanted me to try,' her mother replied, referring to the woman who'd been cutting and styling her hair for probably close to twenty years now.

Delphine had been wearing a bob since her twenties and the style still suited her and framed her striking face.

'You still really suit that hair colour,' Sasha added. She was on the verge of saying something about 'not many women your age would...' but then thought better of it.

'Yes, I don't hold with this modern mania for going grey,' Delphine told her. 'There are now twenty-year-olds walking about with grey hair... Adele, my own daughter, lets the grey hairs sprout from her head. *Tiens!* Grey... I think it is so inelegant, so ungroomed. A sign that one has let oneself go.'

She gave a little shudder at the thought, which made Sasha smile.

'I like your blonde,' Delphine added, 'sometimes it can look a little brassy, but not today.'

Sasha shrugged. That was quite the typical Delphine compliment; it always came with a rider.

Then, perching her reading glasses on her nose, Delphine carefully applied first of all a crimson lip pencil, then, using a favourite lipstick, she filled in her narrow lips with the pillar-box red. She pressed her lips together to set the colour.

Eh bien!

She smiled at her reflection. High cheekbones, beautifully maintained teeth and an aversion to sunbathing meant she looked very well for sixty-eight. She'd applied quality French creams for decades now and she was convinced they worked.

Attention to every mouthful she ate, along with two brisk walks a day in the bracing Norfolk countryside, meant that she hadn't changed dress size in three decades and could still wear all the beautifully tailored skirts, jackets, trousers and dresses that a lifetime of careful and tasteful shopping had bought.

Sasha observed that, as always, Delphine, looked absolutely striking and beautifully put together, from head to toe. Her red lips and nails were the exact same shade; she wore a coffee-brown and black patterned silky shirtdress that looked perfect on her. A lovely gold, jangling bracelet and one of her favourite pairs of gold and citrine earrings completed the ensemble.

'Are you excited about the party?' Sasha asked.

'Oh yes, I'm so looking forward to it, and your father too. He loves a party. He says Chadwell is at its best and comes fully to life with a party.'

'Can I see your outfit?' was Sasha's next question because she knew how much care and attention Delphine would have put into the choosing and the buying of her dress.

'Of course... it's here, on the side of the wardrobe.'

Sasha followed her mother's pointing finger to a wonderful new dress, still in a protective polythene film, of thick, satiny material in shades of pearl and mint green. It had three-quarter sleeves, an elegant square-cut neckline and a flared skirt that ended just below the knee.

'That looks lovely,' Sasha said.

'Oh, it is an absolute joy to wear. As soon as I saw it in the window of Anna's shop – you know the place I mean in Norwich?'

Sasha nodded.

'Yes, as soon as I saw it, I knew it was the dress I wanted to wear tonight. And it will go beautifully with my earrings... you remember? The very special ones given to me by my mother when I left Mauritius and went to Paris.'

Sasha knew the exquisite earrings very well. They had a fat pearl stud at the lobe and then delicate gold wiring was carefully worked into a wide chandelier around more pearls and six sparkling pale green emeralds. Four fat pearl drops dangled from the lowest hoop. Delphine only wore these earrings on the most special of occasions, when they always attracted attention.

The interesting thing about the creamy South Sea pearls was that nowadays, they were still valuable, but much less so than when these earrings were made. Back in the early 1800s, pearls were worth a fortune because divers had to go down onto the bottom of the seabed to search for oysters and only one shell out of hundreds contained the choicest fat pearl. Modern pearls are farmed in wire baskets in the water, but when these earrings were made, pearls like this were rare, exquisite, and extremely valuable.

They had belonged to Delphine's great-grandmother, who was thought to have been born a slave on Mauritius before being freed and marrying Delphine's white great-grandfather. The couple had apparently gone on to become very wealthy, running a string of grocery stores. But apart from the earrings, there was very little evidence left of their fascinating tale.

'I come from a family of merchants in Mauritius,' Delphine liked to tell her children and grandchildren, whenever she was asked. 'That's what they've been for generations and still are... I think they import fancy cars onto the island now. But back in the days of gold and old money... well, I don't like to think too much about what they were involved in. It's all a bit murky... tobacco, guns, sugar, gunpowder, booze.'

Sasha knew that the heirloom chandelier earrings were still kept in the antique polished box made from the white mahogany of Mauritius that they'd been in when Delphine's mother had given them to her. The box was too large for just a pair of earrings and that was because there was still room against the pale silvery-blue velvet for the matching emerald and pearl necklace that had once been there. Apparently, decades ago, it had been swapped by Delphine's grandmother for a valuable piece of property.

There was the sound of a car rolling up the driveway. Sasha looked out of the window and at the sight of a sleek and brand-new Range Rover purring into view with her baby brother at the wheel, she couldn't help feeling her heart sink a little. *He* was obviously not dealing with clients who were refusing to pay.

Delphine jumped up from her dressing table and, with a glance at the window, announced with a clap of delight, 'It's Beau! My little Beau is here!'

She quickly slipped on her shiny, black, kitten heels and trotted at speed out of the room, across the hallway, down the stairs and straight towards the front door.

As Sasha came downstairs, she met her dad in the hallway, who gave her a warm smile and said, 'That will be your brother, then.'

'So I gathered,' she smiled back.

Tony rolled his eyes and Sasha's smile widened. And that was how they dealt with Delphine's overt favouritism. No one said it out loud, but they acknowledged it, eye-rolled, and knew that it was there.

'Beau, how wonderful to see you!' Delphine could be heard gushing. 'And Sura... and my little Pica... and how is the new baby?'

Tony and Sasha went to the front door now, as Sasha tried to work out when she had last seen her little brother, who now lived in Birmingham with his glamorous wife. She hadn't yet seen the new baby, who was only a few weeks old.

As she got to the door, her eyes fell first of all on Sura, who was stepping forward from the car, holding the baby in her arms in a beautiful pale turquoise blanket, and Sasha was suddenly struck by a surprisingly similar flashback.

Her own daddy and mama arriving in their car at the front of the house. Daddy rushing round to open the door for Mama, helping her out, and in her arms this bundle in a blanket.

* * *

'Come and look, girls...'

Sasha and Adele had rushed out, down the front steps, over the gravel to meet Mama, who seemed to have been gone for weeks.

'Mama! Mama!' They put their hands on her waist, took hold of her skirt, but she couldn't put her arms around them right now because she was holding the bundle.

'Just a moment, girls. Let's get inside and then you can have a look at him.'

So Mama went into the drawing room and put the bundle down on the sofa, opened up the folds of the blanket, and there was a real baby. Sasha could still remember staring down at the strange peachy little face with utter astonishment. There really was a baby. And it was so small. And so cute. His little balled fists waved about his face and he mewed like a kitten.

There had been talk of Mama having a baby in her tummy, but up until this moment, Sasha hadn't really grasped the idea... that there would be a baby and he would be a boy, a brother, and he would be coming home to live with them.

'Will he be here all the time?' asked Adele, who was eight at the time, while Sasha was six.

'Yes, of course,' their mother had told them. 'This is baby Beau. He's your beautiful brother.'

'Baby Beau,' Sasha had repeated. 'Hello,' she'd said and reached for his little hand.

'Oh no!' Mama had put her hand out to stop her. 'No touching Beau and not so close. He's very tiny, Sasha, he mustn't get any germs.'

Mama was so focused on the baby. Sasha was only small, but she had seen straightaway that Mama couldn't take her eyes from baby Beau. She'd wrapped him back up in his blanket and said she would take him upstairs to his room. And then she didn't come down again for what felt like hours.

'Your mother is very tired,' their dad assured them, 'she's probably having a sleep with the baby.'

And over the next few days and weeks, Sasha and Adele had had to adjust to this new Mama, who was always carrying the baby, who was always tending to this baby, who was so completely taken up and preoccupied by the little package of fuss and squawk that they were only allowed to look at from a distance because of *germs*.

But it wasn't as if Sasha felt she had lost her mother's attention to this new baby. No, because she hadn't really had her attention before. Certainly not this concentrated, devoted, endlessly delighted and fussing level of attention. When Sasha had seen her mother bestowing all this on baby Beau, she didn't know what jealousy was, all she felt was that she wasn't worthy of this kind of attention; maybe she didn't need it; maybe, unlike this new baby, she wasn't fascinating enough to get it.

And whenever grown-up Sasha tried to think back to before the baby... well, she only had vague and distant memories, but in them, Mama was always sad. Mama was in the little blue bedroom crying and didn't want Sasha to come in. Mama was too tired to make dinner and they were to make toast... and there was one acute childhood memory, which sometimes appeared in Sasha's dreams even now and woke her up with fright – that Sasha's baby bear had been taken away.

In the dream, her family was very sad for her and hugged and held her while she cried, but no one could bring the bear back.

She'd dreamt of this memory so many times that she could no longer tell if it was real or imagined, if she'd ever had a toy bear or not. But sometimes, Sasha did wonder if there was some little drama at the heart of the family that she'd never quite understood; sometimes, as a child, she'd stumbled on words and whispers that hadn't made sense... that had given her a feeling that there was something hushed and hidden that might one day come to light.

8

'Pump! How are you doing?' Beau grabbed her into an enthusiastic hug. Sasha considered asking him for the one millionth time not to call her that, but suspected there was no point.

Always, it was a jolt of energy to see Beau. He was handsome and smiling and fun. He was high energy and always had new ideas and interesting stories to tell and, really, it was hardly his fault that Delphine was so unfairly *obsessed* with him – there wasn't any other word for it.

Sasha remembered once overhearing Delphine tell a friend, 'Of course, one loves all one's children completely, but personality also comes into it, and one can't help getting on better with one of them than with the others. Some people are just more compatible, on the same wavelength, *non*?'

At the time, as a teenager, Sasha had thought, but if you're the *parent*, surely you have to try, don't you? You have to want to know how to get onto the same wavelength as each of your children?

'Hey, Beau, I'm great,' she told her brother with a big grin, because his enthusiasm was infectious. 'And you have a new baby... that's just wonderful!'

'And here he is...' Beau put a protective arm around Sura's shoulder and guided her up to the front door with the baby cradled in her arms. 'Say hello to baby Dokus.'

'Oh, he is so gorgeous.' Sasha concentrated on the little face and tried not to notice her dad tensing beside her.

'Dokus?' Tony asked and there was a whole world of indignation in that single word.

'Yes,' Beau said lightly, as if it wasn't anything.

There was a pause, a sort of dust settling kind of moment and then Sasha heard LouLou pipe up from behind her.

'Is that his *real* name?' she asked incredulously. 'Dokus... *Dokus*?' she repeated slowly.

'LouLou...' Sasha warned, and her eyes met her daughter's.

'I've just never heard that name before... that's all,' LouLou backtracked.

It was Delphine who piped up now as she went forward to hug and kiss both Sura and then her little granddaughter, Pica. 'I love his name... Dokus... it sounds Greek and classical and classy. *J'adore*.' She touched the baby's forehead lightly with her beautifully manicured fingers. '*Bonjour, mon petit*.'

Only after Delphine had ushered Beau, Sura and Pica into the hallway did she register LouLou properly.

'Ah,' she put up her hands in a gesture of surprise, 'LouLou, so wonderful to see you too.' And she wrapped LouLou in her Chanel No. 5-scented embrace.

Tony ushered everyone into the drawing room and busied himself with taking drinks orders and making up the required glasses, while LouLou volunteered to hand out drinks very carefully, one by one.

Sasha sat on the sofa beside Sura and asked about the new baby and how they were all coping. Little Pica, who was three now, sat close beside her mother, peeping out at her auntie now and then.

'Oh, I'm pretty frazzled,' Sura admitted, but she didn't look it. She'd obviously made a big effort for today; her beautiful blue-black hair was fresh and shiny, hanging in styled ringlets against a soft blue sweater. Her make-up was perfect and there in her ears, complimented by her golden Iranian skin, was a pair of elaborate pearl, gold and diamond earrings that Sasha instantly recognised as having belonged to her mother.

'Oh, those earrings look so beautiful on you,' she said.

'Thank you,' Sura replied, looking pleased, 'your mother gave them to me when Pica was born.'

'That was so lovely of her.'

And how nice and how generous of her mother to give Sura such a beautiful and personal gift... but... Sasha had that familiar pang of jealousy that her mother's actions could rain down on her in all kinds of sudden and unexpected ways. In this case because she'd never given Sasha any of her jewellery.

'I have anaemia,' Sura confided. 'I know it's quite common after having a baby, but I'm so tired all the time, I could just cry.'

'Oh no... are you getting treatment?'

'Yes, taking the tablets, drinking iron water, eating steak... but apparently it can take a few months to get your levels back up again.'

'Your little boy looks so well. He's obviously thriving,' Sasha assured her. 'And how about Pica, how is she coping?'

As both Sura, and with a few shy words, Pica replied, from the corner of her eye, Sasha saw Ben coming into the room. She loved how different her husband was to the men in her family. He was almost a head taller than Tony and Beau. He was blonde, while Beau had Delphine's darkest brown curled hair and Tony was salt-and-pepper grey. Ben was fit, long-armed and long-legged with an athlete's build, while Tony and Beau were more compact and barrel-chested. Ben was a skier, runner and cyclist, while her dad and her brother liked to drive and sit at their desks.

Unusually, Ben had a large G&T in hand and Sasha suspected this was to ward off his tension about being here in the heart of the Griffons. Ben fielded Beau's cheerful, 'Hey, Ben, how are you doing? How's the business?' with an equally bright, 'All good, can't complain,' quickly followed by the deflecting, 'And how about you? It can't be easy juggling everything with a new baby.'

'Exhausted, totally exhausted already and it's only week three,' Beau said and shook his head. 'Amazing, though.'

Meanwhile, Sasha could hear Sura saying in an exasperated whisper, '*Huh*? He sleeps in the spare room.'

It occurred to Sasha that maybe Beau had not been having the easiest time with his bar businesses lately with so many new restrictions and regulations. She wondered if he would mention it, or if he was going to gloss over any problems the way she and Ben were planning to do.

'So what's your little boy called?' Ben asked and took a sip of his drink.

'Dokus,' Beau replied.

Completely involuntarily, as he would explain to Sasha later, Ben startled, stalled and then sprayed his mouthful of G&T across the room. For several moments, there was a stunned silence, before it was broken by the sound of Sasha bursting into a coughing fit as she tried not to die of laughter, LouLou issuing a very disapproving 'Daddy!', Delphine's stunned '*Mon dieu!*' and, thank goodness, the sound of a throaty, rumbling engine and wide tyres crunching up the driveway to distract everyone from Ben's faux pas.

'I'm guessing that will be Adele!' Tony said, jumping up from his chair with enthusiasm.

Sasha went over to the big bay window to watch her sister and niece, Sylvie, arrive. She knew they'd flown in from Switzerland this morning, so this was obviously a hire car – a swanky branded SUV, all glossy with flashy chrome trimmings. To Sasha's surprise, the passenger door opened and out stepped, not Sylvie, but a tanned, lean and fit man in his late twenties, early thirties maybe, who certainly wasn't lovely old Henry. This guy had short, sandy hair, a handsome face and was smartly dressed in trousers and a shirt, both pressed to within an inch of their lives. And here was Adele, in a chic grey jumper dress, classy sunglasses and heels. Her hair was shorter than before in an above-the-shoulder bob with a short fringe that really suited her. Sasha felt a rush of warmth and love to see her sister again and an immediate wish to get on well with her this weekend.

Yes, maybe if Adele was also a London-based mum, struggling with her business, they would have a lot more in common. But instead, Adele was on a stellar, international wealth-management career path, leading a stressful but also very luxurious life, and even as Sasha hugged her sister warmly, she was wondering how she would navigate conversations around the gardening business without letting Adele ask too many questions or find out too much.

The thing about older siblings is that there is no time when they aren't there in the family, doing everything first. Adele was always first. The first to go to school. The first to go to secondary school. The first to be a house captain, win prizes, travel to Germany with the hockey team, star in the school play, do a reading at the Christmas service. She was the one who set the bar. And it didn't matter that Sasha had gone on to do many of these things, too, the point was that she wasn't the first, so no one was ever quite as impressed.

Adele was the first to get a grown-up haircut, have shoes with a heel, go to the ball, choose what to study at university. When you're the first, you blaze the trail and Sasha had never felt she could quite live up to all the excitement of Adele's achievements. It was a feeling she still couldn't shake off.

9

'Marla has put some food out in the kitchen for everyone,' Delphine instructed, 'so let's go and eat and talk and have some champagne. And afterwards, I have some chores I need you to help with, so we are all set for the party at 7 p.m.'

The big group of siblings and parents and partners and children made its way into the spacious country kitchen where smoked salmon on bread, little tortillas and all kinds of delicious goodies were eaten with fizz and chat.

Sasha sought out her niece, Sylvie, to talk to. Sylvie, draped in a baggy black sweater and black skinny jeans, swished her long hair over her shoulder and talked to her aunt about the stresses of starting her final year at school and the pressure of the exams ahead.

'But you are so smart, just like your mum,' Sasha told her encouragingly, 'I'm sure you'll do really well.'

And then Adele appeared beside them, along with the tall man of mystery, who had been introduced to the family as, 'Dirk, he's from Switzerland and we've brought him along because he's

Sylvie's tutor and he's never been to Norfolk before, so we thought he'd enjoy the trip.'

'Hello, Dirk,' Sasha smiled up at him. 'I sincerely hope my family behaves and does nothing to scare you away,' she joked.

'Oh!' Dirk sounded surprised and didn't seem to know what to say to this.

'Typical British humour,' Adele said, and Sasha thought she saw something of a little look pass between her sister and Sylvie's tutor... but then she decided that she was probably imagining things. Very quietly, Adele asked her, 'Are they really going to call that gorgeous little honeybun *Dokus*?'

'Yes, I think you'll find that they already have.'

'Is it an Iranian name?' was Adele's next question because Sura had Iranian parents – or when Delphine was telling it, Sura was Iranian *nobility*.

'No... apparently they both just liked it because it was so unusual.'

'But... Dokus?' Adele asked in a whisper. 'I mean, hocus pocus Dokus.'

'We'll probably all get used to it,' Sasha tried to be reassuring.

'Typical Beau,' Adele muttered, 'so determined to show off and be special, he doesn't mind condemning his son to a childhood of playground bullying.'

Beau was heading their way, so it was time to stop the Dokus conversation and turn back to handsome Dirk. Sasha asked him where he lived, and it turned out he lived in Zug, on the outskirts of Zurich, just like Adele, but he had grown up in a small mountain town.

'Oh, I bet you ski really well. You have to meet my husband, Ben. He's obsessed with skiing.'

'Yes, I heard...' Dirk said.

Sasha glanced over at Ben, but saw he was deep in conversation with Marla, probably trying to get the inside track on the desserts that lay ahead this evening.

'Hello, Pump, how is it going? Tell me all about your gardening business. Is it flourishing... blossoming... see what I did there?' Beau arrived beside their little group, already looking a little flushed, as he'd obviously been making his way at speed through the G&Ts and fizz.

'Well... it's been a really busy spring and summer,' Sasha began, all smiles and breeziness, 'and now we'll be winding down a bit because it starts to get cold, people come indoors and stop worrying about their gardens until February.'

'But every single person I know has a fire pit, fairy lights and patio pots... that must be extending your season a bit?'

'Oh yes, of course,' she agreed. 'And there's pruning and tree surgery, lots of that going on in the autumn and winter.'

* * *

Some of the time, she felt nervy to be here – because a family member might suddenly demand to know more details about the business, and she would have to scramble to create the right kind of smokescreen. But it was also quite calming, because when she wasn't being directly asked about the business, she found herself not thinking about it quite as constantly and obsessively as she had for the past weeks and months.

Here at Chadwell Hall, she felt far away from the day-to-day problems and in a little protected bubble, almost. Maybe it was the family home effect. Enormous, draughty and impractical, Chadwell was still the place she'd grown up in, her childhood home, and she dreaded the inevitable day, hopefully well into the future, when it wouldn't belong to her family any more.

'So what are our chores, do we know yet?' Adele asked and as she moved her hand up to bring another mouthful of fizz to her lips, Sasha spotted Delphine's thick golden rope of a bracelet slide elegantly along her sister's wrist.

'You're wearing Mama's bracelet,' Sasha observed, 'it suits you.'

'I know, isn't it lovely?' Adele said. 'She's been opening the treasure chest and handing a few things on. Has anything come your way yet?'

When Sasha shook her head, Adele said, 'Well, stand by, or just ask her.'

But Sasha didn't want to ask. Just like Sura and Adele, she wanted to be surprised by a generous and unexpected gift from her mother.

'Oh, for crying out loud!'

This was the reaction from Tony as he stood by the kitchen window and watched the heavy downpour of rain.

'That's all we need! I've had my eyes glued to the weather forecast for the last two days. Yesterday it looked perfect, but this morning, this bloody rainstorm began to edge in on us. There was only a 20 per cent chance of it hitting us; it was supposed to go a bit further north... but damn and blast, it looks like it has.'

'Is it expected to last for long?' Adele asked.

'Let me see.' Tony took his mobile out of his pocket and began to scroll. 'Well... we'll have to cross our fingers; it doesn't look too good.'

From the kitchen window, the lawn rolled out, lush and green, and standing at an angle to the house was the large marquee all set up for the lavish party, only a few hours away now. Already, the rain was making the pink and white of the tent look a little more grey and saggy, a lot less festive and fluttery.

'I have a list,' Delphine began, 'of all the things still to do.'

'No problem,' Sasha began, just as Beau chimed in with, 'Yes, ma'am.'

So Delphine began giving out instructions of an extremely fussy and pernickety kind, not that Sasha had expected anything else.

'The white linen napkins are to be folded exactly like this one on the table here. Who knows how to do that? And someone needs to go into the garden and cut some of the white and cream-coloured dahlias, well, maybe a few pale pinks as well, but nothing bolder, because the scheme is gentle and pastel. And cut some green branches too... maybe some white hydrangea flowers. There are flowers in the marquee already, but this is to supplement.'

Many other jobs were mentioned: sweeping rain from the wooden walkway, raking the gravel, marking out car parking and creating signposts to the bank of 'posh' chemical toilets.

'And Sasha, I have a special job for you and LouLou. First of all, you need to come upstairs with me, straightaway... *tout de suite*.'

Sasha thought her mother's face looked troubled, so she asked, 'Is everything okay, Mama?'

'You and LouLou... I'm sure you can help,' Delphine said, smoothing her hair down with her hands several times over, the way she did when she was anxious. 'You're always so good at looking for things, Sasha. You're calm and diligent. And LouLou, she can crawl under the bed, check the little spaces, can't you, *ma cherie*?'

'Yes, no problem,' LouLou said, pleased to be asked.

'So, have you lost something?' Sasha wondered.

'Oh, yes, yes.' Delphine began to frown. 'I've lost something very important. So important! And I really need to find them now. Well before the party.'

'Of course...' Sasha soothed. 'And don't worry, Mama, I'm sure we'll find it.'

'Them,' Delphine repeated. 'I've lost *them*. My earrings – the very special, very valuable ones, the ones from Mauritius that my mother gave me, from her mother. The emeralds and pearls.'

'Oh, goodness...' Sasha, of course, knew exactly what her mother meant. Hadn't they been talking about those earrings earlier? They were a family heirloom, a family legend even. Only Delphine was allowed to wear them. In fact, only Delphine was allowed to even handle them.

'Come on, then.' Sasha interlinked her arms with her mother on one side and her daughter on the other.

'I'm sure we can find them. You've probably just done something absent-minded... put something on top of the box, or moved it to a different drawer. You'll help, won't you, LouLou?' Sasha asked. 'Grandma has mislaid her earrings – you know, the ones from Mauritius – she's shown them to you before, hasn't she? So we're going to go and help her find them.'

'Lost her special earrings?' LouLou stopped in her tracks and exclaimed, 'Oh no!'

Sasha was surprised by the shocked expression on LouLou's face.

'It's okay, honey, I'm sure we'll find them.'

But LouLou shook her head and looked quite upset. 'Oh no! Oh no!' she repeated.

'LouLou, what's the matter?' Sasha asked.

Finally, with tears in her eyes, LouLou whispered, 'I think it's very bad luck.'

10

In Delphine's bedroom – she'd stopped sharing with Tony and his snoring many years ago – everything looked neat and orderly and the smell of Chanel still lingered in the air.

It was such a lovely room, painted a pale silvery blue with old-fashioned chintz curtains, blossoming with pink roses, and a velvet bedspread in the same shade of dusty rose. An old, dark-wood double wardrobe was home to Delphine's clothes, along with a matching chest of drawers, which had a mirror on top and the small boxes and trays were filled with her make-up, perfumes and skin creams.

'Okay, let's see if we can find the box,' Sasha said, approaching the chest of drawers and preparing to open the top drawer, where she knew her mother's jewellery was kept in a selection of wooden and velvet boxes and little silken bags.

'But I have a special drawer for the earrings box,' Delphine said, and she perched herself on the edge of her bed and then, with a little silver key, opened the drawer within a drawer at the top of the dressing table.

This inner drawer was empty.

'Oh!' Sasha was surprised. 'But if there's no sign of the lock being broken, or anything like that, then you must have put the box somewhere else.'

'But I would not have done that,' Delphine insisted.

'So... when did you last see the earrings and the box?' Sasha asked.

'I cannot remember,' said Delphine, looking around the room helplessly.

'Today? A few days ago?'

'Oh no,' Delphine said. 'Weeks ago now... weeks ago. But I just can't remember when. Was it when I had bought the new dress? Did I try the earrings on with it? I can't remember!' Delphine sounded frustrated with her own forgetfulness.

'Well, let's look on all the surfaces first,' Sasha suggested, 'and I'll just check inside the top drawer too. Then maybe we should have a look in the bathroom, do you remember taking them to the bathroom? Maybe to try them on in front of the mirror there?'

'No!' Delphine sounded almost angry now, angry with herself, maybe, for forgetting something so obvious.

'It's okay,' Sasha said, 'I'm sure there's an obvious explanation.' But over the next twenty minutes, she searched the drawer and then the room, the bathroom and as many nooks, crannies and crevices in Delphine's bedroom as she could think of... and the earrings did not emerge.

Sorting through some of the contents of the jewellery drawer for a second time, admiring brooches and pendants, chains and entire handfuls of earrings, she asked Delphine, 'There isn't any chance you've given them to Adele, is there?'

'Adele? No!' Delphine said with something close to a snort.

'Well... you've given other pieces to Adele and Sura...' she stopped short of adding, 'but not given anything to me,' thinking that the sentiment surely expressed itself.

'Yes... well, I don't go out as much as I used to. I don't wear these lovely things. Jewels need to be worn. They need to see the light, be warmed by the skin. So, yes, it's time to pass some of them on. And I will give you some pieces, too, Sasha, of course.'

'Well... I didn't mean—' she began.

'But I have been thinking about what to give you,' Delphine added. 'You've got thick fingers, so you won't suit my rings and your neck is quite short, so bracelets are probably best for you, but I only have one or two good ones and I still wear them.'

Did Delphine have to be so blunt, Sasha wondered? *Did she always have to say whatever came into her mind? Couldn't she just keep some of her thoughts to herself? Did she never consider that her remarks might be hurtful?* Sasha didn't feel particularly hurt now, as an adult, but growing up, the criticisms about her 'unmanageable' hair and her 'rather shapeless' legs and her 'straight waist' and so many other 'uncompliments' had been difficult to bear. They'd made her wary of her mother, reluctant to share too much with her, because her mother didn't feel like a true friend or ally.

From underneath the bed came an indignant, 'Mummy doesn't have fat fingers! She has very nice hands,' as LouLou made Sasha's heart soar by rushing to her defence.

'Not fat, no,' Delphine defended herself, 'just not the long, fine fingers that work best for good rings.'

'Well...' Sasha wanted to pull the rug from this in-depth critique of her bad points. 'Right now, we can't find the earrings, which is a bit of a problem. I am sure they will turn up, Mama. But you might not be able to wear them tonight.'

'Oh, my goodness.' Delphine looked agitated.

'And you don't remember putting them somewhere else?'

'No... no... I don't think so.'

'I'm sure they will turn up and I know they are valuable...'

'Oh, *bien sur*.' Delphine's hands flew up in exasperation. 'Worth £150,000, I've been told.'

'What?' Sasha exclaimed.

'Did you say £150,000?' came LouLou's voice from under the bed.

'Well, yes, I've been told... when I described them and their history to a jeweller... they've not been properly valued.'

'But... I thought pearls were worth less now than they were then?'

'Perhaps... but it's the historical value. They're very old.'

'Good grief!' Sasha managed and sat down on the corner of the bed.

She ran the figure through her mind again: £150,000! For earrings? It didn't make any sense at all – £150,000 for something that might slip from your ear and disappear down a gap in the floorboards! Besides, her parents were well off, and very comfortable, but not exactly the kind of people to have £150,000 sitting about in a drawer. Into her mind came the thought: *why on earth am I so worried about asking them for a small loan?* But she brushed that thought away again. She would not ask them. She didn't want them to know. She didn't want to reveal the real situation... she didn't want her parents' sympathy or their inevitable judgement.

'I take it the earrings are insured?' Sasha asked now.

'Well... yes... I think so.'

'You *think* so?'

'What do I know?' Delphine snapped. 'You need to ask your father about insurance.'

Whatever else Sasha might have said, it was interrupted by Beau's shout from downstairs. 'Mama! The cake is here. Do you want to see it? And where shall we put it?'

'The cake!' Delphine jumped up from the bed, looking as excited as a young girl. 'Come on, LouLou, let's go and see *le gâteau*.'

'What about the earrings, Grandma?' LouLou said, sliding herself out from underneath the bed.

'Well, I just don't know. I will just have to hope that they reappear.'

It was a bit odd, Sasha thought, following her mother and her daughter out of the room. They were kept in a locked drawer and her mother couldn't remember taking them out or moving them anywhere else. It was definitely a bit odd.

11

There was of course something of a drama around the cake – Delphine was rarely far from a drama of one sort or another.

At first, she didn't like the decoration. She thought it was too bold and not in keeping with the gentle pastel colour scheme she had arranged for the marquee.

But Adele, Sasha and, especially LouLou, all persuaded her that it was a beautiful cake with its gold, pistachio and cream marbling and soon Delphine had been talked round again.

So the stately three-layered cake was lifted, along with its special table, by Ben and Beau and taken, under cover of an enormous golfing umbrella, to stand in its place of honour in the marquee. But the rain was still falling heavily. The grass was becoming soggy, puddles were forming on the wooden walkway over the lawn to the front of the tent and Tony was on the phone to the marquee company to find out how many hours of rain the tent could take before it would start to leak.

'The forecast does not look good,' he was telling them. 'Heavy rain for the next two hours... and then no sign of any let-up all evening. What I want to know is just how wet can these tents get?

Hmmm... well... yes... Do we need to go round poking at the bulges where the water is collecting? Is there any chance the thing could come down?'

Tony was pacing now and looking extremely concerned.

'Shall we go and look in the marquee, Mummy?' LouLou asked with a gentle pull at her arm. So Sasha followed her daughter outside, trying to dodge the puddles on the walkway and using her hand to try to protect her face from the rain.

'This is *a lot* of rain,' she told her daughter once they'd made it to the marquee entrance.

'I know!' Loulou agreed. 'I'm glad I brought my wellies. Do you think this dress will go with wellies?'

The idea made Sasha laugh.

Inside the tent, everything looked wonderful. She was truly impressed. So much blousy pastel blossom everywhere, the stunning cake, the tables bedecked with pale-lemon tablecloths, elegant glasses and place settings, then the elaborate golden chandeliers glinting from the centre of the tent ceiling made it all look fairy-tale like and utterly party perfect. But there was no escape from the loud drumming of the rain, and the damp grey patches forming on the tent ceiling.

Sylvie was in the tent, doing some last-minute table-laying, and Sasha watched as LouLou sidled up shyly to Sylvie, who greeted her with a big smile and a friendly hug.

Over in the far corner, Adele was talking on the phone and tapping at speed into a laptop... probably a work call, probably an important client having a meltdown that only Adele could talk him down from. Dirk was also in the tent, hovering behind Adele, in a close-fitting T-shirt and leggings combo that suggested he'd been or was about to go out for a run. She suspected he and Ben might find one another over the course of the evening ahead and discuss their favourite ways to keep in peak shape.

Beau appeared briefly at the tent flap to tell them all that it was approaching 5 p.m. and time to spruce up for the night ahead. He had a champagne glass in one hand and a bottle of fizz in the other.

'You're in top party mode,' she said.

'Oh yeah!' he agreed, raising the bottle at her. 'Want some?'

'No, thanks... I'll get into my party gear first. LouLou, I'm going to get changed. Do you want to come with me? Or are you staying with Sylvie?'

LouLou and Sylvie exchanged glances, as if LouLou was asking for permission to stay with her and Sylvie was agreeing.

They looked so alike, these two girls, Sasha couldn't help noticing: same high foreheads, soft, straight hair and that determined expression about the mouth. They looked like sisters, not cousins – the family resemblance was so strong.

Sylvie caught her look and gave her a smile. Sasha wondered what Sylvie was making of it all. She was eighteen, on the brink of leaving school... she'd been transplanted from London to Zug, her parents had split up, and now here she was in the heart of Norfolk, helping to lay out a marquee for a party that would be packed with people she didn't know.

Sasha smiled back.

'Okay, LouLou, if it's definitely okay with Sylvie, I'll leave you with her. But, Sylvie, please feel free to send her back to me any time.'

'It's no problem,' Sylvie said.

'Fantastic, I will go and enjoy a little bit of peace and quiet and party prep,' Sasha said, pulling a face at her daughter, who pulled one straight back.

With that Sasha went back out into the garden and jogged through the rain to get back into the house. She met her father as soon as she was back inside.

'Your mother will not be pleased at all, but I seriously think we might have to move the whole event into the house,' he told her.

'Really? Move everything from the marquee?' Sasha tried to take in what a major fuss and upheaval this would involve – transplanting the chairs, the tables, the flowers, the settings... the cake. Delphine would quite possibly have the meltdown to end all meltdowns.

'I'm going to give it another half an hour before I decide. Where's Ben? He's a practical sort of chap... let's ask him what he suggests,' was Tony's surprising verdict.

'Ummm... well, upstairs, I think. I can go and find him for you, but I really don't think he knows very much about marquees... or rain storms.'

* * *

Up the stairs Sasha went, *number seven, eight, nine and right turn*, that's how well she knew this staircase, she could run up or down it with her eyes closed, and along the corridor on the left-hand side and into the little blue-with-yellow-flowers room that she was sharing with her husband and her daughter on this trip. It wasn't her old bedroom; this room had always been a guest bedroom and it had been allocated to them for the night. It had an odd 'jack and jill' bathroom arrangement. There was a door which led to a bathroom that was shared with the next bedroom along. So you had to always remember to lock and unlock both doors... or there were complications.

'Hello, husband,' she greeted Ben. 'I was just wondering where you'd got to. I thought you might have tried to sneak off for a pre-party jog with Dirk.'

Ben was pulling on his smartest pair of trousers, while a relatively ironed white shirt flapped about, still open, over his chest.

'How are you bearing up?' he asked.

'Not too bad, considering. But I honestly think my mum might have lost those earrings, which is going to be a pretty big fuss. It's not just that they are family heirlooms, handed down from my awesome great-grandmother, that's bad enough, but my mum thinks they're worth about...' Sasha paused for effect, 'one hundred and fifty grand.'

'What?!' Ben stopped in his tracks. 'You have got to be kidding me!'

'Apparently not.'

'Jeeeeeeesus... if I'd known that, I'd have stolen them years ago,' he added.

'That's not very funny.'

'Sash... do you think someone *could* have stolen them?'

'Like who?' she asked.

'Well, a lot of people have been here lately... the caterers, the window cleaner probably, the people who put up the marquee.'

'Oh, about the marquee...' she remembered, 'Dad wants you to go and talk to him about rain and how the marquee is holding up and whether or not we should move the whole party into the house.'

'Wants to talk to *me* about it?' Ben asked, sounding surprised.

'I know! Says you're "a practical sort of chap".' She made quote marks with her fingers. 'He doesn't exactly dole the compliments out, so take them where you can get them.'

Ben buttoned up his shirt and tucked it into his trousers. Then he smoothed over his hair.

'You look so good,' she told him and moved in for a kiss. She put her arms around his waist and tipped her face up towards his. But the kiss he gave her was much more fleeting than she'd expected.

'There's something I have to talk to you about,' he said, stepping back from her.

'Oh?'

'Yes... but let me just go and see your dad. I'll be right back. You get changed. And where's LouLou?' he asked as he headed out of the room.

'With Sylvie... they both seem to be enjoying themselves.'

And he was gone. Leaving her wondering and worrying slightly... *talk about what, exactly?* She began to unzip the garment bag protecting the satiny blue dress that she was wearing tonight. It wasn't new, there were no funds for new anything right now, but it was a favourite of hers and she was looking forward to putting it on. There was one benefit to all this terrible fretting, she had dropped down to her preferred weight without even trying, and the dress would hang well... even if she did have 'a thick waist' and 'shapeless legs' and 'a short neck' and 'fat fingers'... *thanks, Mother.*

Sasha stripped down to her bra and pants and gathering up different underwear, the dress and her make-up bag, she opened the bathroom door. To her surprise, there was an extremely buff, tanned and naked man standing in there.

'Oh... would you like to use the room?' Dirk asked, turning towards her so that he was now full frontal.

'Ummm, yes, ummm, right, just... be right... back, ummm,' she managed, backing quickly out of the room.

'It's no problem, I won't be long,' he said pleasantly, as if she'd just walked in on him tying up his shoelaces or putting on a hat... and now she was imagining him doing both of these things while naked, which made it all worse.

There were moments in life when you realised just how British you were, she thought to herself, even if your mother was from Mauritius and had lost her heart to Paris and had only spoken French to you until you were thirteen, when you'd had an absolutely screaming hissy fit and told her if she didn't stop, you would run away. That had been quite the day of drama...

But for much of the time, Sasha didn't really feel truly British, the way she could see that other people did. Some part of her was held in reserve. Sometimes when she was in France, it felt more familiar... the food was the kind she grew up with, the habits, the customs were part of what she was used to. Having a foreign parent was like being in a permanent state of culture clash.

She gave it a few minutes, then dared to go back into the bathroom, carefully locking both doors. Then she took a quick shower before applying her make-up, heavy on the eyeliner and styling her shiny platinum bob with some wax to make it a little more messed up and edgy. Then she put on the nice underwear and the silky blue dress.

Yes... she was happy with the result, so she unlocked both bathroom doors and went back into the guest bedroom, where Ben was standing and seemed to be waiting for her.

* * *

'What did you decide?' Sasha asked Ben, but she could sort of already tell. This bedroom was directly under the roof and the drumming had gone up to a new level, almost like a constant roar.

'He's being quite calm and sensible about it,' Ben said. 'He's phoning the people from the marquee company and is going to see if they can come out and help. There's a lot of stuff to shift and the first guests will probably be here in... about forty minutes.'

'Oh no! How is my mum taking it? '

'Ermmm... she's in her room getting ready. I don't think Tony has broken the news to her yet.'

'Oh dear,' Sasha said, 'we'll have to go and help... with moving things, with telling her... this is all turning into a bit of a mare.'

'Sasha.' Ben put his hand gently on her bare upper arm. 'You look really nice,' he told her.

'Thank you.' She smiled at him.

'And there's something I really need to talk to you about. It's pretty important.'

'I think it is going to have to wait, Ben,' she said, wondering why on earth he would want to bring the business stuff up now, when they were about to go and party for a few hours and at least try to put on their happy faces and enjoy themselves.

'No... I don't think it can wait. I'm sorry but I need to tell you about this now. I'm thinking about it all the time, I'm grinding my teeth about it at night.'

'Okay... right... so, what's the problem?' Sasha felt her face flush and her heart start to beat a little faster. Her mind snatched at random ideas... was Ben cheating on her? About to leave her? Maybe there was someone else? Their love life had been pretty non-existent lately, but she'd put this down to the stress of the situation.

'Ben?' she asked, and heard the hint of teariness in her voice. 'Okay... well, what is it?'

'Sasha... I haven't told you the full story.'

'Right... okay.' She tried to sound normal, but she suddenly felt hugely nervous.

'When things were looking good,' he went on, 'and we thought we'd get the money from the big housing contract... well, I came across an opportunity...' She heard his voice falter. But she held her breath and waited for him to continue.

'I made an investment in a company that makes sustainable bamboo skis—'

'Sustainable?' She repeated that word, although her brain was actually gunning for the word 'investment'. *Investment* did not sound good... no, it did not sound good at all, investment sounded very expensive.

'Skis made from bamboo,' he said. 'They're amazing, actually, very strong and very light, really flexible.'

'Bamboo skis?' she asked, then with more than a hint of annoyance, she asked, 'But gardeners don't have a great deal of use for skis, though, do they?'

'Well, obviously, I had my skiing head on when I...' He trailed off and at least had the decency to look guilty.

There were about one hundred things that she wanted to say, or make that shout, at him right now. But first of all, she focused on the big one.

'So how much did you invest?' she asked and waited, holding her breath, for the answer. For a fleeting moment, she thought, maybe it's only £50... even if it's £500, we can laugh it off and say, hey, never mind, maybe it will still come good.

But then Ben blew all those thoughts away with the words, 'I've spent £20,000.'

He'd obviously decided to just come out and say it. Not beat around the bush, soften the blow, or explain anything around the circumstances.

For a moment, Sasha's mind reeled... the figure just did not seem to register. She focused on the twenty and tried to blank out all the zeros after. This... on top of all the other money they'd borrowed.

Finally, in a whisper, she was able to repeat, 'Twenty thousand... pounds?'

'Yes.'

'And... and... do we *own* these skis? Do they exist somewhere?'

'Some of them do...'

'*Some* of them?'

'Yes... some of them are in a warehouse in Fulham. But about two-thirds of them haven't been made yet.'

'So, maybe we can explain that you went temporarily insane

and we can ask for some of the money back...?' Oh god, imagine! She pictured a big fat transfer of £20,000 being made into their starved bank account.

'No, we can't get the money back,' he said, sounding understandably glum about it. 'Because I signed a contract and although the company can't make the skis at the moment because they can't get the material, I can't get the money back. I've even spoke to Jason about it.'

Ben's lawyer friend, Jason, had certainly been kept busy lately listening to all their problems.

'So when did you make this *investment*?' Sasha realised her voice sounded a strange mix of trembling, uncertain and withering.

'It was in July.'

'But we didn't have £20,000 then.'

'No.'

'So?'

'I borrowed the money.'

'But we were already up to our armpits by then, so how on earth did you borrow the money?'

And then Ben did a thing she'd never seen him do before. He bowed his head and he looked extremely ashamed and sorry.

'Ben?' she asked, feeling full of dread. Tears were forming at the back of her eyes before he'd even said anything. She didn't want to hear this from him. She didn't want to see him like this. She did not want to be in this position, or anything even close to it. *Weren't things bad enough*? She had thought that maybe there was a hope they could hang on to their family home... but now, another £20,000 in debt, what were the chances of that? A terrible image of the three of them surrounded by packing boxes, about to leave their home, came into her mind.

Sympathy for Ben was competing very closely in her mind with fury.

'It just seemed such a great opportunity,' he tried to explain. 'I thought over the winter, while our business is quiet, I'd go to Switzerland and open a little booth in one of the resorts and do a roaring trade, because people love buying new skis, but they also want to be environmentally friendly and do the right thing.'

'How could you have borrowed so much money without discussing it with me?' she protested. 'How did you even get the loan?'

And then, suddenly, she knew what he was going to say.

'I used that credit card,' he admitted. 'The emergency-only, really high interest rate one, because I thought this would be very short term and I would sell the skis and this would be an amazing boost for us. The idea was to sell the skis for three times what I've bought them for.'

'Oh my god...' Sasha sat down on the edge of the bed.

For a moment, she couldn't think of anything to say. But then she asked, 'How high is the interest rate?'

'I don't know exactly.'

'You don't know? Well, what's the repayment... and where the hell is it coming from?' was her next question, as she realised that she looked at the accounts every day and hadn't seen anything unusual.

'The repayments have been on hold... but I can't keep them on hold any longer.'

Every time Ben opened his mouth, something even worse came out.

'It's going to be about £700 a month,' he admitted.

Once again, she felt as if she couldn't think of anything to say, but then she quietly repeated what she'd heard, just to make sure she'd understood it all correctly. 'So, we're going to be paying £700 a month for some bamboo skis that are either in a warehouse, or haven't been made yet? Ben... that's... that's... that's absolutely insane.'

She closed her eyes and tried to let this sink in.

Finally, she told him, 'I can't think about this right now.' And that was the truth. She felt overwhelmed with anger and sorrow and, quite frankly, rage.

'I just can't think about this right now,' she repeated. 'It's just too much! Absolutely too much to deal with.'

She turned on her heel and stormed out of the room.

12

Downstairs, there was something in progress that could only be described as civilised mayhem. The marquee people had arrived and were bringing tables and chairs into the house as family members tried to direct traffic and decide where everything should go. Meanwhile, the first of the bemused guests had started to arrive.

'Just steer Mama into the kitchen and make her sit down and drink a glass of champagne,' Sasha suggested to Adele, who she met at the bottom of the staircase. 'Tell her it's all under control – it's all going to come together beautifully. Tell her they have to do this at the Queen's garden parties all the time… basically, tell her whatever she needs to hear… and apply champagne.'

'Very good idea,' Adele said and went in search of Delphine.

Then Sasha set to rushing about, directing the flow of tables and chairs and making sure the new set-up across three different rooms was as lovely as it could be.

Sylvie, Beau and Dirk all helped to reposition glasses, vases full of flowers and the cake. Meanwhile, she made her dad stand in the hall and keep guests there, chatting and drinking until the huge game of musical chairs and musical tables had come to a halt.

Despite the enormous shock she had just had, in a funny way, Sasha was almost enjoying trying to put this chaotic party back on track. She was all dressed up, for the first time in months; she was going to see old family friends, other relatives and maybe even try to enjoy herself. More than anything, she needed at least a few hours away from thinking constantly about the very precarious financial situation. But no matter how much fun she might try to have, every now and then, she knew the situation would bubble right up in her mind again. And now this new loan – and a £700 monthly payment – how on earth would they cope?

'Oh, Sasha! You have done such a good job.'

Sasha turned to see her mother, followed by Adele, coming into the dining room.

'Well, it wasn't just me,' Sasha began, 'the marquee people did most of the heavy lifting.'

'I know... but... I think you took charge. I think you've made it much better than it could have been.'

This was all remarkably upbeat for Delphine. Sasha suspected she'd done her wailing and complaining in the kitchen and Adele had just had to suck it up and bolster her mother up enough to come out and try to cope with the new situation.

And the dining room did look pretty. The table and chairs that usually stood here had been pushed right against the back wall to create a sort of buffet area. Then many of the small tables and chairs had been arranged right across the room. The little vases full of flowers and the big arrangements brought in from the marquee had made all the difference, along with putting the dining room's very impressive chandelier on its lowest setting. Then there were battery operated but nevertheless atmospheric candles scattered all around the room.

'So this will be where almost everyone can sit and eat. But we've also changed the library around quite a lot and put more tables in there too. The drawing room will be for meeting and greeting, so it's got a whole flowers-and-candles thing going on too.'

'Pretty impressive for forty minutes' work,' Adele said. 'Maybe you should be doing events as well as gardens.'

Sasha smiled at them both for a moment, quite unaccustomed to this kind of praise from either of them.

'You look so glamorous,' she said, 'both of you.' And this was true.

Delphine's pearl and mint-coloured satin dress was just beautiful, perfect anniversary wear. It was a wonderful nod to wearing a wedding dress and being the star of the show, which Delphine was particularly good at. Her bob was in place, her red lipstick on and glossy gold diamond-studded hoops took the place of the missing chandelier earrings, which Sasha remembered with a lurching feeling that also made her think of the bamboo skis.

She stuck a smile on her face to cover up these stressful thoughts and looked a little more carefully at Adele.

'Love your dress,' she told her older sister. It was a lovely red and black silky, clingy swirl of a thing.

'Thank you.'

'You look so fit,' Sasha added.

'I know... I've taken up mountain biking,' Adele replied. Then, taking a step back from their mother, she silently mouthed 'and sex' to Sasha, whose mind flashed back to walking into the bathroom. *Was Dirk Adele's boyfriend, as well as Sylvie's tutor? Maybe he wasn't even a tutor? Maybe that was purely a cover story.* She'd have to try to find out from Adele in a quieter moment.

'Come on, girls,' Delphine rallied them, 'I can hear more cars arriving and Tony is holding the fort at the front door, welcoming everyone in. It's time to go and help him greet the new arrivals.'

* * *

So, in a swirl of 'hellos' and bright dresses, glasses of champagne and, 'How are you... it's been too long!' the party began to get into full swing. There were so many people from Sasha's past: aunties and uncles, looking older and frailer, cousins, and friends of her parents, who seemed to know every little thing about her.

'So, we heard you'd bought a beautiful new home in south London... and you and the very handsome husband are running a gardening and landscaping business. How wonderful! And I bet business is booming.'

It felt as if this was all anyone wanted to talk about: gardening, landscaping and how well everything must be going.

'How's business going?'

'So, do you do garden design?'

'Have you got regular maintenance contracts? That's where the money is, I'm sure. You want to have it rolling in every month.'

'I heard you'd landed a housing development. Well, that's the big time, isn't it?'

And it just felt so sad to hear all this positive feedback and encouragement. More than anything, she wished it could all be true. She and Ben had worked so hard – they deserved it to be true.

Instead, she had to offer up bland, 'Thank you so much... well, you know, small businesses, we're taking it one step at a time,' kind of statements. And her true feelings, her true anguish at how badly they'd been damaged by a client, were kept hidden.

Even worse was to hear her husband telling white lies about the situation. Whenever they met one another's eye, it was horrible, like being caught red-handed. And if you added one lie, that seemed to propel you down a path of even more.

'Sounds like it's time to expand the business?' some friend of Tony's was telling Ben.

'That's probably a very good idea,' she heard Ben say. 'We've been using freelancers, but it could be time to take on one or two people.'

Then Tony came into earshot.

'I'm very proud of these two,' he told his old golfing buddy. 'Real entrepreneurial spirit. Beau has it too; he's into running bars and property... and obviously Adele has the soar-away career. She's a wealth manager in Switzerland now,' he added with a chortle, beaming with pride. 'Teaching them how to count their gold bars, probably.'

Sasha attempted a chummy giggle, but really, she wanted to run from the room screaming.

How would she and Ben fix this?

How would they get back on track, so that none of what had really happened ever needed to come out? And they could get back to the normality of building their business? All she could think about as she went round the room was what a scorching hot topic of conversation she and Ben would be if news got out that they had gone bust.

All these people busy patting their backs and urging them on would be just as animated talking about how it all went wrong.

'Oh, they flew too high... borrowed too much money... didn't really know what they were doing... made the wrong kind of deal... spent it all when the going was good.'

And oh, lord, if she had to listen to one more conversation about how well the children of her parents' friends were doing, she would burst; genuinely, she had heard enough to last a lifetime.

'You'll remember little Charlie, our youngest?'

And Sasha would recall a small boy with skinny legs in shorts at a birthday party.

'Yes... he's a barrister now... has a beautiful mews house in Kensington... and two children.'

'Oh yes... and how's Lucy?' Sasha asked, flashing back to a shouty squeezer of small guinea pigs.

'She's just sold her start-up business for several million. She's now decided to go into high-end property renovations, revamping country houses for oil barons and that kind of thing.'

What was going on? Did her parents' circle of friends have some sort of secret success sauce that they'd basted onto every single one of their children?

Across the room, she saw the dark head of Beau in a tight knot of friends. Beau had another bottle in his hand. It looked as if he was cracking a joke because the guys around him were laughing and they all seemed to be in a tearing hurry to get out of the room. Standing not far from them, she could see a pale gingery bob and a lovely, familiar face that took her back to a happy time in her life.

She said goodbye to the person she was talking to and headed over to reintroduce herself to Sally Clarke, who she hadn't spoken to for... over a decade, maybe.

'Sally! Hello... remember me? Sasha? I didn't know you were going to be here tonight... how are you doing?'

Sally's face brightened and she looked properly pleased to see Sasha. And Sasha remembered how much she had liked Sally, the mother of an early but still quite serious boyfriend – Finlay Clarke. She'd been with Finlay during turbulent years, when she'd dropped out of uni, couldn't decide on any kind of career path, and been trying to cope with rubbish first jobs and the temptation to just drop out altogether, smoke weed all day and rebel against everything.

Finlay and Sally had been caring and stabilising influences on her and much more of a helpful presence in her life than her disapproving mum and dad. In fact, much to her parents' horror, Sasha had even moved in with Sally, Finlay and his sister, Flo, for about six months.

'Oh, Sasha! Of course I remember you! And you know, I was quite surprised to be invited tonight,' Sally admitted, 'but you know how it is with villages, there's a tipping point and then you have to invite everyone. I came along hoping to see you. It's been such a long time. Come here,' she said, insisting on a hug.

At first, Sasha asked all the questions and listened closely to Sally's news and then, when the turn came for Sally to ask the inevitable, she prepared herself to give answers that were a bit more open than some she'd given so far tonight.

'And how about you? How's it all going?' Sally began. 'First of all, how's your little girl?'

'She's ten now and having an absolute ball tonight! Every time I've seen her, she's been eating, or dancing or grinning,' Sasha said, making a mental note to go and track LouLou down soon.

'And your husband?' Sally asked.

'Ben – he's very well... have you met him?'

'No, so I'll look out for him tonight. The tall, blond skiing instructor, right?' Sally gave Sasha a mischievous smile.

'Yes...'

'And I heard you two are running a gardening and landscaping business now.'

'The way news travels around here!' Sasha said.

'Oh, don't... we are such a bunch of gossips, always discussing other people and other people's children like there is no tomorrow. So how is it going? Lots of ups and downs running your own show, I'm sure.'

Sasha's eyes met Sally's. There was no way that she was lying to this woman, who had shown her such kindness and understanding when she had needed it so much.

'Well,' Sasha said gently, 'I don't mind telling you that it's all a bit touch and go at the moment. But keep your fingers crossed for us and let's not talk about the gloomy stuff when we're at a lovely party and it's so good to meet again after such a long time.'

'Okay, I will keep the fingers crossed and...'

'It's totally between us...' Sasha added in a whisper.

'Of course.'

'So... how is Finlay?' Sasha asked, mentally adding up how many years it had been since she'd seen last seen him.

Sally was looking just slightly beyond Sasha's shoulder and Sasha could sense exactly what she was about to say. Completely involuntarily, all the hairs on the back of Sasha's neck rose up.

'You can ask him yourself,' Sally said, 'he's right behind you.'

13

Finlay Clarke... if Sasha was forced at gunpoint to come up with three highly romantic memories of her time with Finlay, she would probably struggle. But he had been such a nice boyfriend, who had done so very many nice things for her during their time together. He'd introduced her to his favourite music, of course, he'd made her scrambled eggs on toast when she'd come home from work, held her hair when she was sick after too big a night out, and been kind and loyal.

What had split them up had been a growing and understandable restlessness... both had felt too young to settle down and stay together and, in Sasha's case, she was increasingly thinking she didn't want to stay in this corner of Norfolk. She'd wanted to try out what life was like in London.

'Oh my god, Sasha!' were Finlay's words of greeting. He held his arms apart and she accepted a big, warm hug that felt oddly familiar; something that was stored deep in her muscle memory, along with the tread of the stairs at Chadwell Hall.

'Hello, Finlay,' she said, pulling out of the hug and meeting his gaze, 'it's so good to see you.'

'You too.' He was grinning at her and even though, like her, he was approaching forty now, that boyish grin meant his face still looked almost exactly as she remembered it.

'You look just the same!' she said.

'Must be the country air,' he joked, followed by, 'You're looking pretty well-preserved yourself.'

'Oh, thanks… that makes me sound like jam.'

And they both laughed, eyes still following one another closely. Looking for all the little changes on a face they each knew so well.

'So how are you doing?' she asked.

'I'm pretty good, considering. The auction business is going really well. Loads of money, Sasha! So many people wanting to sell so many things. Obviously, the personal life is a bit of a shitshow.'

News travelling the way it did in this part of the world, she had heard who Finlay had settled down with eventually and also that this woman had left him a few years ago. She'd moved back to Poland and taken their two young children with her.

'I was really sorry to hear about—' Sasha said.

'Yeah…' Finlay said quickly, so that she didn't have to finish the sentence, 'but I had broken a few hearts. So maybe it was the karma due to me.'

'Don't say that, Finlay,' she told him gently. 'You were always really kind to me. And it's very sad that your boys can't be in Norfolk.'

'We do go to Poland three or four times a year to see them,' Sally said now, and Sasha quickly stepped back to include her in the group.

'They're lovely, lovely boys and their mum is doing a great job,' Sally added generously.

'I bet you're the best granny,' Sasha said.

'Yes!' Sally said with a smile. 'I am! Best granny ever! Right… I'm off in search of a champagne top-up.'

And she left Sasha and Finlay together once again.

* * *

'Not such a bad little place, this...' Finlay said jokingly, casting his eyes over the huge fireplace, ceiling beams, ornate flowers arrangements and chandeliers.

'You always used to say that,' Sasha remembered.

'I know, what a cheeky prat I was. I hope you've forgiven me.'

'Yes, I have,' she laughed. 'We were young and... kind of... sweet.'

'Yeah... that's a nice way of putting it.'

And then the talk moved on to what they were both doing now and where they were living and how life was going, but that felt on the surface. A way of keeping themselves busy while they took each other in and noticed changes and remembered how it used to be between them.

'So where is your husband? The ski instructor,' Finlay added in something of a silly accent.

'He's not French,' Sasha added, 'he's from *Lundun* and he's lovely.' When he's not *investing in sustainable bloody bamboo skis*, she thought to herself, and out loud added, 'You'll like him.'

Sasha scanned the room but couldn't see the blond head she was looking for.

'Don't know if I will,' Finlay added in something of a low voice. 'He's the one who got the one who got away.'

'Finlay... I don't think that's quite how it was...'

'No,' he admitted, 'but after everything I've been through, I do look back and think that what we had was—'

Then he broke off and gave her such a sad look, such a bittersweet, minor key kind of look that she almost didn't want to hear what word he was going to use, so she finished his sentence with: 'lovely'.

'Yes,' he agreed, 'very lovely. Is there going to be dancing later?'

'I don't know, why?'

'We could have a dance, couldn't we? For old time's sake?'

'Ah...' Sasha was still looking for Ben, but she couldn't see him. Instead, she saw a very anxious-looking Sura. She was holding her daughter, Pica, by one hand and cradling her baby in the other.

'Oh, Sasha!' Sura exclaimed, when she caught sight of Sasha. 'Where is Beau? I can't find him anywhere. Pica's been sick and I need Beau to put her to bed and sit with her. I want to keep some distance between her and the baby. He's very small to have a tummy bug.'

'Oh dear, are you okay, Pica?' Sasha asked.

In fact, Pica didn't look too troubled by the recent vomit and Sasha suspected it might not be a bug, but probably had more to do with handfuls of crisps, sweets, nuts, biscuits and whatever else she and, very likely, LouLou had been scoffing since arriving in the house and turning feral.

'I'll go and find Beau,' Sasha offered and remembered seeing him and his group of friends, bottles in hand, heading out of the room. Maybe it was only when he met up with family, but Beau was always very happy to revert to party animal, teenage mode. He'd probably invited his old gang of friends along tonight – she couldn't imagine that Delphine and Tony had put that bunch of wide boys on their guest list. She remembered what it was like when Beau was a student... and pictured the group of them up on the attic floor of the house, Beau's old haunt, drunk and smoking cigarettes, trying to work out who was the least drunk, so he could get into his bashed up old Ford hatchback and drive to the nearest garage – four miles away – for supplies.

* * *

Fifteen minutes later, Sasha had done a thorough search of the house. She'd found out several interesting things – Marla and the caterers were having something of a panic about ovens not running hot enough, but they promised they could fix it and not to tell Delphine. Sylvie was still promising she was happy to look after LouLou, who was now trying on all her make-up. Adele and Dirk were almost definitely having sex in Adele's bedroom (Sasha hadn't walked in on them, or anything like that, she'd just heard really suspicious sounds when she was passing by). Delphine was holding court in the library with a circle of presumably new friends, who hadn't heard the story before, hanging on to her every word about working as a model for Yves Saint Laurent in the sixties... *it was a weekend, Mother, a weekend.* But Sasha couldn't find Beau and his friends anywhere in the house. So she came to the entirely logical conclusion that they must be outside.

'Oh, for *freak's* sake,' she exclaimed to herself, 'do I now have to go out there into the rain and look for you?' She headed to the back of the house, where all the coats, boots and outdoor wear was kept.

There was a little room beside the back door of the house, which they'd always called by its traditional name, 'the dairy', because pre-fridges, it had been where the cheese, butter and milk had been kept cool, even in the height of a Norfolk summer. She had a dim and unpleasant memory of dead pheasants hanging there, too, when she was much younger and Tony still went on the occasional shoot.

Her heels tapped along the stone-floored corridor until she was inside the small dark room. Now, in the quiet, she wasn't thinking of Beau, she was thinking of the bloody bamboo skis, and an additional £20,000 hole and why? Why? Why on earth hadn't Ben told her anything about this? Why hadn't he consulted with her? Confided in her? Why had he done all of this in secret?

She felt hot and angry and desperately wanted to put her cheek against a cool glass windowpane, but the windows in here were small and a wide stone shelf ran round the room, so she couldn't stand next to a window, even if she wanted to. So she rested her cheek against the plaster wall. She hadn't turned the light on, but as her eyes adjusted to the dimness, she made out the jumble of belongings that had collected in this room over the years. The wall hooks, designed for hanging game, were lumpy with coats, anoraks, hats and scarves. Between the stone legs that held up the shelf, piles of footwear had been allowed to gather – wellington boots, outdoor shoes for winter, outdoor shoes for summer, old slippers, even dog leads and dog toys, although it was over a decade since there had last been a dog in the house. The shelves too were also packed full with jam jars, picnic baskets, garden trugs, tools and even a stack of old LPs and CDs.

She tried to imagine the effort that clearing this stuff out would involve and the memories that would burst out at every turn. The adventures attached to each wellington, the shopping trip for every scarf, the silly dancing in the playroom to every CD. No wonder it went untouched by her mum and dad. Better to leave everything stacked and not let memories – good, bad, sweet and indifferent – flutter up at you if you started to sort through the pile.

She could hear the tread of someone else coming down the corridor. Not the clack-clack of heels, but a softer leather on stone sound. Maybe Ben had come to find her... maybe he'd been looking all over the place for her and this was his final thought.

'Hey, Sasha...'

The voice that followed the opening of the small, square door with the polished and dented brass handle was not the one she'd expected. No. She turned and saw that Finlay was in the doorway.

'I just thought that if you were going outside to look for your brother, you might want company.'

She wasn't quite sure what to make of this, so she made light of it. 'I'm not scared of the dark, you know.'

'Are you okay?' he asked. 'I seem to remember that your family always stressed you out.'

It had been years since she'd last seen him, but his voice was reassuringly familiar, just like his hand on her shoulder... reassuringly familiar.

'Yes, I'm fine,' she said, 'just getting some boots and a coat because it sounds like it's still raining out there. Do you want one?'

'Ummm...'

'Take a coat, honestly. Don't get wet.'

'Okay,' he conceded and she handed him an ancient and stiff waxed jacket.

Then Sasha led the way out of the dairy, out of the back door and into the dim blue of the wet evening. Over the lawns they walked, and down stone steps to the levels of the garden that were further away from the house.

Sasha did look back once over her shoulder at the house. The tall windows were blazing with light as figures passed to and fro in front of them, and it looked like a party in a dream.

There was still no sign of Beau and his friends, so she headed towards the large walled garden where, when she was growing up, there had been raised vegetable beds, banks of lupins and holly-hocks, rose beds, espaliered apple trees and even a greenhouse with a grape vine and tomato plants in the summer.

But now, the area was a large, lumpy green space – not as smooth and cared for as a lawn, but a little more kempt than a field. Dotted about were the plum, pear and apple trees she remembered, but much larger and more wild-looking than in the past.

'How are things with you, really?' Finlay asked as they looked around and tried to see or hear if there was any sign of Beau.

'Not too bad,' was her non-committal answer.

'It's quite hard, this grown-up stuff, isn't it?'

She turned to look at him and nodded.

'I was telling your mum,' Sasha began, 'well, to be honest, I don't want to say too much about it, but our business is having a pretty rough time and I don't know if we're going to make it.' And it did feel like something of a relief to be able to be open.

'I'm really sorry to hear that,' he said. 'It's been a very difficult time. Everyone seems to be dealing with something.'

'I'm really sorry about your boys being in Poland.'

'Yeah... that is definitely not ideal. Oh, look over there – the old potting shed is still standing. We're going to have to poke our heads in there for old time's sake.'

'Are we...?'

The little potting shed, with its earth floor, which had once contained garden forks, spades and deck chairs, was where she and Finlay had kissed for the first time.

'Why not?' he asked.

As they approached the little brick building that jutted out from one corner of the wall, he put his hand lightly on her waist to steer her towards the door, still the same rustic wooden one with a heavy metal latch. She couldn't make it out in this light, but she suspected the door was still painted the same shade of pale green that it had always been.

Sasha lifted the latch, put her hands on the smooth iron door handle and pulled. It was something of a struggle to open the door as it caught and dragged on the long wet tufts of grass. But when it was properly ajar, she stepped inside, Finlay at her back, his hand still on her waist.

The smell caught her by surprise, she'd not smelled this scent for such a long time, but it was so familiar, spinning her in time travel back to her childhood and now, of course, the vivid memory of being in here with Finlay.

It was the smell of engine oil on fresh earth. That smell. She could still catch just the hint of it down on the underground train sometimes. And it made her feel young and vividly alive. This was where she and Finlay had once come to hide from everyone in the house when they were young adults, and kissed each other for hours.

'Oh, my goodness...' she managed, looking into the darkness inside the shed, although she could only make out the vague outline of plant pots and garden tools. She'd thought about Finlay, now and then, in the years since they'd broken up, of course. She'd even met him a few times since then too. But she'd not stood alone with him right here in the potting shed of passion before.

'Well...' She thought she wanted to say something, but then she wasn't sure where to begin. And then she didn't want to say anything that might spoil her memories of their time together in here.

'It smells just the same,' he said, and his voice sounded a little hoarse.

She put her hand on his hand at her waist.

'I have only good memories of... this,' she said and tried to sound light and breezy about it.

'Me too...'

She had turned to face him and now they were standing too close together.

'I missed you for a long time,' he said.

'Yeah... me too.'

His hands were on her back and quite suddenly, with the tang of oily earth in her nostrils, she realised that she could definitely kiss him, because all these powerful memories were being stirred now.

And he definitely looked as if he might want to kiss her.

But... what good would come of that? Sasha asked herself. It didn't matter that her and Ben's business was in trouble, it didn't matter that Ben had made a reckless decision about some stupid bloody sustainable skis, Sasha loved Ben and wanted to sort all this mess out with him. Going on some nostalgic snog-fest with Finlay – who, by the way, was not nearly as sexy as Ben – would only be a terrible mistake.

'Finlay.' Her voice wasn't much above a whisper. 'This probably isn't a good idea.'

'Couldn't we just...?' he began.

She tipped up her face and saw his neck, his chin, his lips just above hers.

'I'm sure you've been very lonely,' she said gently and gave him a hug, putting her head against his shoulder and letting him hold her tightly. But then she let go and fell away from him.

'It's not a good idea,' she said again. 'It wouldn't be fair... and I think we should enjoy remembering how it was... and go back to real life.'

For a moment, he stood there, staring at her, breathing a little more intently than before as the blood subsided for both of them.

'Yes... probably right,' he agreed finally. 'I'm sorry, Sasha...'

'No, really, don't be...'

She and Finlay would most likely have headed back to the house; her to find Sura, Finlay maybe to find another bottle, but they were stopped in their tracks by the sound of laughter from the other side of the high garden wall: loud, excited, whooping laughter.

Sasha went to the little arched doorway on that side of the wall and stepped out into the woodland beyond to see who it was. One of the laughs, she'd thought straightaway, had sounded a lot like Beau's.

One whiff of the distinctive sweet, rubbery smell coming from the same direction as the laughter and she thought it smelled a lot like Beau's younger self too.

'Hello?' Sasha asked.

An explosion of high-pitched laughter followed.

'Where are you?' she wanted to know. In the darkness, she could only see a clump of young trees and couldn't make anyone out.

In a silly sing-song voice, someone replied, 'We're over here...'

This was followed by more laughter.

Sasha and Finlay headed in the direction of the voices, just as two young men in suits stepped out from behind the trees. Sasha recognised them as two of Beau's friends from school, Charlie and Will. As she approached, the whiff of weed and alcohol got even stronger.

'Oh, hello, are we gate crashing your private party?' she asked.

'Something like that,' Will replied. 'I think Beau may have got a little carried away.'

'As usual,' Charlie added.

Their remarks were met by a loud burst of Beau's laughter.

'Where is he?' Sasha asked.

'Right here.' Charlie pointed a bit further back into the woodland.

Sasha stepped towards the trees, glad that she'd thought to change out of her lovely suede heels and into wellies. She could just make out a pair of shoes and a pair of legs lying on the ground. As she approached, she saw Beau, flat on his back in his good suit, a glazed grin over his face.

'Oh, Beau!' She couldn't help laughing.

Both she and her brother had known how to party back in their twenties. Before she'd become a responsible mother with a business to co-run... before he'd become a dad with two bars and a string of properties to look after.

Beau propped himself up on one elbow and gave her one of his charming smiles.

'Hey, Sasha,' he said, 'left the old cronies to come and have some fun with us?'

'I'm supposed to be looking for you,' Sasha told him. 'Sura wants you to help with Pica, and Mum and Dad will soon be missing their golden boy.'

At this, Beau lay back down flat on his back again and gave a long sigh.

'But I'm having such an *unbelievably* good time,' he said, 'and I think you and your friend there should join us. Is that you, Finlay Clarke?' he added. 'Don't think I've ever seen you in a suit before. You look the business.'

'Hello, Beau,' Finlay said.

Sasha saw three of her dad's prized champagne bottles lying empty on the ground beside her brother. Beau and his friends had obviously exited the party with a bottle each, come to the woods to smoke themselves into oblivion and Beau was clearly succeeding.

'Beau, it's Mum and Dad's big party. I think you should probably come back into the house and drink some... coffee... or something,' Sasha said.

This caused a raucous round of laughter, from Beau and also his partners in crime.

'Noooo, Sasha, I think you should come and sit down beside me...' he took off his jacket and put it on the ground at her feet, 'and have just a little puff,' he held out his joint, 'because, I promise, it will help you to enjoy this whole thing so much more. Sit...' he patted his jacket, 'sit beside baby Beau,' he joked.

For a moment, Sasha stood still. Yes, her late teens and twenties had definitely been about working hard and partying hard. She'd had quite her share of alcohol and illicit substances. But all that had changed when she'd met health-conscious, athletic Ben and they'd had their daughter. But there was that tantalising joint and the prospect of taking just a pull or two and letting everything she was so uptight, so stressed and on edge about – the business, the debt, the bamboo-bloody-skis – letting it all go, blur, fade away... even for a few hours. That was a very, very attractive thought. How long had it been since she'd felt totally relaxed, totally chill, totally 'blissed out'? That was the phrase she remembered from the party days... that was always the aim, to be blissed out.

Blissed out.

It was so tempting to try to reach for that feeling... even for an hour or two, hell, she would take even for a moment or two.

'There you go,' Beau said handing her the joint.

'Sasha, is that such a good...?' Finlay began, but too late. Sasha was already sitting down beside Beau and inhaling... once, twice and then a third time.

She closed her eyes and waited for the effect, which didn't take long to arrive. *Woah*... this was like drinking at speed. Things were blurring and melting and spinning slightly.

'Slow down, Sasha,' Beau warned, 'it's probably been years, you need to pace yourself.'

'Like you have?' she retorted. 'Flat on your back, sozzled on weed and champagne!'

Beau took the joint out of her hand and inhaled deeply.

And Sasha, feeling light and floaty and free, lay down beside him on the wet grass.

'Stars,' she said, looking up into the night sky.

'I know,' he replied.

She saw Will offer Finlay a swig from a champagne bottle. As

Finlay took a drink, Sasha called out, 'If you can't beat them, join them, huh?'

'Ha!' Finlay replied.

'This is fun,' Beau said. 'Remember our night out in London? When LouLou was a baby?'

And Sasha was thinking way, way back to her last night out with Beau. It was years ago now, when LouLou had been about six or seven months old, and Sasha had been at peak new mother exhausted.

It was at that moment in her life that her baby brother Beau had arrived on her doorstep, down from Birmingham for a work trip. Beau's work back then was in the nightclub business, so he had a list of the hottest places he was planning to go to, and he thought it was a great idea for Sasha to dig out her long-forgotten dancing clothes and join him.

For the first hour he'd been in her flat, she'd just laughed and listed all the reasons why she couldn't possibly leave her new baby and go out. Meanwhile, Beau had sat quietly on the floor in the centre of the room, picked things up, folded them and found much better ways to put them away.

'You're so creatively neat!' she'd told him.

'I know, tidying up and arranging things is my super-power. You should come and see my new place, I have an open wardrobe and it is so beautiful, like walking into a Ralph Lauren shop. I think it's all those hours I used to follow Irena, our cleaning lady, around. Do you remember? And then think of all that time I spent with Mama arranging her shoes, her earrings, her clothes on the hangers.'

'I think you were probably supposed to be gay,' Sasha remembered telling him.

'Yeah... probably... but the lure of the ladies proved too strong.'

Beau had gone all around her London flat, tidying, folding, putting things beautifully away. Then he had thoroughly vacuumed and dusted. And then he'd gone to Sasha's wardrobe and dragged out the slinky things that she had almost forgotten all about.

'Just one evening off mama duties, surely that's allowed?' he'd asked and looking at those forgotten velvety, sequinned and sparkly things strewn across the bed, Sasha hadn't immediately said no. Sensing the vague possibility that she might say yes, he'd kept at her.

'I won't fit into any of those things,' was Sasha's first objection.

'So, we take these low-slung white jeans... and this drapey pink top and we put this silky bomber jacket on top. C'mon. That is a winning combo right there. What's not to like? Practical, slinky, camouflaging, cosy... I can hold your jacket when you dance... you can put it right back on if you get too cold.'

'So where do you think you'll go tonight?' Sasha had asked and had the feeling, as soon as the words were out of her mouth, that Beau wasn't going to let her back down now.

He was on the guest list for everything that was incredible in London that weekend. He had an expense account for taxis to take him from place to place and he promised her that every single drink would be on him. Then Ben had joined in to persuade her to take the night off, loving the idea of Sasha getting dressed up and going out while he stayed home alone with his baby.

'I can manage,' he'd assured Sasha, 'we'll get the little cup and LouLou can lap up her milk... and that's *if* she even wakes up before you're home.'

So, finally persuaded, Sasha had washed and styled her hair, applied make-up for the first time in months, dressed and given baby LouLou one last feed. Then she'd headed out of the door, into a taxi and just one night of Beau's glamorous life of guest lists, the VIP area, free drinks, celeb spotting and nightclub hopping. Yes, for the first hour or two, Sasha had felt completely out of place, out of fashion and out of her depth and she'd had to message Ben every fifteen minutes to make sure LouLou was okay. But then, as the steady flow of cocktails had begun to take effect, she'd started to enjoy herself. By hour three, she was on the dance floor, by hour four, she was on the dance floor with a crowd of admirers. Hour five was a giddy flash-past of different clubs, different people, and standing up, whooping in the backseat of a convertible car as it sped down Pall Mall. Inevitably, hour six was spent in an extremely fancy nightclub toilet throwing a lot of those cocktails back up, while Beau had soothingly held her hair and told her nice things like, 'I'm so jealous you can be this sick. You are basically going to have no hangover tomorrow. Zero!'

Meanwhile she'd wailed about not being sure if she'd pumped enough breast milk to make sure she didn't make LouLou drunk as well.

The next stop on the nightlife tour had been a very low-key jazz lounge, where Sasha was given restorative chai tea while Beau talked to the manager about his favourite performers. Only in the tiniest hours of the morning did they finally get a taxi home, with Sasha recovered enough to be able to gossip about all the famous people they'd seen.

She still counted it up there as one of the best nights out of her life. And yes, in later years, they had done cool London things as a foursome – her, Ben, Beau and Sura – but small children had made the logistics of everything so much harder. And besides, on that night, when it had been her and Beau out together, it had felt as if they were sharing a slice of the teenage years they'd never actually shared because of their age gap – not that Beau had behaved like a teenager that night. In fact, for the first time, she'd seen her baby brother as the grown-up he'd become and realised how perfect the nightclub business was for him, because he loved to enjoy himself and help other people to have a good time. Plus, for Beau, striking up conversations and talking to people was like breathing air. That night, she'd seen what a success he was likely to be at what he did. And she had forgiven him slightly for being such an annoying brother and their mother's favourite.

* * *

Opening her eyes now and returning to being just a little bit stoned round the back of her parents' garden, Sasha remembered, 'Beau, I came out here because Sura's looking for you. Pica's been sick or something and Sura wants your help.'

'Oh dear...' Beau slurred, 'but she's so capable, Sura. I'm sure she's doing totally fine. We can be here for a bit longer.'

'I don't know if we can,' Sasha said, 'there's a whole party thing going on in there. We probably need to get back to it.'

'Probably,' he agreed and raised his head off the ground, but then obviously thought better of it and let it fall back down again. 'But sometimes... sometimes, you've got to get well and truly arse-holed to cope with it all! Don't you? Well and truly arseholed-hold-ed...' he slurred.

Sasha pulled herself to her feet. She felt good... relaxed, a little woozy, not blissed out exactly, but definitely less freaked out than she had been earlier.

'Okay, we have to get you back to the house,' Sasha told her brother.

'Nah!' Beau protested.

'He's fine,' Charlie added, 'we'll look after him.'

'Totally,' Will agreed.

But Charlie and Will did not have a beloved life partner wondering where on earth they were while she put their pukey toddler to bed and breastfed their new baby. Beau needed to get indoors and sober right up before Sura saw him like this.

'Finlay, can you give me a hand?' Sasha asked. 'We need to get Beau up on his feet and back indoors.'

'No... no... I'm not going to go inside just yet,' Beau protested, 'it's so nice out here and there are so many boring people inside... I just don't know if I can take it! If I go back in there, someone will probably make me play a game of bridge or something.'

But Sasha and Finlay stood at either side of him, got hold of an arm and an armpit and lifted him carefully to his feet.

There was some more protesting, but now that he was on his feet, Beau seemed to go willingly with them towards the house. In fact, as the lighted windows loomed up ahead of them, he even appeared to be sobering up slightly.

But he was also beginning to feel pretty rough.

'Oh my god... why did I go out there with those guys?' Beau asked. 'Why did I agree to smoke *anything*? I feel absolutely terrible. I don't even drink much these days...'

'I don't think you can just blame Will and Charlie,' Sasha reminded him, 'you seemed to be well up for a party.'

'Oh god... do I look presentable?' Beau asked, voice still slurry and still leaning heavily on her and Finlay's shoulders for support.

Sasha dusted some of the earth, grass and other bits from Beau's jacket, but then had to admit, 'Ummm... not really. You might want to get to a bathroom and check yourself over.'

'I feel terrible,' he repeated and shook himself loose of both Sasha and Finlay's grip. Then he meandered in an unsteady line towards the back door of the house.

'Sasha? Is that you? I've been looking everywhere!'

Standing in the dim light at the corner of the house, she could now see Ben. And it felt like a happy relief to see him.

'Ben!' she called out.

'Hi,' he replied as Sasha and Finlay drew closer. 'And who is this you've got with you?'

'Ben, hello... how nice to see you,' Sasha said with a big grin.

'Have you been drinking?' Ben wondered.

'Yes! And it's been amazing. I'd forgotten how much I loved drinking *and* smoking!'

'Smoking?' There was no ignoring the disapproval in Ben's voice.

'Don't worry, not cigarettes,' Sasha said, but that didn't seem to make it any better.

'I'll just go check on Beau,' Finlay said and headed off towards the other door.

'And who was that?' Ben asked.

'That was Finlay,' Sasha said, 'old family friend... used to be my boyfriend.'

'You've been outside drinking and smoking weed with Beau and your old boyfriend?' Ben asked and he didn't sound too amazingly cheerful about it.

No longer in the happy or relaxed place she had been for the past little while, Sasha couldn't resist replying, 'Yes, and I had a great time and... guess what, I didn't spend twenty grand.'

14

Back in the house, all the little tables were packed full of guests, who were now sitting down to delicious-looking plates of food. Sasha realised how hungry she was, but she also realised what a long time had passed since she'd last seen her daughter and the need to make sure LouLou was eating a wholesome plate of food came to the front of her mind. So a quick tour of the house followed before she found LouLou and Sylvie, both in their party dresses, in front of the little TV in the cosy little sitting room, still known as 'the playroom'.

'Hello, are you taking a break from the party?' was how Sasha announced herself.

And then they chatted about food and whether or not LouLou had eaten any.

'I have,' LouLou announced. 'I had fish and potatoes and salad. And I'm leaving some room for Grandma and Grandpa's cake.'

'Good idea,' Sasha agreed. 'How are you, Sylvie?'

'I'm fine... just enjoying some chill time.'

Sylvie was wearing a long, slim column of a dress in palest grey-blue that was beautiful, but somehow it didn't really suit her. It drained the colour from her pale face. But hopefully it had been the dress Sylvie had wanted and Adele had been happy to let her have.

'LouLou can come and hang out with me,' Sasha offered, 'that will let you go and have some fun out there, Sylvie. There are lots of nice people here... I can introduce you to a few friendly faces if that helps.'

'No...' Sylvie said. 'I'm honestly happy here with LouLou. We'll just watch some TV for a bit, then come back out again.'

'Well, if you're sure,' Sasha said.

'I'm sure, honestly. We'll come out in a bit.'

Sasha left the room and felt properly hungry now, she really had to go in search of a plate and the buffet and a comfortable little seat to park herself for the few minutes it would take her to wolf everything down.

Suddenly, she found herself thinking about the overdrafts. What if they properly ran out of money? What would they actually do about food? She tried to imagine having to tell LouLou that there wasn't anything in the fridge and no they couldn't go and buy something. She frantically tried to remember what was in the kitchen cupboards... tins of beans? Pasta? A jar of sauce?

But what would they do?

On a hiding to nothing was one of the phrases that regularly haunted her thoughts.

Robbing Peter to pay Paul was another, as she used one overdraft to pay for the minimum repayments on another credit card. And the interest rates on all these loans were high and accumulating. They were paying too much money in interest every single month. She'd spent hours with a calculator boiling it down. She had rung every company and asked for repayment freezes and smaller monthly repayments... and sometimes it had worked and sometimes she'd felt that she was simply alerting the sharks to the smell of blood.

She was exhausted with the worry of it. She couldn't watch TV shows without thinking how lucky everyone was to have steady jobs and income... even some thriller where someone's life was in danger, she'd find herself musing about his pension benefits and life insurance. All too aware that she and Ben were completely winging it and it could take years to recover from this trauma.

She knew there were solutions, of course there were. Anyone looking from the outside in could see there was obvious solutions: she could get a job, Ben could get a job, and they could sell their flat to clear the debts. All of these things would make the situation much better very quickly.

The problem was, every single one of them required you to spend some money, or spend some time looking at alternatives, or make applications, decisions, effort. Everything required the things they didn't have: time, money, mental clarity, optimism, 'get up and go'. They had burned through all of these things. And now it was not at all obvious how they would get back on their feet.

'Gosh, Pump, you look like you have the whole weight of the world on your shoulders. Have you had any dinner yet?'

In one of the corridors between the playroom and the dining room, Sasha had bumped into her father.

'Just on my way,' Sasha told him, as cheerfully as she could, forcing a smile onto her face.

'Everything okay?' he asked.

'Totally... the party's going so well. Great atmosphere, amazing food.'

'Well, how do you know if you've not had any yet?'

She was never quite sure if questions like this were her father trying to be witty or pointing out that her attempts at compliments were lame.

She left it unanswered.

'Right, must get on,' he said. 'I need to bring another case of red up from the cellar. It's getting drained at a rate of knots.'

And Sasha was on a path to the dining room again, until she reached the hallway and once again saw Sura, baby in one arm, looking frazzled.

Her relief at seeing Sasha was obvious.

'You look as if you need a hand,' were Sasha's opening words.

'Oh, Sasha... Beau's in the room with Pica. But he's not well. I think he's got the stomach bug too. Could you come and see him, please? I just don't know if he's okay.'

Stomach bug... entirely unlikely. Eight solid hours of drinking plus some very unwise drug-taking decisions... highly likely.

'Yes, sure...' Sasha said and was once again diverted from the groaning buffet table, which she could just catch sight of through the ajar dining room door.

Upstairs, in Adele's old bedroom, which had been given over to Beau and family, Beau was sprawled across the double bed, face down, groaning. Meanwhile, a very perky looking Pica was sitting in the little armchair in the corner of the room playing a game on an iPad.

'Pica, you should be in your bed,' Sura said, pointing to the little camp bed that had been set up.

'But I'm not tired and I want to go to the party,' came the determined response.

Sasha went to the bed to take a look at her brother. His face looked pale and sweaty with that tinge of green around the mouth that did not bode well.

'Beau,' she ventured, 'do you need some water?'

'No...' he mumbled. 'Fine.'

'He does not look good,' Sura said, looking anxiously at her husband.

Where did Beau manage to find all these endlessly supportive and caring women? First, of course, had been Delphine, for whom nothing that Beau did or wanted was ever too much trouble.

Looking back, his big sisters had indulged him just as much. 'He's just little.' 'He can have that, it won't do any harm.' 'Just let him do that.' It didn't help that if you ever didn't give Beau, or for that matter Delphine, exactly what they wanted, there was likely to be a tantrum.

Sasha felt a little conflicted about it all – on the one hand, there were so many times growing up when she'd thought: this isn't fair, why can't I have that amount of fussing too? But also, being left on the sidelines had cultivated her fiercely independent streak. She was still determined to sort things out for herself, without her family.

Sura was exactly in the mould of the over-caring, over-protective women who had taken on the looking after and nurturing of Beau. Although, as Sura now had two little children, Sasha could only imagine that caring for Beau was probably getting a little old. Probably Sura was about ready for Beau to start caring both for himself and for them.

'Sura,' Sasha began, deciding that maybe a bit of the truth might be helpful here, 'Beau has had way too much to drink. That's what's wrong here. He's probably going to be sick quite soon and he might feel a lot better afterwards.'

Just as Sura pulled an astonished face and shook her head sadly, as if to say how could Sasha even think such a thing about the amazing Beau, the man in question suddenly picked himself up and, at quite an astonishing pace, flung himself at the door of the adjoining bathroom.

They watched as he made the five steps to the toilet bowl at record pace, dropped to his knees and began to vomit hard.

'He's so ill,' Sura said, looking alarmed.

'He's drunk,' Sasha countered, 'give him some water and let him sleep it off. Shall I take Pica to find LouLou? She probably won't want to watch this.'

'No, she'd better not watch,' Sura said and was at least starting to look slightly more annoyed than worried.

'Hey, Pica, would you like to have something else to eat?' Sasha asked the little girl, who was now jumping up out of the armchair, ready to find LouLou. 'Because I don't know about you, but I am starving!'

But once again, just as Sasha got within sight of the dining room and its wonderful plates piled high with all kinds of delicious-looking things, she was stopped in her tracks.

'There you are,' Tony announced with relief. 'Could I ask you to round up the family and then... everyone else, really? The food's all done and dusted, and Delphine and I are getting set for the speeches and the cake.'

Just as Sasha was about to protest that it couldn't possibly be time for the speeches, the caterers wheeled past a heavy trolley loaded with cups, plates, and the coffee urns.

'Good grief, chop, chop,' Tony urged them. 'Can't have coffee without cake... can't cut the cake until the speeches are done.'

Was that right? Sasha wondered. It wasn't a wedding; it was a wedding anniversary... was anyone going to mind about the order of cake or speeches? Would anyone really want to hear speeches, was her next thought... but probably not a good idea to air that right now.

With Pica still holding her hand, Sasha went from room to room and found Ben and Adele and got them to round up further guests to the dining room, where cake and speeches were to happen. She also found Sylvie and LouLou and was a little disappointed when Pica wanted to transfer her hand grip from Auntie Sasha to cousin LouLou.

Then, as everyone began to make their way to the dining room, she decided that she would go back up to Beau and Sura and see if Beau might now be in some kind of state to come down and listen, at least briefly.

She went up the stairs and knocked on the bedroom door. It took a moment, but then there was an urgent, 'Yes, come in!'

Sasha could tell immediately that things had gone wrong when she saw Sura looking wildly round the room, as if for help.

'What's up? Is everything okay?'

'No! No! It's not okay at all. I closed the door to the bathroom so I wouldn't have to listen to him doing all that vomiting... I can't stand the sound! I can't stand the smell. But now, listen! All I can hear is water running... I can't open the door because I think he's fallen against it and he's not answering!'

Sasha went to the door and listened to the unmistakable sound of a tap running at full volume.

She tried the door. It wasn't locked, but she couldn't budge it by even a centimetre.

'Beau!' she called.

There was no reply.

'Oh my god!' Sura cried. 'He's passed out. What if he inhales his sick? What if there's a flood in there and he's lying on the floor? He'll drown!'

15

Sasha put all the effort she could into pushing against the door, but it didn't move.

'Beau!'

'Beau!'

Both she and Sura were shouting in unison, which caused baby Dokus to wake up with a startled cry.

And still the gushing tap sound.

'Okay... just hold tight, hold tight,' she tried to reassure Sura. 'I'm going to go and get some help.'

She raced down the stairs and into a dining room packed with Tony and Delphine's guests. Tony and Delphine were standing together beside the cake; Tony's arm was around Delphine as she beamed up into his face. For just a second, Sasha saw that look and couldn't help thinking how special it was that, after all these years, her mother clearly still adored her dad. But then she scanned the room for the blond head that she needed right now.

'Now, where are my children?' Tony began, scanning the room himself. 'Adele? Oh, yes, I can see you. Sasha?' Tony cast around.

'Back here,' Sasha said. 'Look... umm...' Good grief, this was so embarrassing. In front of all these people, she had to say, 'Can you just hold fire for a few minutes? I'm going to need Ben and we're just going to get Beau.'

'What?' Tony sounded his very own mix of affable and appalled. 'Where the hell has he got to?'

'Slight problem with a bathroom lock...' was the best that Sasha could come up with under the circumstances.

Ben had turned his head in her direction and read the 'Please! Now!' expression on her face, so he made his way quickly over.

'Well... let me tell my lovely friends here how Delphine and I met. The children have heard it all before, so I daresay it won't matter if they miss the intro... bloody kids,' he added and that earned him a laugh.

'What's up?' Ben asked as he and Sasha headed out of the dining room.

'You won't believe this – Beau is stuck in the bathroom, passed out cold and the tap is jammed on.'

'Jeeesus. I'll get up there now. Do you think you can find a toolbox?'

'I think so...'

So Ben headed upstairs, while Sasha rushed towards the kitchen because she suspected the toolbox was still under the sink, where it had always been kept in the past.

Should she turn off the water in the house? Would she even know how to? No... surely Ben was going to manage to get the tap turned off once he'd got into the bathroom.

* * *

By the time Sasha was back up in Adele's old bedroom, with the toolbox in her hands, the panic seemed to have upped to a higher level. Ben had managed to open the door by a few centimetres, but this only afforded a view of the floor, which was completely under water. The sink tap was still gushing, and Beau was wedged firmly behind the door out of sight. It would not have been an exaggeration to describe Sura as pretty het up.

'Beau! Beau! Are you okay?' she cried, while jiggling the crying baby in her arms.

Ben was knocking loudly on the door at the level he was hoping Beau's head would be at. 'Beau!' he was saying loudly. 'I need you to move forwards so I can open the door.'

Sasha put the toolbox down at Ben's side.

'I don't want to have to take the door off its hinges,' Ben said, with remarkable calmness, 'because that is going to take ages. Look at all those layers of paint on top of the screws. I could be there for an hour.'

'Come on, Beau,' he said with another loud volley of knocks on the door. 'Move forwards! We need you to move away from the door, okay?' he said in that calm, authoritative way Sasha remembered from his lessons on the slopes that could still make her feel slightly weak at the knees. 'Just nudge over so we can get in.'

There was something of a groan from Beau and the sound of movement, so Ben kept up his pressure on the door.

'Come on, Beau,' Ben encouraged him, 'just a bit further along.'

There was another groan and, sensing the opportunity, Ben gave the door a hefty push. A good bit of movement was achieved this time and the door opened to almost thirty centimetres or so.

'That's good,' Ben said. 'Sasha, do you think there's any chance, if I keep pushing, that you can wiggle in there?'

'Bloody hell,' was Sasha's response to this, but she took off the lovely suede shoes, bought when the developer contract was signed, her racing thoughts just *had to* remind her, and then she started to try to get into the room. She wriggled and struggled as Ben pushed hard at the door.

She squashed one shoulder, one boob, one hip and a leg through and paused for a moment, halfway, aware that if Beau moved heavily back against the door, she would be stuck and it might also hurt quite a lot. Also, her foot was now in cold, wet water and that water was escaping out onto the bedroom carpet. There was nothing for it but to heave in her other boob and hip, scraping and scratching herself and her dress as she did it, through the narrow opening.

And then she was in the room. Beau was slumped in a sitting position on the waterlogged floor between the bath and the door, water pooling around his legs, his trousers soaked, his head resting on his chest, his eyes closed, vomit all down the front of his white shirt. But he was flushed pink and breathing. Alongside her annoyance, she also felt strangely protective of him. It was so strange to see him all boyish and helpless one again – this adult Beau, who usually drove around in swanky cars and couldn't help telling you how well he was doing. This thirty-two-year-old Beau, who she usually found it a bit hard to be around. There he was in a puddle of water and sick, desperately needing some care and attention.

Before going to help sort him out, she had to first of all turn off the tap. She sloshed through the water to the sink, which was completely blocked with vomit. Chunks of it were swirling in the water and in the water on the floor too, she saw as she turned the tap.

Back to Beau she went. She wiped his face with the corner of a towel and wiggled him forward so that Sura could also get into the room along with Ben, who quickly started to heap towels onto the floor to try and soak up some of the water.

'Which room are we above?' was Ben's urgent question as he

and Sura tried to lift Beau onto his feet and Sasha's attempt to mop up just resulted in the towels becoming completely sodden as the surprisingly deep water still sloshed around.

Sasha knew immediately that they were directly above the dining room.

'Oh, dear god... more towels,' she said, opening a small cupboard where she suspected more would be stored. She hauled them out and threw them randomly across the bathroom floor, trying to soak up the flood.

It was a lot of water on the bathroom floor of an old and fragile house.

'We're going to need more towels... and a mop, bucket, maybe some cups to bail... I think I'd better go and get supplies,' Sasha said, stepping across the room towards the door.

She hurried downstairs and on her way to the kitchen, had to just peek into the dining room to see what was happening.

Tony was standing up, Delphine at his side, holding forth before a rapt audience of friends. Sasha wasn't looking at her father, though. Her eyes were immediately drawn to the pale brown stain on the ceiling, currently the size of a small puddle. Galvanised, she headed to the kitchen for the supplies she needed.

Sasha had hardly made it back to the bathroom when she could hear the roar of her father's voice from the other side of the door.

'What the bloody hell is going on up here? There's water dripping from the ceiling onto the bloody cake of all things!'

Tony flung open the bathroom door and his eyebrows shot right up into his forehead at the sight of the small catastrophe.

'What on bloody earth?' he gasped. 'What is going on? And what the hell is wrong with Beau?'

'Beau is drunk,' was Ben's simple explanation.

'He's ill!' Sura exclaimed.

'He's blocked the sink with sick, left the tap on, collapsed against the door and this is the situation,' was Sasha's addition. Being on her hands and knees on the floor, mopping, with her father looking on in a fury was making her feel about eight years old. She suspected that an enormous telling off was about to rain down on everyone's heads and, really, this was only Beau's fault and, even then, it was an accident.

Glancing at her ice-cool husband, she realised she loved that, unlike her volatile dad, Ben hardly ever got angry and only when it was completely justified.

'What the bloody hell were you thinking?' Tony shouted. 'Of all the nights... I can't believe what I'm seeing...'

He was getting more violently red by the moment.

Sasha looked at Ben and hoped that somehow he could come up with a way of sparing them all from any further ranting from her dad.

'Tony,' Ben began, in a tone of absolute calm, 'if you could send up some buckets, mops and more towels, that would be extremely helpful. We're doing the absolute best we can to clean this up as quickly as possible.'

With a disgusted expression, Tony turned and stormed off.

'That was brilliant,' Sasha told her husband, who gave her a just-between-us wink.

Sura had managed to get Beau out of the bathroom, but she needed Ben to come and help her take off his wet and stained clothes.

'No cake and speeches for you, my friend,' Ben said and couldn't help adding, 'and I don't envy you tomorrow's hangover, either.'

Beau just groaned as they steered him over to the bed.

Sura went to the cot and put the crying Dokus down, her face completely furious.

Although Sasha was in the bathroom mopping, she could still

hear Sura's rant. 'Look at the state of you! Do you think I've got the time, let alone the energy, to deal with you like this? I should be asleep! You should be asleep! The children will wake us up at 3 a.m. and 5 a.m.!'

At this point, Ben, minus his shoes and socks and with his trousers rolled up, came quietly back into the bathroom to help with the mop-up. He didn't say anything to Sasha, just gave her a look that said, 'You can hardly blame her.'

'And don't think you're going to loll around in bed all day tomorrow with a hangover while I do everything,' Sura went on, 'you total tosser...'

Unfortunately, Tony was then back, with another mop and bucket, plus an armful of towels.

'You're not soaking it up quickly enough!' were his opening words to them. 'It's still dripping out of the ceiling and you know how fragile the plaster is in this house.'

At these words, there came the sound of somewhat alarmed cries from downstairs.

'Oh my god, I need to get down there!' Tony exclaimed. 'These are ancient lathe and plaster ceilings. Once one piece goes, the whole lot can come down. We need to get people out.'

Sasha made the decision to go too. In her wet bare feet, she suspected she could get down the stairs at pace, quicker than her father. So she raced out of the bathroom, overtook him and hurried down the stairs two at a time. The memory of that staircase and how to run down it was completely ingrained. One hand on the banister, racing down the curves, then sharp left into the dining room at the bottom.

* * *

The room was crowded, and all eyes were raised upwards to what was now a hole in the white plaster, leaking a substantial trickle of water onto the floor. The cake, its top layer soggy and ruined, had been pulled out of the way, but the water was splashing up onto it from the carpet and no one was going to enjoy another mouthful of that no-doubt-heavenly gateau.

Beside the cake stood Delphine. Her eyes were fixed on the ceiling and there was a look on her face again of extreme upset. Sasha didn't want to use that sexist 'hysteria' word, but Delphine was standing there, definitely on the brink of a meltdown.

'Hello everyone, okay, let's just move out of the room, please,' Sasha commandeered, 'just to be on the totally safe side.'

The crowd dispersed quickly out of the dining room, into the hallway and then on into the other rooms. There was animated and polite chatter, with everyone being very 'let's get on with things and not spoil the party'.

Sasha wove through the people heading out of the room to get to her mother's side.

'Come on,' she said, putting her arm round Delphine and almost tearing her away from the scene. 'The leak has been sorted and they're mopping like mad upstairs. Once it's cleaned up and this has dried out, it really won't be so bad, I promise.'

Delphine accepted the arm round her shoulder and the gentle steer out of the room.

'I love this house,' Delphine whispered to her. 'I love it so much. I never want to leave it.' Delphine's eyes were full of tears and her voice was trembling. 'This house has made England bearable for me. This house and Tony, otherwise I would never have stayed. Please don't make me leave it.'

'Mama, it's okay,' Sasha soothed, 'no one's going to make you leave.'

'Yes,' she exclaimed, 'your father. I've seen the estate agent brochures. He's thinking about selling... maybe he wants us to move to a bungalow in the town.'

'What?' Sasha stopped in her tracks. She'd never once heard talk of her parents selling up. This was a completely unexpected shock.

With a dramatic toss of her head, Delphine declared, 'Over my dead body.'

16

_____

After the ceiling drama, the ruined cake and the interrupted speeches, it was difficult to keep the party spirit alight. Rain was still drumming down heavily and guests, worried about waterlogged roads and tricky journeys home, began to leave.

Within forty minutes or so of the dining room evacuation, most of the big public rooms in Chadwell were empty, apart from the drawing room where Tony and Delphine had asked their children to join them for a nightcap.

'I suspect that might mean one final lecture before bed,' Sasha told Ben.

'Do you want me to come along too?' he offered.

'Yes, please.'

'What about me?' LouLou asked, although she was already face down on her bed, party dress still on.

'No, honey, you get into your pyjamas and we'll be up really soon... I hope,' Ben told her.

The drawing room had a post-party air. The surfaces were cluttered with used champagne glasses, smudged with lipstick and fingerprints; small bowls with just the last few broken crisps and little silver trays with one lone vol-au-vent, two curled up canapés, or a wedge of squeezed-out lemon. Sasha even spotted some mashed-up crisps in the velvety rug. The fire was burning low, and the hearth was full of ash.

Delphine was seated on the beautiful antique chaise longue, which coordinated perfectly with her dress, and she looked as though she had been crying. Meanwhile, Tony was still completely wound up and agitated. And sure enough, once all of his three children were in the room, he started ranting at them indiscriminately.

'My god... I've never seen such a fiasco! Get stark, staring drunk on my £80-a-bottle champagne, why don't you, Beau? Completely flood my bathroom? Bring down a great chunk of my ceiling?

'And as for the rest of you, rushing about like completely headless chickens, frightening off every single guest, who might have otherwise had the sense to stay! I've never seen anything like it. And let's talk about the cake, shall we? That cake alone that your mother had put so much effort into – finding the right baker, deciding on the flavours, and the fillings, and the colour of the sodding icing! The whole thing was completely and utterly ruined. I don't think more than five people got a slice and I certainly wasn't one of them.

'What an absolute fiasco!' he said. 'What a total farce from beginning to end. Good god! Why do I bother? Why do I even bother to organise these things? Putting in all the time and the effort? And let's not even get started on the money. Did you even want to come? Hmmmmmm? Any of you? Well, did you? Adele spent most of the party in her room with her daughter's tutor, who's obviously her new boyfriend.'

'Dad!' Adele protested, but the blush on her face suggested their dad may have guessed correctly.

'Well, he's only about two decades too young for you,' he added.

Before anyone could even react to this insult, on he went with,

'And then Sasha – the rebel – was out in the garden with that oaf Finlay, god knows why...'

'We were looking for Beau, thanks very much!' Sasha broke in, wanting to put her foot firmly down on this rant-athon.

But Tony carried on regardless. 'And as for Beau. He was so sorry to be here, he had to go out into the back garden and get so completely wrecked – no doubt on my vintage Pol Roger – that he brought down the dining room bloody ceiling. So, thank you very much, my beloved children. Thank you for being so supportive.'

For a moment or two, there was a stunned silence.

Oh, for god's sake... Sasha couldn't help thinking: *are we really going to let our dad just shout at us like this? We're grown-ups. Surely we get a say, don't we?*

The rebel? She frowned at the thought. Her parents only believed she was 'the rebel' because she had never agreed with them half as often as Adele and Beau had... or at least had pretended to.

Still silence... okay, she was going to have to say something. Maybe her brother and sister expected her to... maybe she was supposed to be the fall guy.

'Steady on, Dad,' she began, trying to keep her voice calm and level, thinking of how she always admired Ben when he held it together. 'We're all here. We all came. And there were hours of the party that were really lovely... despite the rain and despite having to move it in from the marquee. Accidents happen... bathrooms flood and that's life. There's no need to completely lose your cool and start tearing into us all. That's just upsetting.'

Her dad looked at her, gave something of a sigh and an eye-roll, as if to say, 'What does she know about anything?' then turned to Beau.

Beau, sitting at the far end of the sofa from Ben, who probably wished he was anywhere but here in the middle of his family-in-law's row, was already in his pyjamas. He was hanging his head and looked pale, washed out, still pretty green and rather sorry for himself.

'What's the matter with you, Beau? Forgotten how to hold your drink?' their dad asked bitterly.

'Well, Dad, I think you know exactly what's the matter with me,' Beau said, slowly raising up his face to look his father in the eye.

Delphine also looked up and as if she was ready to jump to her son's defence.

'Oh yes, I forgot, unfortunately, business isn't going too well, so you've had to run to Mum and Dad for a cash top-up,' Tony went on in a harsh tone that mixed both anger and disappointment.

Sasha's eyes went from Beau to her father to Ben and back again. This was surprising news... Ben's business wasn't going well? Despite the brand-new car? And he'd had to ask their parents for money? But before she could even really digest this, along came the next revelation.

'But unfortunately, Mum and Dad could only help a bit because they weren't very liquid, were they?' was Beau's acid reply. 'Because they'd already given most of their cash to the golden girl.'

Sasha suspected she had made an audible gasp at this even more startling piece of news.

Glancing over, she saw Adele tensing visibly, then she glanced back at Ben, who was now looking just as astonished as Sasha most likely did.

'That was an investment, Beau,' Tony said, his tone now steely. 'Adele gives financial advice. That's her job.'

'Yes, but so far the investment has been terrible, hasn't it?' Beau went on. 'That's why there's hardly any money left and Chadwell will probably have to be sold and Mama's heart will be broken.'

Sasha felt as if she was having a weird out-of-body experience. *What was going on? No, seriously, what was going on? Was this honestly happening? At Chadwell? In the drawing room?* Had her dad honestly just admitted that he'd given all his money to Adele to invest? And she'd lost it? And Beau needed money too? And Chadwell would have to be sold? *What was going on?*

Her sense of her family... her sense of the family home as something that would always be there... everything was suddenly rocking beneath her feet and feeling far less certain.

Her parents not having money... her parents lending to Beau... trusting Adele... having to sell up... she was having a hard time trying to keep up with all this information.

'What on earth is the point in keeping this place if not one of you is interested in running it?' their father asked harshly. 'Not one of you has made enough of your lives to be able to afford to run it.'

Having delivered those words, he sat down and faced them all, as if daring them to challenge him.

For several moments, again no one said anything... maybe Adele and Beau were too humiliated to make any kind of answer, while Sasha was too stunned. But then, finally, she was once again the one who broke the silence. She wanted to make sure she had heard and understood the current situation, everything, correctly.

'So, Beau... you've had to borrow some money from Mum and Dad?' she asked her brother.

When he nodded, she asked, 'How much?'

'Fifty thousand,' he said simply.

'Right...' She tried to keep her voice steady, when in fact, she felt shocked. That was a lot of money... couldn't he just have not bought his Range Rover?

'And, if no one minds me asking, how much did Adele invest for Mum and Dad?'

After Adele and their father seemed to exchange glances and a nod, Adele replied in a formal and expressionless voice, 'Three hundred and fifty thousand.'

Although Sasha might have wanted to say, 'How freaking much?' she instead went with a much more level, 'And how much is the investment worth now?'

Again, Adele's reply was strangely neutral. 'Currently about £120,000.'

'Oh my god,' Sasha heard herself reply because she still could not believe this was all happening. 'Oh my god,' she repeated.

The first wave of shock was quickly being replaced by a wave of anger.

'Why hasn't anyone said anything about this?' was her next question.

When this was met with silence, she realised that most likely, they'd all been discussing these issues for weeks, maybe even months, but not with her.

'Okay... so obviously what I should have asked was, why did no one think to mention any of this to me? I mean it's quite a big deal, surely, deciding to make a major loan to one child and deciding to invest most of your money with another.' She directed this at her parents. 'Didn't you think I might have been a useful sounding board, at least?'

There was a long and brooding pause.

Then her dad made everything so much worse by saying, 'Well, but you're Pump... what do you know about investing...? Or the property business?'

Sasha felt a fresh and much bigger wave of anger. It was in her chest, in her throat, in her head.

Why was her family always like this?

How did they always manage to upset her so much?

She looked at the door. It would just take a moment or so and she could be across the room and out of the door. She could leave without saying anything else. She could swallow the situation, as she had done when her father had refused to lend her and Ben anything at all to start their venture up, and as she had done in the past after so many arguments and difficult conversations before. Then she would be left to deal with her complicated feelings about her complicated family alone – and she could try to ignore the feelings; she could bottle them up, parcel them up and try to bury them in some corner of her mind; she could numb them by drinking a bit too much, bingeing on treats... or all the other ways in which she'd tried to cope with these difficult family feelings in the past.

Or...

What had Ben said in the car? When she felt like doing one thing, maybe she should try to do the opposite.

So... maybe this time... maybe right now, she should try to tell them how they made her feel. She should put her feelings out there on the table and let them cope with her for a change, instead of her always trying to cope with them.

She stood up.

'What's up, Pump?' Beau asked. 'Do you need a handout too? Unfortunately, it doesn't look like there's any left.'

'Whoa.' It was Ben who made the first response to this. 'Easy, Beau, these are very personal topics.'

Usually Sasha would walk away, she knew that. But she was too upset, too angry, too worn out with her own problems, too fed up with her family's problems and too bloody hungry as well. She'd not had one single mouthful of food since a smoked salmon canapé at two o'clock, for goodness' sake!

'I'm really, really angry,' she began, trying hard not to cry. 'I'm really angry that you've not told me about any of this. You've not asked for my opinion, you've not valued my opinion. Yes, sorry I'm not a wealth manager, or a hotshot bar owner and property developer. But I still have an opinion... But don't bother asking me what I think because I'm just Pump. What am I supposed to know? And for god's sake, I'm thirty-eight years old. You just can't call me

Pumpkin any more. You can't, I'm not allowing you to. You have to call me Sasha.'

Then turning to her parents, she said, 'Adele is Daddy's girl, Beau is Mummy's boy, neither of them can ever do any wrong in your eyes. Well, you know what? I'm completely fed up with feeling like the spare part. And yes, Ben and I have worked really, really hard at our business. But, very *unluckily*, we're not going to get paid for the work we've been doing pretty much all year, so we've got a really difficult time ahead.

'And the worst part is... I didn't even want to tell you that, because I didn't expect to get any support from you at all – not financially and not emotionally. I thought you'd just judge me, judge us, as not as good, or as incredibly smart as you all think you are.'

Struggling to keep control of her voice, she added, 'I really need a break. I need a break from you all. I think you've been unbelievably rude to me.'

Then, shaking with anger, Sasha finally let herself run out of the room and away from them.

17

Somehow, it wasn't enough to run upstairs to the bedroom. So instead, she ran to the back of the house, found the coat and boots she'd worn earlier and then let herself outside into the darkness.

Yes, it was cool, damp and calming, and she felt her breathing and her heart rate return towards some kind of normal again, but it was also still pouring with rain, so after just a few minutes, she had to turn and head back to the house. As she made her way through the downstairs hallway, she listened out, hoping not to meet anyone on her way up to the bedroom. If she did, she decided she would just blank them and walk straight past.

Lights were still on, but she didn't meet anyone and couldn't hear any talking as she passed the big reception rooms. Sasha went as quietly as she could through the hall and up the stairs, taking them two at a time. Then left and along the corridor and into the bedroom that she, Ben and LouLou were using.

It was such a relief to close the door behind her, not having run into anyone, and to see Ben checking on a sleeping LouLou in the little bed set out for her in the corner of the room.

'Oh, hello, Sash,' he whispered. 'I'm so glad you're back... I was about to go and look for you.'

'Thank you,' she whispered back.

'That was... very painful,' he admitted. 'I left pretty much straight after you and thought you'd have come up here. I think everyone else went their separate ways not long afterwards.'

'I still can't believe everything we've heard.' Sasha kept her voice low, but felt a fresh wave of anger washing over her. 'All that money to Adele... and two-thirds of it has just gone! I still can't believe it... and £50,000 to Beau. I hope there's some chance that he can pay it back.'

She tried to understand what was upsetting her the most. There right at the top was the old, nagging feeling of being excluded, of unfairness – the feeling of being second best. Her family had given her all those feelings for so long now, it was almost how she expected to feel and not just when she was with them. These feelings probably coloured much of her everyday life: the feeling that she wasn't ever quite good enough.

'Are you okay?' Ben asked and put his arm around her.

Usually this would feel supportive and so reassuring. But tonight, her heart was bruised and broken and Ben, her beloved Ben, he'd let her down too, she remembered with a horrible lurching feeling.

'I'm so angry about the bloody bamboo skis too, absolutely bloody furious. Bamboo freaking skis!' she was shouting, but still in a whisper, so that their daughter couldn't hear her.

'I thought it was going to be such a good idea,' Ben whispered back.

'If it was such a bloody good idea, why didn't you tell me all about it? Why didn't you want to share everything about it?'

This whisper-shouting was killing her throat. *How did stage actors keep it up?*

'It's always been *our* business and we've done everything, made all the big decisions together. So, what possessed you?' she demanded. 'And who is the owner of the bamboo ski company, by the way?' she asked and suddenly had quite a horrible feeling about what Ben might say.

Sure enough, he looked away, he looked embarrassed and then in an even lower whisper he added, 'Scarlett Smith.'

'Scarlett Smith? And who the hell is *she*?'

'She's someone I met... an excellent skier, who has a company making bamboo skis.'

Dear god... if Sasha was going to make up someone for Ben to have an affair with, she would be an excellent skier, with a sustainable ski company, called Scarlett... was this some sort of cosmic joke?

'So do you have anything else to confess to me about Scarlett Smith, apart from the fact you've given her £20,000 of *our* money?' was Sasha's next question.

'Not really...' was Ben's reply after a telling pause.

'Not *really*? Right. Well... this is rapidly shaping up into one of the shittiest days of my life to date.'

'Sasha, I am on your side,' Ben said emphatically.

'It doesn't feel like that right now. And I don't even want to talk about this!' she declared, completely stressed out.

But she couldn't go back out into the house in case she ran into a relative, so there was only one place she could retreat to – the bathroom.

'I'm having a bath,' she announced and began to go all around the room gathering up her toiletries. But when she pulled open the bathroom door, the lights were on and once again, she was confronted with a stark-naked Dirk.

And once again, he felt it was okay to turn to her and let her know he wouldn't be long.

'No problem,' she mumbled and backed a hasty retreat.

What was the matter with that man? Didn't he know about bathroom locks? Didn't he care about privacy – at least other people's, if not his own?

'Dirk...' she explained as she sat down on the bed again. 'Whenever I try to go in, he's already in there, completely bollock naked.'

'It's a Swiss thing,' Ben said, 'they're very comfortable in their skins.'

'I'm still unbelievably angry with you,' Sasha said, 'but I'm too tired to argue any more. And too drained... I didn't get one mouthful of that lovely dinner or the sodding cake... make that, the sodden cake.'

'What?' Ben sounded genuinely shocked. 'That's terrible.'

'Don't you dare suggest that's why I'm so angry.'

'No, of course not. Look...' He sounded so warm and sympathetic, she couldn't help looking up and meeting his eyes. 'I'll go down there, heap up a plateful of leftovers and bring it up to you.'

'Good grief, we should be down there helping to start the massive clean-up. We should all be helping.'

'No, *you* definitely shouldn't go down there. There's been quite enough drama for one day. And anyway, Delphine said the caterers are back first thing tomorrow to look after the clean-up,' Ben said. 'So, shall I go and get you some food?'

'No, I've completely lost my appetite with this entire fiasco. I don't want their food. I really feel I've had it, with all of them!' Sasha said. She felt weird and shaky. Her hands were trembling. 'God, I'm so angry, Ben, with you and with them. I'm so angry, I can't even have a good cry! I just want to get packed up right now and get out of here first thing.'

18

When the alarm went off at 7.30 the next morning, Sasha totally regretted setting it. She felt as if the bleeping noise was dragging her up from the bottom of the seabed. Her head was throbbing and now as she took in her surroundings, the memories of last night all came flooding back. Yes, that row with her family had really happened. And all of those painful revelations had been made. And, yes, they had said all of those hurtful things to one another. And now, despite her throbbing head, she just wanted to leave.

Ben's very groggy voice came over to her from the other side of the bed. 'What time is it? It can't possibly be time to get up.'

'It's 7.30,' she replied. And after all the booze, emotion and drama of last night, it did feel ridiculously early. Even LouLou, who was usually such a reliable alarm clock, wasn't up yet.

'Could we just stay in bed a bit longer?' Ben pleaded. 'I'm sure not one other soul will be up yet.'

'No.' Sasha was firm, and already pushing her corner of the duvet away. 'We're getting out of here before anyone else is up and about. I just want to get away and as quickly as possible.'

So they got up and washed and dressed. Then they woke

LouLou and explained to her that they had to be back in London for work, because something unexpected had come up, so they were going to sneak out of the house and not wake anyone up.

LouLou was predictably very grumpy about this. She wanted to stay and see her cousins again. She wanted to at least say goodbye to her grandma. She definitely wasn't going to leave the house without breakfast. That was just child cruelty, she informed her harassed parents.

'We'll stop on the road and get a nice breakfast,' Sasha promised rashly, without much of an idea about where that would be.

But this did at least seem to buy her some cooperation from her daughter, who put on her clothes and brushed her hair without complaining any further.

'Okay, have we got everything?' Sasha asked, scanning the room once again carefully.

When both Ben and LouLou nodded, and Sasha had made a last check under the beds, they picked up their bags and all filed out of the door.

'Quiet, remember,' Sasha whispered to LouLou, 'we don't want to wake anyone.'

There was no one in the upstairs corridor and when they got to the top of the staircase, there was no one there either, so down they went. As Ben headed for the front door, Sasha said in a whisper, 'We'll go out of the back door. It makes less noise and it's closer to the car.'

Unfortunately, just as they got to the door of the kitchen, it was obvious that both the lights and the radio were on. Sasha tried to hold LouLou back but her daughter, excited to see someone else before they left, burst through the door to see who it was.

'Grandpa!' she announced. 'Mummy said everyone was still asleep, but you're up. Can I have some toast?'

'Hello, LouLou, of course you can have some toast.'

When Sasha heard her dad's voice sounding so warm and kind to her daughter, she almost relented... at least a little.

But then he ruined it by adding, 'And where is your very irritating mother?'

'She's here,' LouLou said, 'and she's not irritating, and we were going to leave without waking anyone because she says we have to get back to London early because of their work.'

'Oh, you do, do you? Well, 7.30 on a Sunday morning is pretty early to have to leave for work reasons.' This was obviously being said for Sasha to hear, so she and Ben followed LouLou into the kitchen.

'Good morning,' her dad said, in a completely frosty tone. 'Well, that was quite an end to the night.'

'Dad...' Sasha warned. 'I don't think we should kick it all off again.'

'Well, did you honestly think it was a good idea to bring everyone's dirty laundry out into public and give it a jolly good airing?'

Sasha couldn't believe what she was hearing.

'I think you were the one who provoked that,' she said, defending herself before he started to re-write the entire situation.

'Round and round the room,' he went on, as if he hadn't heard her, 'dragging all the painful stuff from everyone. Getting everyone more and more upset. Is that what you wanted? I mean, don't you think Adele and Beau feel ghastly enough about what's happened?'

'Dad, that's not how it—'

'And your poor mother, she's so upset about everything – she keeps trying not to think about it all. And you have to go and remind her.'

What was her dad doing? Did he honestly not remember how the conversation had gone? How he had got furious with his children first? How on earth was it now her fault? Why was he trying to make her out to be the problem here?

Maybe just so he didn't have to blame Adele and their mother didn't have to blame Beau... that was certainly how it seemed to Sasha.

'Dad,' she began firmly, 'if you're not going to listen to me, then I'm not going to remind you how the conversation actually went. You stick with your version if that makes you happy. We're going to leave now.'

And Sasha somehow, clutching her bag, stumbling through the familiar stone-floored corridor, made it to the back door where she turned the large metal key in the lock and got out, LouLou pathetically calling out, 'But what about my toast?'

Over the wide gravelled courtyard at the back of the house they crunched, Sasha's head whirling. She wondered if she wanted her father to come after them, but then she decided that she didn't want that. It would make everything much more complicated. What would he say? What could he say? And she would have to walk away from him again.

But then she felt very angry that he didn't come after, not just her, but after them. Did he really want her to do this? Walk away in a fury? Taking Ben and LouLou with her?

As they bundled their bags into the back of the car, then got into their seats, she caught Ben's eye.

He didn't say the words out loud, but she caught the meaning of his look: 'Are you sure?' he seemed to be asking her. 'This could be difficult to repair...'

She nodded. So they buckled their seatbelts and Ben started the engine.

He reversed the car, turned it and they began to drive away.

'What a bunch of absolute... *imbeciles*,' Sasha said, managing to restrain herself from using the worst words because of LouLou.

'Who is?' LouLou asked from the backseat.

Sasha didn't answer, just stared out of the window at the oh-so familiar driveway, the familiar trees and anticipated the familiar bends in the road.

'Let's just get out of here,' she said through gritted teeth and eyes that were beginning to feel blurry.

The tight corners of the very narrow road that led on from Chadwell's driveway were opening a little now and they were on to the wider, tarred, but still single-laned road that would carry them to the next, bigger road. Ben was taking it just a little faster than he would usually, but she didn't say anything. It felt like a relief to put distance between them and Chadwell. Her anger felt perfectly expressed in the speed.

He swung the steering wheel hard right into the next bend and for a moment she couldn't understand what she was looking at. Then her brain processed, and she saw a wall of red earth, coming far too fast, filling the entire windscreen. She screamed at the top of her voice and instinctively turned and put her arms out to somehow protect her baby. Ben was standing on the brake, shouting with fear, and in a horrific chaos of screeching, shattering, smoke, bang, ricochet and an awful crumpling sound, they crashed into the road blockage.

For a moment, there was a red-black, eyes-shut, utter panic and then, when Sasha dared to open her eyes again, she saw white – a white, fluttering, smoking cloud.

She was aware that someone was saying in a very high-pitched voice 'ohmygodohmygodohmygod...' over and over again. And when the highest pitch of her panic had subsided, she realised it was her, and she was still here in the car seat but in a cloud of white dust. She immediately craned her head and was overwhelmed with relief and happiness to see LouLou. There she was, strapped firmly into her chair in the middle of the back seat, looking pale, looking shaken, but also looking untouched and totally fine.

And also there, breathing, right beside her, covered in the white powder that she was working out now was from a burst airbag, was Ben.

'We're all okay,' she said in a whisper.

'Yes, I think so.'

'We're really all okay?'

'LouLou,' Ben asked, turning round to his daughter, 'how are you doing, darling?'

'Okay,' said LouLou.

'Does anything hurt? Anything at all?' Sasha asked.

'No,' LouLou said, quite decidedly. 'Nothing hurts. But why is it snowing inside the car?' And then she let out a little giggle.

Sasha wanted to laugh along with that giggle. But instead, she found herself bursting into tears.

'It's okay, Sasha... it's okay... oh, bloody hell, we've been so lucky,' Ben's voice broke through her crying.

'Mummy? Are you okay?' LouLou asked.

And Sasha nodded and, after a moment or two, tried to stop her tears by blowing her nose.

'Without airbags... or ABS brakes... it doesn't bear thinking about,' Ben said, unfastening his seat belt and gingerly trying the door. It opened, but groaned on its hinges.

'Out of alignment,' Ben said, which struck Sasha as a reassuringly blokey thing to say. Yes, no doubt the door was slightly 'out of alignment', having just pounded at speed into an enormous... what exactly? Sasha got out of the car slowly, registering her shaking legs, and opened the door at the back so she could unbuckle LouLou and give her the big hug they both needed.

Together, the three of them took in the scene. The car was totalled, no doubt about that. The bonnet was completely wrecked, the wheels were at an angle, the windscreen shattered but still in place. They had run into a landslide, a huge mound of red Norfolk soil at least two metres high that had slipped down from the steep banking at the side of the road, maybe loosened by the heavy rainstorm last night. The road was completely blocked.

'We've been so lucky,' Ben said again. He put his arm around Sasha, who had her arm around LouLou and for a moment or two, they stood there and Sasha really did count her blessings. Unlucky things had happened to them lately; imagine if this had been more dreadful luck. Imagine if one of them had been killed or injured in this crash... as Ben had said, it didn't bear thinking about.

Giving the side of the mound a hard pat to try to establish its solidity, Ben decided that he would take a little scramble up and see how wide the landslide was.

'Please be careful,' Sasha instructed as he kicked a foothold into the earth and stepped up. She realised that she felt shaky and strange with shock. Her hands were numb, her knees actually trembling, and she thought she might quite like to be sick. But she tried to hold onto LouLou and breathe her way through it.

'Good grief,' Ben said when his head was above the edge of the mound, 'it's really bad – five or six metres wide. They'll have to bring diggers in to shift this.'

'So what are we going to do now?' Sasha asked once Ben had scrambled down again.

Ben let out a deep sigh escape.

'What are we going to do now?' he echoed Sasha. 'I'm just trying to keep up with events. Okay... well, first of all, we're going to phone the police to report a huge landslide and the fact that we've crashed our car into it,' Ben said. 'Then we're going to phone the insurance company that, I suspect, you will have on your phone under "car insurance" and you'll have updated it to the company that's given you the best deal at the last renewal, because that is how good you are at admin.'

Correct, she thought and gave him a smile. It was probably a very good sign that her husband's sense of humour did not appear to have been damaged in the crash.

'And then,' Ben went on, but cautiously, 'we're going to have to walk back to Chadwell... tell them what's happened and... wait it out for a bit, I suppose.'

'Oh no,' Sasha began. 'I'm not going back there! Not after everything that's happened! Not after everything I've said. I can't go back to them, Ben.'

'So what do we do instead?' he asked.

'Well... we wait for the diggers,' she suggested. 'And maybe they can clear us a path through it and then we can walk out and... hitch a lift and... get away like that.'

It sounded pretty improbable, even as she said it.

'Mummy, that could be ages,' LouLou pointed out, 'and what if one of us needs the toilet?'

But Sasha had to get away from here. That was exactly what she wanted to do. Get away from her family at Chadwell.

'Well...' Ben ran his hand through his hair, which meant he was exasperated and didn't know what to say. 'Let me ring the police, anyway. That's the first thing we have to do and that makes sense.'

So Ben looked up the number for the local station and began the call.

'Do you know the names of any of the roads?' he asked.

Sasha was just about to reply when she heard the unmistakable drone of an engine... another car was approaching.

'Oh no!' she shouted and, pushing LouLou deftly to the side of the road with a firm 'stay there', she ran along the verge with her arms waving, to try to create some kind of warning. But as she rounded the corner, she could see that she was offering far too little and too late. Her dad, in his Audi, was approaching at a speed that was going to make...

There was an abrupt braking sound and then not exactly a bang... more of a scraping, crunching, crumpling sound as the Audi smacked straight into the back of their car.

19

'Dad!'

'Tony!' Ben exclaimed, wrapping up his call to the police with, 'Make that two cars... I've got to go.'

Sasha was the first to get to her father's side.

He looked a little shaken, but otherwise fine.

'Good god!' was his first reaction. 'Why didn't you move your car?'

'Are you okay?' Sasha decided it was more important to ask that than to answer her dad's question. 'You haven't hurt your head or your neck?'

By now, her father had stepped out of his car. He rather comically looked himself up and down and replied, 'I certainly seem to be okay, which is more than can be said for my car.'

Then he looked at Sasha and Ben's vehicle, and beyond it to the enormous dump of red soil across the road.

'Good god,' he said again, and for a moment gaped in astonishment at the landslide, as he tried to take it all in. Then he went to the front of his car, where there was some minor bumper damage;

after this, he walked calmly around their car, perhaps to gather his thoughts as well as to examine the full extent of the crash damage.

'Good grief, it's absolutely wrecked. Are you all okay?' he asked. 'What about LouLou?' As Sasha saw the genuine concern pass across his face as he registered what a horrible experience they'd just been through and with their daughter on board, she could feel her anger at him subsiding just a little.

'We're fine,' Sasha assured him, 'but it's been a very big shock.'

'Have you told the police about this?' Tony asked next and as Ben said that he had, Tony pulled out his ancient mobile and said that he would get onto a local councillor friend to report it and find out when the road could be cleared.

'Well, maybe you should put your suitcases into my boot and we'll try and get my car to limp back to the house with us.'

As LouLou gave an excited cheer at this news, Sasha looked at Ben uneasily. The one thing she did not want to be doing right now – well, aside from dealing with a written-off car, overdrawn bank accounts and a failing business, obviously – was to go back to Chadwell.

'It's completely, 100 per cent up to you,' Ben said quietly.

But what else could they do? Sit here beside the car wreck until a digger arrived?

'God knows how long they'll take to clear the road,' Tony added, 'might not be able to get anything started today, knowing the coun-cil... it is Sunday, after all. And you'll have to get another car organ-ised by the insurance company... what an utter disaster. Right, let's see what we can get into the back here.'

He opened the boot of his car and Ben transferred their bags.

Sasha quickly got in to the back seat beside her daughter, leaving Ben to sit in the front with her dad. She was not in the mood for the 'let's all pretend we didn't have an argument' small talk. The prospect of being forced to spend more hours in her fami-

ly's company was making her feel extremely tense. As the car trav-
elled along the road and the thick hedge came into sight, she tried
to plan how she would handle it – would she go and hide in her
bedroom? Stay silent? Carry on as if nothing had happened? Or
maybe re-start the argument? What was the correct etiquette for
being forced back into the bosom of your family after you'd
stormed out?

The weird thing was how normal her dad was being over there
in the front seat. Going on about the landslide and the state of the
embankments and so much heavy rain these days.

And now they were pulling up at Chadwell Hall... and getting out
their bags... and walking reluctantly back to the house with LouLou
rushing to the door ahead of them, openly delighted with this
change of plan.

In the corridor between the back door and the kitchen, Sasha
could smell coffee and toast and now that she was feeling a little
less shaken, both of those things seemed like a very good idea. She
pushed open the door gingerly, wondering who she would find at
the table. First of all, she set eyes on Dirk, who was, mercifully,
dressed in a crisp white shirt and jeans.

'Hi,' she said simply.

Then the very rough and groggy voice of her brother asked, 'Is
that Pump?'

'Actually, it's Sasha,' she said, getting as much indignation into
the words as she could.

As she came into the kitchen properly, she saw Beau at the
table, looking like a very pale-green vision of death. His dark
stubble and inky flop of hair only served to make him look even
paler and more ill.

'How are you doing?' she couldn't help asking, despite her promise to herself that she would not pretend that nothing had happened.

Beau rested his head on one hand and half-heartedly sank a spoon into a plateful of leftover pavlova. 'Completely dreadful,' he admitted, 'serves me right... trying to party like I'm twenty-five.'

He put the spoonful of pavlova in his mouth and the expression on his face told her that he wasn't sure if that had been a good idea or not.

'Would you like a cup of coffee, Sasha?' Dirk asked. 'And how about you, Ben? And maybe a slice of toast, yes?' he added in his very clipped and precise English.

And because it was Dirk asking, and not a family member, Sasha felt she could say yes without betraying her cause.

The coffee mug, a worn blue-and-white striped mug that had been doing duty in this kitchen for years, was put into her hands as she sat down. She took a sip and contemplated Beau's sickly face. At least she wasn't feeling as bad as him – that was some consolation.

'So, there's been a landslide,' Ben began, 'about two miles away on whatever that road is called...'

'A landslide?' Dirk repeated.

'Yes... and we've crashed our car into it. Completely totalled it. So, until a digger can come out and the insurance can give us another vehicle, we're stuck here... and, unless you can book a helicopter, you're probably all stuck here too.'

'What?' from Dirk.

'You're joking,' from Beau.

'They're not,' from Tony.

'But I've got to be at the bar tonight,' Beau said, 'staff meeting.'

'Better organise a Zoom link,' said Ben.

'Bloody hell.' Beau sank the spoon back into the pavlova.

At this point, Sura came into the kitchen, holding the baby and with Pica clinging to her hand. She looked even more tired than Beau.

When Dirk asked if she would like some coffee, Sura looked at him blankly as if she'd forgotten what coffee was, she was so beyond receiving any help from it.

Beau briefly and very gloomily brought her up to speed about the whole stuck/landslide situation. Once again, she looked as if she was struggling to register this.

'You know,' Sasha began, full of sympathy for these exhausted new parents, 'since we're all stuck here and can't get back to London, why don't Ben and I look after Pica and... Dokus,' she said the name uncertainly, 'and let you both get some sleep? You really look like you could do with it, and we'll be fine. If there's any problem, we'll just come and get you.'

And that was when Adele came into the kitchen and pretty quickly caught up with what was happening. She pulled a very silky dressing gown more tightly around her, took a seat at the table and seemed to take a moment or two to process before asking, 'So the road is completely blocked?'

'Totally,' Ben confirmed, 'first by a landslide and second by our crashed car.'

'God, I'm really sorry,' she said. 'I'm sure you don't need a wrecked car, right now... not that anyone ever needs a wrecked car,' she added. 'So *no one* can go *anywhere*, until someone comes and digs the road out? And that's going to be the council, most likely?'

Now it was Tony who chimed in. 'I've been on the phone to my friend, Frank, you'll remember him, been on the council for years. He says there's flooding and all kinds of problems all over the county. He doesn't think there's any hope of sending a digger over this way until Tuesday.'

'*Tuesday*! That's ridiculous!' Adele was the first to say it, but it summed up everyone's feelings.

'Well... Frank thought Tuesday was being optimistic,' Tony added.

'Oh, for crying out loud,' Adele added, 'so we're all stuck here together, glowering at each other while trying to get a phone signal?'

Sasha stared down into her coffee cup, it would be fair to say that her first attempt at getting everything off her chest and out into the open had completely backfired. Yes, next time, she'd probably stick with keeping everything bottled up and repressed in the Griffon tradition.

'What about food?' Beau wondered.

'No need to worry about that,' said Ben. 'I'm guessing there's a small mountain of profiteroles to get through, plus vol-au-vents, biscuits and cheese, not to mention three tiers of a very damp cake.'

20

Sasha found her mother in the dining room, sitting calmly at one of the small tables set out there for the party, drinking her usual morning cup of black coffee and tall glass of warm water with a squeezed quarter of lemon. She swore this was the secret to her exceptionally good health. Lemon was detoxifying, while black coffee contained antioxidants and kept one 'regular', she claimed. Like many a Frenchwoman, Delphine was a stickler for proper meals, and religiously sat down to eat her lunch and dinner contemplatively over several small courses. Dumping all the food onto one large plate was a no-no for Delphine, who would remark, 'Comme les fermiers,' whenever she saw this.

The dining room looked understandably rumpled after last night. There was a tea-coloured stain on the ceiling and the hole left by the missing chunk of plaster in the centre. There were abandoned glasses, balled-up napkins and empty dessert plates on most of the tables across the room. The sideboard against the wall was still strewn with empty wine bottles, diminished platters of biscuits and cheese and crystal bowls still half-full of desserts.

Delphine looked up and when she saw Sasha coming into the room, she said, 'I heard you leaving this morning, without even saying goodbye. Who leaves their parents' house without saying goodbye?'

If she had wanted to answer completely truthfully, Sasha would have said, 'Someone who has had a huge row with their family because they've been undermining and undervaluing that person for years... especially around money.'

But instead, she went with the more tactful, 'I didn't want to start another argument, so I thought it was better to leave and take some time to think about... everything.'

Delphine rolled her eyes and added, 'And now you can't leave because of a landslide. Tony has already told me. I always thought there was a danger something like this would happen. In fact, I even told—'

But Sasha was in no mood to listen to another story about how her mother could have saved the day if only people had paid attention to her.

'Yes, I'm sure,' she interrupted, then added, 'The caterers won't be able to come in, so I'm going to start the clean-up along with Adele. We've sent Sura and Beau back to bed because they both look exhausted. LouLou is playing with Pica and Dokus is in the kitchen, asleep in his pram.'

'Oh yes, Beau and Sura both look ill, they're so tired. I'll take care of this food over here,' Delphine said, gesturing to the buffet table. 'I'll need to find room for it all in the fridge and the freezers. You girls can take care of the dishes. Make sure you put the dishwasher on the short cycle. Then it will clean more loads more quickly.'

Her mother downed the rest of her coffee, then left the room with one of the platters of profiteroles in her hands.

As Sasha began to gather up the remaining plates and pieces of cutlery and stack them together, Adele came into the dining room. She was carrying a large tray that she set down on one of the tables, then she began to collect glasses to put onto it.

At first the sisters worked around one another, not saying much. Sasha suspected that Adele had something of a hangover, and she wasn't particularly used to it. There was also a lot of upset hanging in the air between them.

Finally, Adele broke the silence with a terse, 'Well, this is not exactly a very happy family get-together, is it?'

'Not after last night, no,' Sasha replied.

Adele didn't make any response to this, so Sasha finally had to ask, 'Why do you always leave me out?'

'Did it have anything to do with you?' Adele asked sharply. 'Me handling Mum and Dad's investments, Beau taking a loan from them – what did either of those things have to do with you?'

There was of course truth to this, Sasha had to admit. What did it have to do with her? But she couldn't help feeling that in loving, close-knit families, surely these things would be discussed between family members? And wouldn't that foster more openness and warmth, instead of all this secrecy and tension?

'You always, all of you, make me feel left out,' Sasha countered, 'like my opinion never matters.'

'You're the one who was always so scathing about my "boring" career. I've worked really hard to get where I am today,' Adele snapped.

This cut Sasha to the core.

'Running a business takes a lot of hard work too,' she fired back, 'and there's no holiday pay, no pension plan, no perks, no job security. We've had very bad luck. It doesn't make us bad people who are bad at what we do. And, by the way, when we were starting up, we asked Dad for a really small loan and he wouldn't give it to us. Didn't trust us. But no problem giving £50,000 to Beau and letting you make a big chunk of their money disappear.'

The words were spilling from Sasha faster than she wanted. Her heart was racing, hands shaking, and she knew she had gone too far.

Adele set her tray down and turned to face Sasha. 'That money has not disappeared!' she said furiously. 'I've invested it for them. And yes, that investment has plummeted in value, but it may still come good. It might just take some time. And to be honest, I hope this makes them face up to the fact that none of us wants to live in this place and they're getting too old to live here. I mean, it's enormous and how will they manage to keep it up?' She pointed to the hole in the ceiling. 'It's literally falling down around them.'

'There's a reason for that mess,' Sasha reminded her. But it was true, she realised with a lurch, she had never really thought about her parents leaving Chadwell... but she had also never thought about how it would feel to be an old person rattling about in this place... or, shudder at the thought, a single old person. She'd never wanted to think about the loss of the family home and now here was Adele pointing out what was clearly obvious. It was far too big for them and, although it was comfortable, it really needed something of a renovation and she doubted that either of her parents could be bothered with the hassle of that, let alone the expense.

But then what about the enormous bother and hassle of packing up, paring down and moving? Could her parents face that? Looking around just at this dining room, Sasha's eyes fell on all kinds of items – paintings, candlesticks, silver sauce boats, crystal vases – that she knew Delphine absolutely treasured. The concept of 'downsizing' would be extremely difficult for her mother to grasp.

'What about the heirloom earrings?' Sasha asked her sister. 'Would they not help? They're supposed to be worth £150,000.'

'Of course they would help,' Adele replied, and Sasha noted that Adele was talking much less angrily now and it did feel as if she wanted to move on from the argument. 'We all know they're incredibly valuable, but where are they? Mama is sure she locked them away in her usual drawer, just as she always did. She's never wavered in that version of events. So what's happened? Can they honestly be lost? Or has someone who knew exactly where they were, taken them? Or... has she already sold them?' Adele asked, her voice dropping. 'Maybe to give the money to a certain favourite son?'

'Is that what you think?' Sasha asked, feeling that uncomfortable mix of emotion that talk of Delphine's favouritism always brought on... anger, jealousy, frustration and even resignation too – this situation would never change, so what was the point in even thinking about it?

'Beau had asked them for a bigger loan,' Adele explained. 'He needed £100,000 to get a property finished and ready to sell. But they could only give him £50,000 because they'd let me look after... invest...' she corrected herself, 'the rest.'

'I see,' was all the response Sasha made.

At this point, Ben came into the room with another big tray and for a time there was no more talk, just a concerted clearing-up effort that moved from the dining room and out into the hallway, then into the other rooms.

All the while, Sasha couldn't help thinking about what Adele had said. Her mother would, of course, have wanted to help Beau, but really... would she go through so much drama and deception for the sake of her son? Insisting she couldn't find the earrings... convincing everyone that they must be lost? On balance, Sasha came to the decision that perhaps Delphine would. But would Beau have let her go through all this?

But then, when the desserts, plates, cutlery and glasses had all been cleared away, the floors vacuumed or mopped and the dishwasher switched on with yet another load, Delphine took Sasha completely by surprise by seeking her out and telling her that once again, she would like Sasha's help to search for the lost earrings.

21

'This is the locked drawer,' Delphine once again pointed to the small drawer in her antique dressing table, 'where I always keep the earrings.'

'Yes, I know, Mama. You showed this to me yesterday, and it was empty. Where do you keep the key?' Sasha wondered.

'The key is very small, and I keep it here.'

To Sasha's surprise, her mother held up her left wrist with the thick gold charm bracelet that she usually wore on it. Sure enough, Delphine was now pointing to a small brass key that dangled from one of the links.

'Oh, I didn't know that,' Sasha said.

'No!' Delphine said, then after a moment of thought, she added, 'I believe only Tony knows about this key... and, of course, Beau.' She flashed an indulgent smile.

Of course, Beau... no surprise there. Sasha thought about Adele's theory that the earrings had already been sold for him.

'Mama, is it worth us looking for these earrings?' Sasha asked, fixing her gaze directly on Delphine's.

'What do you mean?' Delphine asked, eyes widening. 'The earrings are very valuable and of huge sentimental value too.'

'Yes, I know they are... but what I want to understand is, are they really lost?' Sasha asked gently, putting her hand over her mother's. 'Or do you, in fact, know what's happened to them?'

'What do you mean?' Delphine repeated.

'Mama... no one would blame you for wanting to help... have you already sold them? Maybe to give the money to Beau?'

'Sasha!' Her mother's face clouded over. 'Is there no end to the trouble you want to make? The earrings are lost! No one has sold them, certainly not me. And no one has taken them. There is no sign that anyone has forced the lock or anything like that. I'm the one who must be to blame. I've forgotten to put them back into the drawer. I must have put them somewhere else! And I don't know why I can't remember!'

This time, Sasha heard the sincere upset in her mother's voice and was convinced that she certainly believed the earrings were lost. So, once again, she helped her mother search the bedroom, even more thoroughly this time. They opened drawers and emptied them out onto the bed; they searched carefully through all the jewellery, real, costume and otherwise; they brought boxes out from under the bed and the bottom of the wardrobe and checked the contents carefully.

Both Delphine and Sasha were a little overwhelmed with all the stuff that they managed to unearth. Sasha couldn't help assessing it as she was searching. From the posh hats to the leather handbags, the thick cashmere sweaters to the tweed jackets and satin skirts, from the gold chains to the alligator-strapped watches... everything was absolutely top quality. Sasha had always known her mother to be a consistent and expert shopper, but she hadn't realised just how much one person could accumulate in their lifetime. And she thought of the racks packed with coats, jackets, shoes and boots at both the front and back doors of the house, not to mention the drawers and cupboards and sideboards groaning full of stuff in every other bedroom, sitting room, dining room and kitchen. This was a house that had every single thing that you could possibly want. There were silver and mahogany wine bottle holders to grace the dining room table. There were initialled silver fruit knives and cake forks. There were paintings on every wall and antique vases in every alcove. There was a library, begun when Sasha's grandfather owned the house, with floor-to-ceiling shelves packed full of hardback, often leather-bound books.

'You do realise that you have a fortune's worth of stuff inside this house?' she asked Delphine. 'If you gathered the jewellery, your best handbags, silverware, cutlery, the oldest books, the best paintings and all those kind of things together and sold them, you'd probably make tens of thousands of pounds – enough to make any repairs and redecorations and even the senior adjustments that you might need. Have you ever thought about that?'

Delphine looked down at the neatly stacked piles of sweaters and the row of designer handbags. She put her small hand, with its deep red nails and familiar decoration of gold, diamond and pearl rings onto the nearest of the handbags.

'Senior adjustments!' Delphine said, with a roll of her eyes. 'I can still get out of my bath, and up the stairs, thank you very much. And I love my things. I need my things,' she added, 'these are the signs of a civilised life. A life well lived.'

A life well spent... Sasha couldn't help thinking to herself.

'Chadwell Hall needs its things too,' Delphine insisted, 'imagine the library without any books, or the walls without the paintings, or not being able to set the dining room table properly.'

'But does anyone really need a silver and mahogany wine bottle holder, though?' Sasha couldn't help herself from asking.

Delphine's look suggested that anyone who didn't need a silver and mahogany wine bottle holder still had a lot to learn about life. Then she said indignantly, 'Those were a wedding present from your father's cousin, Florence. They've been part of the household for forty years and I'm now supposed to flog them off at the auction house, am I? Also, you have no experience of auction houses…'

Sasha might have added that she actually did have a pretty good idea how to run a successful sale on eBay, Etsy and various other sites, and she was once pretty close with Finlay, who was a partner in the local auction house, so he would certainly look after any sale of Chadwell items, but instead she let Delphine continue, 'They take 15 per cent of everything plus VAT on top. I heard all about it from Joan. It is absolute daylight robbery! She sold some of her furniture when they moved from their lovely farmhouse to that pokey little bungalow on the edge of the village. And another thing, my physio told me that as soon as older people stop going up and down stairs many times a day, their muscle tone just disappears, withers on the bone. So, no, I know you mean well, Sasha, but there will be no fire sale here at Chadwell.'

'So what do you plan to do?' Sasha asked her mother, feeling a prickle of anger. 'Because houses don't repair themselves and it is a very big place for you and Dad to live on your own.'

In response to this, Delphine gave a truly gallic shrug and tossed her sparkling hands up into the air.

'Something will turn up. And I think it will be the earrings. We just need to keep looking.'

'We've looked everywhere in here… is it worth having a look in Dad's bedroom?' was Sasha's next suggestion.

Her mother looked non-committal and merely said, 'Well… if you think it might help.'

'Do you ever use the wardrobe in that room?' Sasha wondered. 'Is there any chance you could have put the earrings there?'

'I suppose sometimes... there's one cupboard where I store out of season things.'

* * *

When they went into Tony's room, Sasha was surprised to find Ben there, squatting down on the floor in front of the big bay window with Chadwell's ancient old toolbox beside him.

'Hello, what are you doing here?' she asked her husband, 'I thought you were on Dokus duty?'

'No... Sylvie and LouLou have taken charge, so I'm doing stuff,' was Ben's cheerful reply.

'What kind of stuff?'

'I thought I'd better make myself useful,' Ben said, glancing up from the task he was attending to at the bottom of the window, 'so I've basically asked Tony for a list of all the small jobs that need to be done around the house... I mean, there's always something to be done in every house.'

Delphine came over to look at the draught-proofing tape that Ben was carefully reapplying to the old wooden sash window.

'And what is this?' she asked.

'Tony said that a draught comes absolutely whistling in from this window, across the room and straight into the side of his neck when he's lying in bed. He said if I only sort one thing out in the house, this should be it. Apparently, nothing else annoys him as much as this. But first things first, I noticed that two of your electrical sockets were pretty much hanging off the wall downstairs, so I put them on properly. That was a bit of a priority.'

'Oh, how clever of you, Ben,' Delphine said, as she came closer to examine the work on the window. 'I knew the sockets needed work, but I hate to call out the electrician because he charges so much money and he never comes... he's always on holiday in Barbados.'

This made Ben laugh. 'Maybe I should retrain,' he added.

'And how much insulation tape do you have? Would you be able to fix the draught on my bedroom windows too?'

'Once I've finished this one, I'll go into your room and see what I can do,' Ben promised.

'How clever!' Delphine repeated. 'I didn't realise what a practical man you were, Ben. I mean... if I sat down and thought about it, I could probably come up with a list of jobs as long as your arm. I could probably keep you busy here for days on end.'

'You're very welcome to keep me busy,' Ben said generously.

'How very lucky you are to have a practical husband,' Delphine said, turning to her daughter. Sasha smiled – yes, Ben was practical, loving, kind, generous and uncomplicated. She thought that maybe her parents were beginning to understand all the good things about Ben, but she was still a long way from forgiving, let alone forgetting, Delphine's snide comment about marrying one's skiing instructor.

'Tony is absolutely hopeless around the house,' her mother added, 'the last time I asked him to hang up a picture for me was just before our twentieth wedding anniversary and he knocked a piece of plaster right out of the wall, about fifteen centimetres square. It cost £500 to replaster and repaint. And I thought, that's it, my darling, no more DIY for you.'

'To be fair, lathe and plaster walls can be very unpredictable,' Ben added kindly.

'We were going to take a look in the wardrobe,' Sasha reminded her mother.

'Oh yes... so we were.'

And so Delphine opened up the thin double doors at the end of the long bank of fitted wardrobes. There was a clothes rail at the top of this wardrobe, packed with blouses, tops and camisoles, then there was a row of six drawers underneath this. When Delphine pulled open the first one, it appeared to be full to the brim of carefully folded scarves.

'The problem with having such a big wardrobe, and such a big house, is that you end up keeping everything,' Sasha said.

'Yes,' her mother agreed, then with a girlish giggle, she added, 'And I can't remember what I have, or where I put it, so I go and buy another one.'

One drawer after another was carefully pulled right out, so they could look through the contents. But although they found scarves and more scarves, squashed pillbox hats, shiny patent handbags and a yellow cashmere sweater with a stain, there was no pale mahogany box and no sign of the earrings.

'Is there anywhere else you could have put them?' Sasha asked, aware that she'd come back to this question almost too many times now.

'Anywhere in the bathroom... or the library?' she prompted, shuddering at the thought of having to look through that enormous room. 'The dresser in the kitchen? Is there somewhere else where you keep private, personal things?'

Delphine just shook her head and looked visibly distressed once again. 'Sasha, this is what I don't understand. Those earrings are very precious to me and I only *ever* keep them in one place – in my bedroom, in the locked drawer. And I'm certain I put them back there. And I'm *certain* that I have not worn them since I last locked them away. I'm honestly not losing my marbles yet.'

'Well, I suppose we might as well check this last drawer, down here,' Sasha said, gesturing to the bottom of the wardrobe, 'since we're here.'

'No, no, the earrings will not be in there,' Delphine insisted, but Sasha had already pulled the drawer open anyway.

Inside was a random assortment of items: a small gold clutch bag with a broken strap, an intricately knitted pale-blue baby's blanket, a box of pillar candles and a photograph in a silver frame.

Sasha picked up the frame and took a look at the photo. She couldn't remember having seen this picture before, but the funny thing was, it was of the memory that had been stirred yesterday when Beau had arrived at the house with his new baby. The photo had been taken at the front of Chadwell, but facing away from the house, so the person who'd taken it must have been standing at the front door. In the centre of the picture stood her mother and father, and behind them was a glimpse of the garden in full bloom and the long silver car her parents must have had at the time. In their arms, wrapped in a blue blanket, was baby Beau and there, standing beside Delphine, in a shiny white pinafore with a dinky blonde bob and an uncertain smile on her face, was little Sasha.

'I haven't seen this picture of us before,' Sasha said, but her mother took it from her hands and pushed it back into the drawer.

'It wasn't a good one... I don't know why it was framed and that's why it's ended up in here,' she said and shut the drawer abruptly.

'Sasha... without the earrings, is there really a chance that we would have to sell the house?' her mother asked in a voice that sounded far less confident than it had before.

'I don't know, Mama,' Sasha said gently. 'You and Dad probably need to take some really good advice... independent advice,' she added, to make clear she didn't mean Adele, 'because independent advice would be neutral, far less emotional. I'm sure there are lots of different options.'

'The house and all its memories,' her mother said, very wistfully.

But Sasha couldn't stop thinking about the photo she had just seen, with the garden in full bloom... and her in the little white pinafore. She held it all in her mind's eye for another moment. It was funny, but that was not at all how she remembered the day that Beau had come home.

She didn't want to ask her mother about it, though – it would be another one of those moments when Delphine would snap, 'Sasha, that's just not how it was!'

But that photograph... it was *not* how it was. Sasha was sure of that.

22

Somehow, the fractious and hungover Sunday wore on. Beau and Sura did go back to their room for more sleep, while everyone else took turns to hold, rock and entertain Dokus and Pica. LouLou turned out to be by far the most successful at this. Pica hung on to her every word and even Dokus in his little carrycot seemed to be listening to her voice and following her darting and cartwheeling around the room, as if she was the most fascinating toy ever invented.

Sylvie and Dirk went to the library to do battle with Maths; Tony blustered off to read the *Telegraph* undisturbed; Delphine decided to supervise Ben's ever-lengthening list of home repair chores, and that left Sasha in the sitting room with LouLou, Pica and Dokus.

But then Adele came in, and again, as in the dining room earlier, the expression on her face was soft and quite friendly.

'Hello, P... Sasha,' she began.

'Hello...'

'Can I come and sit with you?'

This was a surprising question.

'Yes, of course,' Sasha replied, 'if you promise you're not going to reveal any other big family dramas I don't know anything about.'

'Not likely,' Adele said, placing herself down on the other side of the sofa from Sasha and tucking her legs up, which gave Sasha a powerful flashback to teenage Adele and their occasional chats on most of the sofas dotted around the house.

'How are you doing?' Adele asked.

'Still pretty angry, to be honest,' Sasha replied, though in a lower voice, so that LouLou wasn't in on their conversation. 'I don't know how this family always manages to make me feel like the odd one out – the one who's outside the inner circle. Why do you always do that?'

'I don't know,' Adele said, and fiddled with her rings. The wedding ring and beautiful antique engagement ring were no longer there, Sasha had already noticed, but they'd been replaced with shinier and flashier gold and diamond rings on her other fingers.

'I thought you kind of liked being different – the family rebel,' Adele said finally.

Sasha thought about this for a moment; was she really the family rebel? In her teens and early twenties, she'd sported punky bleached-blonde hair, three earrings per ear, a lot of tight black clothing, and gone to far more drunken parties than Adele, but surely Beau with his ecstasy-fuelled nightclubbing lifestyle had been much more the rebel child than her?

No, it was more that the family dynamic made her seem like the family misfit: Delphine loved Beau and then Tony best, Tony loved Delphine and then Adele best. Beau loved Delphine best, Adele loved Tony best... and then there was some leftover love from everyone for Sasha. But she was everyone's third best. And she loved them all equally, but in a wounded, not as much as she should kind of way.

She'd not been able to see any of this clearly until she'd got to know and love Ben, and Ben's family – where it was all loving, generous and uncomplicated, without all these hurts, resentments and complications.

'You won't have any favourites in our family,' Ben had told her. 'You'll love me and our children to bits, so it will all be fine. We'll put all of this right.'

And so far, she did love Ben and LouLou equally and fiercely, but she was still afraid of what she might feel for a second child.

There, she'd thought it out loud to herself: she was frightened that she couldn't split her love in three. And what if she loved a new baby less than LouLou? Or more than LouLou? She would never forgive herself for making another person feel the way her parents had made her feel.

'Maybe I felt pushed into the rebel role,' Sasha told Adele now, 'maybe I felt that it was a way to get attention... did you ever think about that?'

'No... I suppose I didn't.'

'We all want attention when we're growing up,' Sasha went on. 'And we'll sometimes do stupid things to get it.'

'Yes, I suppose so.'

There was a pause, and Sasha thought it might be helpful to change the subject, so she asked, 'How is Sylvie doing?'

'Well, if you mean is she coping with the move, being in exam year, and our divorce... it's not been a walk in the park. But she is seeing one of the most expensive psychiatrists in Switzerland twice a week.'

'Oh well, as long as it's the most expensive psychiatrist, then that's bound to help.' The words were out of Sasha's mouth before she had time to consider how badly they might land.

Adele looked momentarily furious. And Sasha totally expected her to say something nasty in reply and get up and walk out of the room, further fuelling the horrible tension between them all.

But instead, Adele seemed to flush slightly and cast her eyes upwards. She clenched her jaw and seemed to be trying hard not to cry.

'I'm sorry,' Sasha said immediately. 'I'm sorry, Adele. That was a really stupid thing to say. Is it helping Sylvie?'

'It's been really, really hard,' Adele admitted, still on the verge of tears. 'She thinks it's all my fault... it is all my fault. Henry is a lovely man who just wants to be with his family. He would take me back in a heartbeat... but what am I supposed to do? I've only just turned forty; I don't want to live in a sexless marriage with a lovely, comfortable old cardigan of a man. If I was sixty, it would be different.'

'I'm so sorry,' Sasha said again, 'that sounds really difficult.'

She felt shaken seeing Adele so upset. Adele's vulnerable side was hardly ever on display, but here it was. Her sister, showing she was actually human. It made Sasha warm to her more than she had for years.

'Does Sylvie like the psychiatrist?' Sasha asked, hoping this would be a positive thing to mention.

'Yes,' Adele replied, 'and the sessions are going well. So that's probably the most I can ask for at the moment.'

'And is Henry okay?' Sasha had wanted to ask this since she'd first set eyes on Adele, because she had always been so fond of her brother-in-law.

'He could be better,' Adele admitted. 'He's very sad about how things are. Family life with me and Sylvie was the most important thing to him. And now Sylvie is about to leave home and I don't want to be with him any more. He feels as if it's the end of the world. I can't bear to see him so upset, but I know this is what I want.'

'And Dirk?' Sasha asked carefully.

'Yes... he is my boyfriend, but that's all. It's a lot of fun... but I'm keeping it as quiet as I possibly can for Henry and Sylvie's sakes. Does that make me the worst person?'

'No, of course not... and I'm sure it's all really difficult.'

'Yes... it is. And not how I expected life to be, but there we go. And I'm so sorry about what's been happening in your business,' Adele added, 'because that must be really difficult too.'

'Yeah,' Sasha said simply. And now she felt as if *she* might cry because she still wasn't used to the problems being definite... and they definitely weren't going to get paid. And it was a hard truth to share with others. There was a scratchy lump forming in her throat. 'It has been very stressful and very unfair,' she managed.

Sasha felt Adele's hand land comfortingly on her forearm.

'Your little family is all together. You're all in great health and you and Ben are so good together and such hard workers,' Adele said encouragingly. 'I know it seems difficult now, but I really believe you're going to be okay. You'll work out how to tackle this and what you need to do next. If you want to tell me more details and see if I have any ideas, I'd be really happy to do that.' Before Sasha could say anything, Adele added, 'I'm honestly pretty good at my job. What happened to Mum and Dad's money is really unusual, really very bad luck – a once in a lifetime market rotation. I feel terrible about it. I'm still hoping that I can turn it around for them, at least a bit. There's always the possibility in investing that there could be a rebound.'

Sasha swallowed her pride and said, 'I think a fresh opinion, a fresh set of eyes over it would be a really good idea, but let me ask Ben first and make sure he's happy.'

Then she couldn't help herself from confiding, 'I don't want to lose our home, Adele. I feel I can cope with everything, so long as that doesn't happen.'

'No!' Adele said, sounding shocked. 'No, that definitely doesn't have to happen. We'll make sure that doesn't happen. Put your mind at rest on that one.'

And it was comforting to hear her big sister, the financial bigwig, telling her that. Maybe Adele could really help them.

'What's the current cashflow situation?' Adele asked.

'Dire,' Sasha admitted. 'All my cards got declined at Waitrose the other day.'

'Oh my god... how stressful. Well, that I can definitely help with. Give me your bank details and I'll sort you out with a £5,000 loan. No strings attached.'

'Really? That's a lot!' Sasha spluttered. 'And very generous of you. We'll obviously pay you back as soon as we possibly can.'

'I know you will, Sash. Don't worry about it. I know you'd do the same for me.'

'Thank you,' Sasha said, but felt a wave of guilt. Adele seemed to have much more warmth and affection for her than Sasha had even realised. Maybe Sasha had painted her big sister as much harsher than she really was.

'I'm so sorry you're going through this,' Adele added, 'but you know, lots of businesses have ups and downs. It's honestly part of the process. You learn, you get stronger and better.'

'That's very kind of you to say... because it definitely doesn't feel like that... it feels like a big, fat fail.' Sasha could feel an unwanted tear slipping down her face.

'Please don't say that... Dad's business had a lot of ups and downs that I only found out about years later,' Adele assured her. 'They had to re-mortgage the house to meet the school fees and all kinds of things like that. Business is hard sometimes... like life.'

The two sisters held one another's eyes. It was a long time since they had been holed up on a sofa and talked to one another about important things.

And Sasha felt much more comforted and supported by the conversation than she could have imagined.

'What if the heirloom earrings don't turn up?' was Sasha's next question.

In a watered-down version of their mother's gallic expressions, Adele shrugged her shoulders and raised her hands, palms facing upwards. 'Would that be *so* awful? If they had to make some big decisions and go and live somewhere a lot more practical?'

Sasha's head reeled at the thought. This house... it had been the family home for her entire life. The Griffons had been in this house since before she was born. Her grandfather had bought the Hall and her father had grown up here. He had always lived here, and she'd thought it would always be here. To be honest, she'd not thought very deeply about Tony, Delphine, the next ten or twenty years and the house. She'd not wanted to think about that.

'I love Chadwell,' she told Adele.

'Of course, me too, and I'm sure Beau does too, but we have to be honest, not one of us is going to live here, are we? Our lives are based far away from Norfolk and any one of us would struggle to buy the other two out of their share. And this is not exactly a practical home for two elderly people who don't have a lot of cashflow between them.'

'No,' Sasha had to agree, 'but can you imagine them moving out? I've spent most of today going through the cupboards and drawers in just two rooms and that was pretty bad.'

'I can imagine... but other people get through this process... other families. What makes us think we won't have to? We would just have to help them through it.'

'But... imagine driving away from here for the last time. Imagine not coming back here? It would be so sad,' Sasha said, not even wanting to picture it. And where would her parents go? To the village? To Norwich? Maybe they'd want to move close to one of their children... Beau, most likely. She wasn't sure if Tony would like Birmingham.

'Don't, Sasha, please!' Adele said.

'Sorry.'

And then Sasha decided she would ask her sister about the other set of questions that was whirling around her head. 'Adele, can you remember a time when we were really small when Mama was sad? Really, properly sad? And she would sit in the little blue bedroom on her own and tell us to go and read a book whenever we came in? And she didn't want to cook any more? Or do anything really?'

Adele looked at Sasha with an expression of surprise.

'No,' she said, 'I don't think I remember that. Didn't we start having those soup dinners when I went to school and had lunch there and Dad used to eat nice lunches for work?'

'Maybe,' Sasha said, 'but then Delphine's dinners returned when Beau came along, don't you remember? She was always making him cottage pies and crème caramel because those were his favourite.'

'Well... maybe Dad stopped eating out so much,' Adele suggested, 'and Delphine does love to cook.'

Sasha had given a lot of thought to the photo she'd found in the wardrobe drawer with her mother. She wasn't ready to go back to her mother about it yet, but she did want to sound out her sister and see if she had shared any of the suspicions Sasha was now having.

'It's just that... when I was helping her to look for the earrings, I saw this photo in a drawer and it was of Beau being brought home from the hospital...' Sasha began carefully.

'Oh yes! Remember how Dad picked us up from school and we were at home waiting and we were so excited,' Adele said.

'Yes! Exactly,' Sasha agreed, 'but in this photo, I'm not in school uniform, I'm in a pinafore I had before I went to school. And you're not there. And Delphine is carrying this bundled up little baby and all the leaves are on the trees and the garden is in full bloom.'

Adele turned to look at her sister with full attention, an expression of astonishment across her face.

'But Beau was born in November,' Adele said, 'no chance of leaves or the garden in full bloom.'

'Exactly...'

'And... it doesn't look like anyone else is there? A friend with a new baby?'

'No, definitely not. It's Mum and Dad and the baby, the car and me. They are coming home with a new baby.'

'In the summertime? Before you were at school?'

Sasha nodded.

'So...' In a low voice, Adele asked, 'Do you think there was another baby?'

23

Just then, Ben's head appeared round the door. 'Here you are! I don't know if anyone's getting hungry yet—'

'I am!' LouLou announced and came down from the handstand against the wall that she'd been holding for a concentrated and determined length of time.

'Well, that's good, because Sura and Beau have set all kinds of lovely food out from last night and there's a big feast spread right across the kitchen table for us.'

'What time is it?' Sasha wondered, all sense of where in the day she was completely disappearing.

'Nearly 7 p.m.,' Ben told her.

'Seven? You're kidding!'

Adele got to her feet. 'I need to tell Dirk and Sylvie. They've been studying for hours, probably had absolutely nothing to eat or drink.'

And so the whole family convened in the kitchen and although the mood was still subdued, due to hangovers from both drinking and arguing, it was much more friendly and conciliatory than Sasha had expected.

Maybe it was possible to make a fuss, have an outburst and be quickly forgiven. Maybe the family dynamic had shifted a little after her blowout and maybe they would now settle into at least a slightly better arrangement. She would only know when last night's difficult conversation was revisited and some of the problems it had brought up were discussed again. But she had some belief now that however difficult the members of her family could be, there was a bedrock of love that nevertheless held them together.

'Still no sign of the earrings then?' Sasha heard her father ask her mother, but he asked in a quiet and gentle voice, not wanting to upset her any further.

She shook her head and added, 'I am certain they are in the house, Tony. Something odd has happened. But I have a feeling that we will solve the mystery. We will get to the bottom of this.'

Sura and Beau looked much more smiley and rested than they had done at breakfast time, which was good to see. Another smiley face at the table was Sylvie's. She put a carefully considered slice of cold roast beef onto her plate, along with a spoonful of salad and a small heap of potato salad. Then she turned and told her uncle Ben that she had finally figured out algebra.

'I really have got it. In fact, what a complete idiot I've been about it!' she said and smacked her lovely forehead lightly. Her cheeks were flushed, and she looked delighted to have at last worked it out.

'She worked really hard,' Dirk told Adele with a smile. 'It's important to keep practising, so that it sticks. But I think we had a breakthrough, didn't we?'

'Definitely,' Sylvie agreed, smiling first at Dirk and then at Adele.

Does Sylvie know about Dirk and her mother? Sasha wondered. Surely she must at least suspect... even if Adele was trying to be low-key.

'Don't eat too much first course,' Beau warned, 'because there is a load... and I mean a *load* of pudding left. A small mountain range of profiteroles and pavlova has been discovered in the dairy, along with bowls and bowls of tiramisu... buckets of the stuff.'

'It has all been kept cold enough?' Adele asked. 'I mean, it will be fine, won't it?'

'Oh god, yeah...' Sasha told them confidently, 'the dairy is amazing. Even on a hot summer's day, it's wonderfully cool. That's how they managed for centuries without the help of a fridge.'

* * *

At 2 a.m., Sasha was woken by a tight, sharp pain in her stomach. The hot, sweaty wave of nausea that followed let her know that she was just about to be sick. She threw back the cover and raced to the bathroom.

'Ben... what are you doing in there?' she hissed when she realised that her husband was already hunched over the loo.

'What does it sound like?' he hissed back and then gave another wrenching heave.

'I'm going to be sick—' she groaned.

'The sink,' he directed her.

And for several dreadful moments, they heaved and retched together, getting rid of the offending pudding.

'Raw egg...' he said when he could finally talk. 'Tiramisu has got raw egg in it. We should not have taken any chances.'

'Oh god...' Sasha gave another heave just at the mention of the dessert.

'What were we thinking?' Ben ran the cold tap on the bath and washed his face and hands.

'How are you doing? Are you okay?' he asked.

'Oh god,' she groaned. 'I've got a chunk up my nose...' she told him, 'eurgh, why does that always happen? It's so horrible.'

'I'll go downstairs, get some bowls and a rubbish bag,' Ben offered. 'We'll need to clean up that sink... don't want a replay of last night.'

'No... and thank you.'

There was a tap on the other bathroom door, the side where Adele's room was.

'Can I come in?' she wailed. 'I think I'm going to vom.'

Sasha opened the door and Adele sprinted to the toilet.

Sasha stood by to help her sister.

'Shall I hold your hair?' she offered.

'Oh god... I haven't been sick for years... what's the matter, have we all caught a bug?'

'Ben thinks it's the tiramisu.'

Once again, this word had a triggering affect and Adele heaved violently.

When she'd finished, Sasha took her over to the bath to wash her down.

'You can't use the sink,' she explained. 'I had to throw up in there while Ben was using the toilet.'

'Dear god... when is this weekend of horror going to end?' Adele asked. 'Who else ate the tiramisu, Sasha? Do you remember?'

'Me... Ben... you, obviously... Beau... poor Beau... he's going to be spending a second night hurling. Not Sura, she doesn't do lactose... not Sylvie... I'm not sure about Dirk.'

'I've just come from his room, he's fast asleep,' Adele said, matter-of-factly.

'Wow... it's been some time since I've played musical beds at Chadwell.'

Adele managed a laugh, despite everything. 'Yes... oh no... I think I'm going to hurl again.'

Sasha helped her get in position beside the toilet.

'Did Mum and Dad have any? Do you remember?' Sasha asked, when her sister had her head above the rim once again.

Adele ran a hand over her forehead, then said, 'Not Mum... I'm pretty sure. And you know, I don't think Dad had any either. He was on the profiteroles.'

'Well, that's at least something. Salmonella poisoning is probably more serious at their age.'

'Hello, Adele,' Ben said as he came back into the room. 'I see this has turned into a puking party. I have bowls for all, so why don't you both go back to bed and let me deal with this crime scene?'

'Ben, you are a total saint,' Adele said weakly.

'Agreed,' Sasha added.

* * *

The rest of the night was rough. There was another heaving session about an hour later, when all three systems ejected the glasses of water that had been drunk in a final attempt to purge the germs. Sasha returned to bed groaning and took a long time to fall back to sleep. When she finally woke up again, light was streaming in through the curtains and a quick look at her phone told her it was just after 9 a.m. She couldn't remember when she had last slept in so late. Looking around the room, she could see that Ben was still asleep in bed beside her; an empty bowl was on the floor beside a glass of water. LouLou's bed was empty and the pile of clothes that had been at the foot of her bed was also gone.

LouLou must have realised that her parents were ill and had mercifully decided to let them sleep. Or maybe she'd not been able to wake them.

First of all, Sasha needed a shower. So, in the bathroom, with both doors carefully locked, she stood under the warm water and tried to revive herself. She still felt fragile, with a tender stomach, but it was already a big improvement on how she'd been in the middle of the night. It was now Monday morning, she realised. She would have to phone LouLou's school and then try to get on with some work from Chadwell: chase down some invoices, check all the accounts. Make sure some cash could be found to keep their shows on the road. Maybe she shouldn't accept the money from Adele... at the end of the day, it was yet another debt that would need to be repaid, but this one came with family strings. It was one thing not to be able to pay your credit card back, quite another to not repay the sister you were going to be in a relationship with for the rest of your life, hopefully.

And then there was the car. Someone from the insurance company was going to have to come and look at it, but only once they could get past the landslide. With a heavy sigh, she realised that because of the car, they were probably stuck at Chadwell for at least another day, even if the road was cleared today.

She turned off the water, dried herself and went into the bedroom to dress, where she saw Ben pulling on his running clothes.

'Do you honestly feel up for a run? After all the puking?'

'Yup... it's my version of hair of the dog, I suppose. Plus, I'm aiming to run down the road and see what's happening at the land-slide. See if there's any sign of action.'

* * *

Down in the kitchen, Sasha was relieved to see her mother looking fit and well at the kitchen table, drinking her black coffee and her warm lemon water. The party's vivid red nail polish had been replaced by a more daywear shade of caramel and Delphine was smartly dressed in pressed camel-coloured flannel trousers and a classy white blouse. At her neck was the Delphine touch, a red statement necklace that looked like a vivid scarlet version of coral cast in glass.

'Morning, Mama. Are you well? You didn't eat any of the tiramisu?'

'No... I heard from Adele, who had to get up early for work calls. So you were all ill. *Mes pauvres, je suis désolé.*'

'Oh no, Beau and Sura too?

'Sura is fine. Beau is still in bed. Poor Beau... and when he's so worn out with the new baby too.'

'Yeah... and so soon after his awful hangover,' Sasha couldn't resist adding.

Her mother arched her eyebrows and pursed her red lips.

'It *was* a hangover,' Sasha insisted and realised she was just being childish, trying to persuade her mother to disapprove of her beloved Beau.

'Would you like some coffee?' Delphine asked.

'No, I'll make some tea, thanks. Would you like anything?' she asked, although she knew already the answer would be no. The black coffee and the lemon water were enough.

'I haven't even seen LouLou this morning,' Sasha said. 'Is she playing with Pica and Sura?'

'Oh yes... they'll be in the little sitting room. They are having such a lovely time; little girls are always so fascinated with babies. And isn't Dokus just adorable? He looks just like baby Beau did.'

As Sasha made her tea, she thought again of that silver-framed photo in the drawer and felt that slight intuition that there was something that didn't quite tally... but nevertheless she sat at the table and drank her tea calmly. Yes... calmly... she was feeling quite unusually calm, calmer than she'd felt for weeks and weeks. This was sometimes the Chadwell effect when everything was going smoothly. It was so far away from London, from bank accounts that were too overdrawn, from all the questions around what they needed to do next.

She drank her tea, smiled at her mother, felt her shoulders lower a little and her breathing deepen and slow.

'Are you okay?' she asked her mother.

'Oh... *comme ci, comme ça*,' Delphine replied. 'I'll miss my yoga class in the village tonight if the road doesn't reopen. And we'll all have to eat party leftovers once again. But no tiramisu this time... I've thrown it all in the bin.'

'Is there any word on clearing the road?' Sasha asked. 'Has Dad heard anything?'

'Speak of the devil...' her mother joked as Sasha's father came into the kitchen.

He settled into his chair at the head of the table and gave them an update. Yes, there was supposed to be one digger coming today, but it might not be there until the afternoon and it might not make enough progress to actually open up the road today. But probably by tomorrow morning things would get going again.

Then Sylvie came in, looking sleepy in pyjama-like leggings and a long, loose jumper. She wanted lemon water, to Delphine's delight. And she also made herself toast and buttered it carefully before adding a thin layer of jam.

Sasha chatted to Sylvie about exams and how her schoolwork was going and about the plans she was starting to make for after school. And so a very amiable hour had passed in the kitchen before Sasha decided that she really must go and find LouLou and see what she'd been up to with her little cousins since 7 a.m.

She put her dishes in the dishwasher, tidied up some stray breakfast things, took a long look out of the kitchen window and felt that strange melding of memories that could happen at every turn at Chadwell. She could be looking out and suddenly remember standing here as a very little girl, remembering the thoughts she'd had then. She would remember the different trees – the ones that were much smaller back then, the ones that had been removed, or blown down. It was sometimes lovely to feel the past so close and interwoven like this... but sometimes it was a little eerie too, and a little too nostalgic, pulling her back here, holding her just slightly back from where her life was based now.

But then she turned her head from the window and went off to the cosy little sitting room to hang out with her daughter and Sura and the delightful little people. When she opened the door on the lovely south-facing room, she saw Sura feeding Dokus, while Pica was cuddled up closely to her on the sofa, being read a story.

Saying a quiet hello, Sasha cast her eyes about the room for LouLou, expecting her lively daughter to pop out from behind the curtains or the back of the sofa, cartwheel across the carpet and land at her feet.

'Hi... how are you doing? I'm looking for LouLou,' Sasha said gently. 'Mum said she'd be here with you.'

'Oh...' Sura sounded surprised. 'She left here a little while ago now. Said she was going to look for you or Sylvie, whichever one of you she found first.'

'Oh.' Now it was Sasha's turn to be surprised. 'I've been in the kitchen with Sylvie for an hour or so and we've not seen her. Okay... well... I'll have a look around the house and see where she's got to.'

First of all, Sasha looked in every obvious room. Then, she doubled back on herself and looked in every obvious room once again, calling LouLou by name and asking her to come out and please not to play hide and seek. Then she looked in every single room in the large house, checked every other corner, nook and cranny that she could think of, but could not find LouLou. Ben came back from his run, soaked with sweat, and met her anxious explanation with his usual reassuring calmness. Together, they checked the house all over again and went out into the garden. They searched and they called LouLou's name over and over. But still no sign of her.

As every minute passed, all Sasha could think was: *at what point is it logical to panic?* Because she was already beginning to panic, but she didn't know yet if she was overreacting or not.

'Do we need to phone the police?' she asked her husband, thinking even as she said it that the road was blocked, so how would the police even get here? But if they couldn't get here, how would they be able to find her?

Her dad was out in the garden too now. Dirk and Adele came out of the house with Sylvie, and everyone was desperate to help. Tony said he and Delphine would thoroughly look through the house once more. Adele said she would take the garden and then the sheds. Ben, Sylvie, Sasha and Beau were all going to spread further out, each taking one of the main paths that led out into the fields and countryside that surrounded the house.

Sasha, who was almost crying with fright now, was given warm and reassuring words by her father.

'Sasha, remember, this isn't London,' he began. 'You children used to wander around here on your own all day long. It's very safe. It's lovely. And she's such a smart and sensible little girl. Please try to be calm. We will find her. She'll pop up back here and wonder what all the fuss was about.'

Sasha tried to smile at the thought, but she couldn't help adding, 'But she's never done this before. Never, ever once. She doesn't go anywhere on her own. She always tells me where she's going. She always lets me know... It's not like her.'

'Maybe she just wanted a little bit of independence,' her dad replied. 'She wanted to go for a little walk on her own. She knows her way round here really well. You all do. Sylvie used to roam all over the place when she was that age. You go out onto the paths and I'm sure you'll find her. We'll look all over the house again. I'm sure, in half an hour, we'll have her back safe and sound.'

It did help. These calming, wise words really did help. They took away the top notes of panic, so that Sasha could at least breathe and concentrate better on finding her daughter.

* * *

At first, Sasha and Ben jogged together along the path that headed east. They were looking, shouting and veering off the path into all the interesting-looking spots. Sasha had not been able to find LouLou's orange anorak at the house, so she was primed to look for orange and when she thought she saw a flash of the anorak, she raced towards it, heart dancing with relief. But when the scrap of flapping orange turned out to be a piece of torn fertiliser bag caught on a fence, she burst into tears at the revelation.

'Oh, Ben! It's my fault, it's all my fault,' Sasha cried, giving full rein to her fear. 'I should have gone to find her before I sat down for breakfast... what was I thinking? Why did I rely on someone else to look after her? I never do that. I'm always the one. I'm always responsible. I've never, ever let LouLou down for one minute. And now I've let her wander off... where is she? Oh! Where is she?'

If it wasn't so important to keep moving and keep looking, she would fall down to her knees right now and weep herself sick. She was so frightened.

'Please, Sash, I think Tony is probably right,' Ben insisted. 'So let's just keep moving and looking and thinking about that...'

But Sasha could hear in Ben's voice that he wasn't quite as sure as he wanted to be.

Everything that had been a problem before this morning just

shrivelled up and shrank away in Sasha's mind. The fact that she'd
been so worried about mere money made her want to slap herself.
Money! Money was all around. She and Ben could both go and
deliver pizzas, who cared? Who cared about status and overdrafts?
Just let LouLou be okay. Just let her have her little girl in her arms
and it would be easy to sort out every other little problem.

24

When the path they were on forked in two, it was time for Sasha and Ben to part ways, so they could search in one direction each. Ben gave her a tight, bolstering hug. 'Keep calm, keep your eyes peeled,' he said, 'she can't be far.'

And then Sasha headed uphill on her own, towards the brow of the small hill and from there, she would head down the gentle slope towards the fields and woodlands beyond.

She was going at a light jog and looking around carefully. She tried to tell herself that there was no way that anything awful had happened... because... because they were in the middle of *nowhere* – the one road to the house was currently blocked with several tonnes of red Norfolk earth, so the chances of some sort of child abduction had to be millions and millions to one, didn't they?

But still, her heart jumped at even the thought.

She could not think about the worst possibilities right now. She had to keep calm and focus on searching for LouLou in the here and now. She was almost at the top of the gentle hill now and from here, she was hoping she would have a good view all around and would be able to scan carefully for that bright-orange anorak, or any other sign of LouLou at all.

And now that Sasha was up here, she realised she'd forgotten all about the old clay pit down at the bottom of the hill on the left-hand side. She'd hardly ever walked down there with her parents or her daughter, but occasionally when she had, her parents had always issued stern warnings about the pit and never to go near it as it was a steep drop with water at the bottom and it really was about time the farmer fenced it off or filled it in.

As Sasha jogged down the other side of the hill towards the clay pit, she told herself that LouLou would definitely, definitely not be in that pit – absolutely no way. But then there was just this little frightened thought, hardly even daring to want to be a thought... that what other explanation was there for the complete disappearance of LouLou, other than that she was down at the bottom of that thing? And just even thinking about that thought was causing her to run faster and faster down the hill.

When she was down at the bottom, she was still some distance from the pit when she started to call LouLou's name.

'Are you here?' she shouted. 'Where are you?'

And just as Sasha had almost convinced herself that she probably didn't need to go over there and even look, because this was ridiculous, LouLou would never be down there, a very surprising thing happened.

A little rock seemed to jump up from the rim of the pit and then disappear down again. *What?* Had she just imagined that? But she left the path and went towards the pit, feeling incredibly nervous. The ground was wet and heavy and clung to her shoes in clumps. She thought about bogs and landslides and imagined the heavy red mud moving under her feet and pulling her towards the mouth of that hole in the ground.

To her astonishment, another little rock jumped up from the

surface and fell back down again, followed a split-second later by a splash.

'LouLou?' she called out. 'Are you there?'

Her words rang out in the windy empty space.

No reply.

Then came that thought that she was being ridiculous again. *But stones didn't throw themselves, did they?*

Sasha inched carefully towards the mouth of the pit, feeling the ground wet and slippery beneath her feet. As she got very close, she decided it would be best to lie down on her stomach and wriggle towards the edge. Surely that would put the least weight on the slippery soil and mean that she had much less chance of falling in. Her parents' warnings were ringing in her ears: 'Never go near that old thing... the edge is crumbling, you could easily fall in and it's very deep. It's boggy at the bottom, there might even be several feet of water if there's been a lot of rain... it's very dangerous. Stay away.'

It was wet and muddy and cold to lie down and wriggle towards the edge. But finally Sasha was carefully craning her head over. It was a wide, deep and dark hole. She couldn't see anything at all.

'Hello?' she called out, feeling stupid. What had she honestly thought?

No reply.

She put her right hand down into the pocket of her jacket and fished out her phone. She sought the torch setting and once the beam had been switched on, she cast it round the deep hole, more out of curiosity really. She wanted to see how deep it was and if she could see the bottom. Her first sweep of the beam took in the muddy red walls and some metal rungs, widely set apart, that must have been hammered in at some point to make a sort of ladder. Her second sweep of the beam gave her such a shock that it was a relief to be already lying down. Right down there at the bottom of the pit was a bright orange bubble.

Her hand was shaking so hard she was frightened to drop her phone, but Sasha cast the light back down, terrified at what she might see.

There was the orange bubble again, it was an anorak hood bobbing in muddy wet water. She moved the phone frantically around and oh, there, there! There was LouLou's face, squinting at the light, looking up at her. LouLou was standing in the water up to hip height. Her cheeks and her lips looked a blue shade of pale and even from this height, Sasha could see the streaks of tears on her cheeks.

The anorak must have fallen into the water and floated away from LouLou; it was horrible the way it looked like her, spread out in the muddy water. Shudder, shudder at the thought.

'LouLou! Oh, darling!' she called down. 'We've come to find you. We've come to get you!'

LouLou managed a tiny bit of a smile, but mainly looked strained, exhausted and just so cold. She opened her mouth and tried to say hello but only a husky croak would come out. Sasha realised at once that LouLou had been shouting for help for so long, she had lost her voice.

'You were so clever to throw the stones,' Sasha said. 'So clever.'

This brought another attempt at a faint smile.

'Okay, I'm just going to phone everyone now... so the light will go away for a moment, but then I'll be right here again. Okay, I'm not going anywhere, I'm going to be here.'

Sasha looked at her phone screen with its hopeless one bar of signal. She tried to call Ben... nothing. Then she tried Adele, the Chadwell landline... but nothing. She couldn't even get a ringtone. There was just not enough signal.

'LouLou,' she called out, 'I can't get a signal, so I'm going to have to go and run for help. I promise you I'll be so quick. I'll try and bring everyone back in ten minutes.'

She watched as LouLou's face crumpled and she began to cry almost silently accompanied only by those little rasping croaks. It was just terrible to see.

No. she couldn't go. She couldn't leave LouLou's side not even for a minute.

'No... look, please don't cry,' she began. 'I'm going to send them a message and then I'm going to come down there to be with you. Okay, my darling? Please don't cry. I'm coming right down, okay.'

Then Sasha called up her own voicemail and changed the message to: 'Please listen – it's me and LouLou is at the bottom of the clay pit. She's okay. I'm going down too. Get help as quickly as you can.' Then she diverted her calls to voicemail.

Once that was done, she felt a surge of energy and determination. There was no one else here to help, so she would just have to work this out. LouLou was counting on her. She switched the torch beam back on and carefully launched herself over the edge of the pit and onto the rungs. The metal felt cold and slippery in her hands, and worse, when her feet landed on the rungs they wobbled, and she didn't like the odd spacing between them.

Carefully and slowly, she began to come down the fifteen feet or so towards LouLou. But then LouLou began to croak and rasp, trying to tell her something. She looked at LouLou, who was pointing to the bottom of the rungs and mouthing: 'Broken.'

Sasha continued to come down anyway, very carefully, foot over foot, hand over hand. She saw that the rungs were becoming more wobbly and increasingly spotted with rust. LouLou was stepping very carefully towards her, desperate to be closer to her mother and the beam of light.

And then Sasha was groping with her foot for another rung, but it wasn't there.

'Broken,' LouLou whispered.

Sasha reached down with her hand, but she couldn't even touch

LouLou's outstretched hand. She was still too high up, and LouLou was too far down. Sasha tried very hard to calmly consider her options when all she wanted to do was just get to LouLou and gather her into her arms. Should she just jump off the last rung and into the water? But then they would both be trapped down here. And it was a horrible, chill cold. LouLou was already shaking and distressed.

Sasha clung to the rail and tried to work out what to do next. Surely someone would get her message and be here very soon?

LouLou began to cry with her damaged rasping voice, and it was terrible to hear. *How long had she been down here?* Sasha wondered. *An hour? Longer?* It was hard to estimate when she had left the house and landed up down here.

'Hello, my darling,' Sasha said in her most comforting voice, 'it's so good to see you.' She gave LouLou her warmest smile and got a smile back. 'Try not to worry. Everyone will be here really, really soon. They'll get a rope down, or a ladder. They'll maybe call the fire brigade. That would be cool, getting a fireman's lift out of here.'

Again LouLou managed a smile. But even as Sasha was saying the words, she was remembering that the road was blocked. So there would be no fire engine. And would her parents have a rope or a long ladder? If not, how would they be able to get to them down here?

And what if LouLou was getting hypothermia? She was shivering and shaking, and her teeth were chattering too. Her feet and her legs were in this horrible water and mud. *What if she suddenly collapsed into the water?* It was really cold down here.

If this was a film, Sasha would somehow just reach down that little bit further and scoop LouLou up, with miraculous upper body strength, and then within moments they'd be up, up, up at the top and this nightmare would all be over.

Think, Sasha, think! What could she possibly use to help

LouLou get out? Her jumper? Her jacket... nothing seemed strong enough. She needed something long and strong. And then she had an idea... yes... could that possibly work?

Holding tight to the rungs, it was the work of a few awkward minutes for Sasha to wriggle out of her jeans. Then she tied one ankle of the stretchy skinny jeans to the rung that her foot was resting on. She tied it on as tightly as she could and wrapped it round once again for luck. Then she sent the rest of the jeans, a length of almost five feet of denim, down towards LouLou.

Yes, there was enough material, but it was not going to be easy. LouLou would have to grip onto the denim and Sasha would have to pull her up to just within reach of that first rung. LouLou would have to hold on so tightly and trust her. And Sasha would have to bear the weight. LouLou was ten and Sasha hardly ever lifted her these days. But occasionally, LouLou sat on her knee and it was still okay. And this was only for a few moments... and surely adrenaline would give her the extra strength she might need?

'LouLou, darling, you've got to hold on to the jeans really, really tightly,' Sasha began. 'You're going to use both hands, and then you're going to put your feet on the wall. I'm going to pull you up and you're going to step up the wall until you can get hold of the rung. Does that sound okay?'

LouLou nodded and took hold of the jeans with one hand.

'Your hands and arms might burn and you might get scraped along the wall a bit, but you've just got to keep holding and stepping and let me pull you up. You've got to just keep holding on. Do you understand me?'

LouLou nodded again.

Now Sasha could see that there was already something else in her daughter's other hand. But she pushed whatever this was into the waistband of her trousers. Then she took hold of the jeans like a

rope, faced the wall, gritted her teeth and there was a very determined look on her pale, blueish face.

Sasha got into the best position she could, braced against the
rungs, and she began to pull. She tried to calm her thoughts, to not
think about what could go wrong, and to just get on with bringing
her daughter out of here.

LouLou felt so, so heavy. It was as if the water and the mud had
her in their grip. There was a sucking, popping squelch as her first
foot came out of the water and onto the wall, and an even bigger
sound with the second.

LouLou held on tight and moved her frozen feet slowly and
clumsily against the wall. Meanwhile, Sasha pulled for dear life,
terrified that she would fail, or LouLou would let go and fall back
into the water... bump her head, or even drown. The muscles in
Sasha's hands and arms were burning and straining; in her chest, she
could feel her heart absolutely thudding. Just let LouLou get to the
rung, she told herself, just to the rung... nothing else would matter.
Never mind the business, never mind the debt, never mind Ben's
sustainable skis, or her sibling and parental money problems... just
let LouLou get to this rung. Please, please. That's the only thing that
matters. Sasha was so weak. She would pump iron after this, grow
enormous muscles. Just please, *please* let LouLou get to the rung.

Sasha's hands and arms were shaking with effort and her eyes
were fixed on LouLou's hands, holding tightly to the jeans,
bumping against the wall, almost there... almost there.

'Grab it!' Sasha yelled. 'Grab!' And now LouLou had one hand
on the rung, one hand on the jeans. 'That's perfect, very well done,
LouLou. Very good! Now keep your hands where they are. One on
the metal, one on the jeans and we'll start going up, really slowly,
bit by bit.'

Sasha was very concerned that these wobbling rungs were

going to give way, so they were going to move slowly and steadily. Coming down the rungs had been the work of a few minutes, but now, making their way up, Sasha felt as if it was going to take hours, that it was fraught with danger, that at any moment, a rung could give way, or LouLou could lose her grip.

She wondered if it had been a reckless decision to try to bring LouLou up herself. LouLou was so cold and so exhausted that this was almost impossible work for her. Her hands seemed to be working stiffly, but moving her legs and her feet was very slow and difficult.

'Hold really tight, LouLou, and if you need to rest, that's fine,' Sasha assured her.

Sasha thought now that she should have done it all differently, should have manoeuvred so she was behind LouLou and could support her. But it was too difficult to rearrange everything now. They both just had to get out before any other rungs collapsed or fell off.

'Hold tight, tight, tight,' Sasha kept repeating, terrified that LouLou would fall now from this height.

So they moved, painfully, excruciatingly slowly from one rung up to the next. Then the next... then one more...

Every so often, Sasha would glance up, hoping that there would be a face at the rim above them. But no... they would just have to keep on going.

At last, Sasha put her hand on the slippery mud at the top of the pit. She knew careful concentration and effort would now be needed to get them both safely out. So she tied her end of the jeans to the top rung, then used her hands, elbows, whole arms to scramble herself over the edge.

Now she was free to concentrate on pulling up LouLou, who was just behind her.

'You're almost there, my darling, just hold tight to everything and come slowly, really slowly...'

Now that she could see LouLou properly in the light, Sasha realised how ghostly blue-white she was. Her daughter's teeth were chattering, and she was shivering so much that holding on, concentrating and making these final moves was going to be difficult.

Sasha just wanted to get hold of her daughter. She felt that if she could just get a tight grip on LouLou's hand, and then LouLou's arm, everything would be okay.

'Come on, my darling,' she urged.

LouLou was almost there. The hand clutching at the jeans was almost at the rim of the pit and was able to grab hold of it.

'Nearly there,' she cried.

Sasha took hold of LouLou's other hand too and pulled. For a horrible moment, she lurched forwards, as LouLou lost her footing maybe, or a rung gave way. But then, realising what was happening, Sasha threw herself backwards, and as she stumbled and fell over into the mud, LouLou slithered over the top of the pit.

Mother and daughter scrambled across the wet mud to get clear of that awful pit and then collapsed in a heap into one another's arms.

'Oh, LouLou, LouLou! Are you okay?' Sasha asked as she put her arms around LouLou and felt how bone cold and stiff she was. LouLou curled up as small as she could into Sasha's lap and in her rasping, hoarse voice began to cry. Sasha's bare legs were cold on the wet ground too. She could feel her pants and her top both soaking wet next to her skin.

'Please someone, come!' she shouted as loudly as she could. 'Hello? Hello! *We are here!*'

She tried to dial her phone, but her fingers were too cold and stiff. She looked around wildly, wondering what she could do and there, at the top of the hillside, at last, were some figures. They were waving and now they were starting to run.

Sasha pulled LouLou right up onto her lap, to give her as much warmth as she could. She cuddled her arms tightly around her and put her face right against LouLou's stone-cold face.

'You're okay,' Sasha told her. 'Mummy is right here with you. Daddy is on his way... and everything is going to be okay now.'

LouLou managed to turn the corners of her blue lips up at this news.

Cuddling tightly against her, Sasha could feel that there was a hard, square lump on LouLou's stomach underneath the soaking wet pink and yellow jumper she was wearing.

'What's that?' she asked, almost to herself, not expecting LouLou to be in any state to explain.

But LouLou moved her hand to the top of the square lump and clutched it protectively.

With what was left of her ravaged, rasping voice, she forced out the words, 'It's a secret.'

25

Ben was running so hard and so fast down the hill, Sasha was worried that some muscle or tendon might give out before he got to them.

But then, within moments, he was there, hugging them fiercely, gasping for breath, and listening to Sasha's hurried explanation.

'You got her out,' Ben was saying, delighted, astonished. 'You got her out! Oh, LouLou, it's so good to see you. And clever, clever Mummy.'

Beau was hot on Ben's heels, running down the hill in a comical outfit put together from pyjamas, wellingtons, and what looked like Delphine's hastily snatched raincoat and he was carrying an armful of tartan rugs.

'Everyone is on it,' Ben explained. 'As soon as we got your message... Dirk is bringing more coats and blankets, Delphine is making hot drinks that Adele will bring. Tony is speaking to 999. But first we need to warm you up and check if we can move you, LouLou.'

And that's when Sasha remembered. Ben, of course, was a

professional skiing instructor. He had training in accidents, broken limbs and hypothermia.

'You've done so well, Sash,' Ben was saying. 'You deserve a medal. C'mon, let's get some blankets down and sit you both on them and Beau and I will huddle in beside you.'

As he talked, he was laying down two blankets and moving Sasha and LouLou gently onto them, then he took off his sweatshirt, sat down close to Sasha and got LouLou right onto his lap, his sweatshirt on top of her. Then Beau sat on Sasha's other side and tucked the remaining blankets on top of them.

'This is cosy,' he joked. His arm was around Sasha's back and she felt the warmth and the comfort of it.

'Help is on its way,' he said. 'You'll both be in a safe and warm place very soon.'

Sasha watched as her husband scanned LouLou over.

'Huddle up nice and close to Beau, Sasha. Is anything you're wearing wet?'

'My knickers and the bottom of my top,' she whispered.

'Okay... not too bad... get your legs right beside Beau's. Okay, we have to get LouLou's trousers and socks off, they're soaked.'

So somehow, in the huddle under the blankets, they peeled off filthy sodden socks and the once-pink pair of cords. Meanwhile LouLou, who seemed hardly awake, clutched tightly to her jumper and what appeared to be a box underneath it.

'What have you got there?' Ben asked, as he pressed LouLou's freezing feet against his hands and inner forearms, trying to impart some warmth into the solid, white, waxy skin.

LouLou didn't answer, just held her hand more tightly against the square.

Dirk and Adele were hurrying down the hill now, laden with blankets, coats and thermos flasks.

And far in the distance, Sasha could hear a clattering, roaring kind of sound. When she looked up, there was a yellow dot in the sky, but it seemed to be approaching at speed.

'A helicopter?' she said, looking at Ben in bewilderment.

'Air ambulance,' he replied. 'Quickest way to get here while the road is blocked.'

'Air ambulance?' Sasha's brain didn't seem to be connecting the dots. Here was LouLou... and Adele, Dirk and Sylvie were also here now, hugging them all, wrapping more blankets around them and opening up flasks full of steaming juice.

Wasn't everything going to be okay now? What was the need for an air ambulance?

But then there was a tumble of events... the helicopter landing in the field with an immense clattering sound, mud splattering and wind and noise. People running out of it in bright anoraks carrying big boxes.

And all the quiet urgency as LouLou was bundled into a foil blanket from head to toe, until she looked like something ready to go into the oven, and a drip went into her arm, too, and Sasha just held LouLou's hands and eyes so tightly with her own. Their gaze didn't break all the time that LouLou was being tended to.

Then the efficient, wonderfully cheery ambulance crew was telling Ben and Sasha that there was only room for the patient and Sasha began to cry. 'But how will I get to the hospital? The road is closed! I'm stuck here... I don't even know which hospital you're taking her to!'

One of the crew told her the name of the main hospital in Norwich once again and promised her LouLou would be well looked after and she could phone any time for updates and to speak to LouLou.

'I will get to the hospital, LouLou,' Sasha told her daughter. 'I'll just walk over the landslide and hitchhike. I'll be there, LouLou, just as soon as I can.'

So the helicopter took off and climbed up into the grey sky, Sasha watching it with tears streaming down her face. When it was just a speck in the sky, Sasha put her arms around Ben and buried her face against his shoulder.

'Is she going to be okay?' she asked her husband.

'It looks really good, really, really good...' he assured her, 'really good.' And she could hear the held-back tears in his voice.

'I have to get to the hospital,' was Sasha's next thought. 'I have to get to the hospital!' she said out loud.

'But the road isn't open yet,' Ben reminded her.

'No, Sasha's right,' Adele said. 'She has to get to the hospital and we'll just have to find a way.'

26

While Ben, Beau and Dirk shouldered all the blankets, Sasha linked arms with Adele on one side and Sylvie on the other as they walked up the hill towards Chadwell. Sasha was so grateful for the support as her arms and legs ached and she was both numb and exhausted, but still jittery with adrenaline.

'You know how sometimes you don't really want to share all the details of a drama with Mum, because... well... she can make it even more of a drama?' Adele said.

'Oh yes,' Sasha agreed, imagining just how her mother was going to react to this story: rant about the farmer who'd never filled in the clay pit, chastise Sasha and Ben for not having brought LouLou up well enough to know not to go into a pit, and so on.

'I think this could be one of those times,' Adele said. 'I'm just warning you. She's probably in the kitchen, making a huge pot of coffee and getting ready to let loose.'

But instead, they found their father in the kitchen, offering tea to whoever needed it. He was quiet, subdued almost, and clearly very worried about LouLou.

'So they've taken her to the hospital... anything broken? What about concussion?' he wanted to know, and they tried to set his mind at rest as best they could.

'Where's Mama?' Adele asked.

'In the playroom,' he told them. 'She's been very upset by this, very shocked. Maybe best go and pop in, tell her LouLou is going to be okay.'

'Are you up for that?' Adele asked her sister, as Sasha realised how cold and tired she was, she was also smeared with mud, wrapped in a blanket and in quite desperate need of some sort of warming bath or shower. She also needed to get to the hospital.

'Yes, let's go and see her,' she agreed.

They found Delphine in the playroom weeping, eyes streaming, make-up over her face.

'Hey, it's okay, Mama,' Sasha said. 'LouLou's gone to the hospital, but that's just to check her over. We really think she's going to be okay.'

'Oh dear... you're so upset,' Adele said, sitting beside her mother and putting an arm tightly around her.

'I know... I know... it could have been a tragedy,' Delphine sobbed, 'It could have been the most terrible loss... I know, I know what that feels like. But our lovely LouLou, oh, I could not bear it. I could not even bear to think about it.'

'Is there something we don't know, Mama?' Sasha asked, very gently, kneeling down in front of her mother now. 'You've had to face it, haven't you? I think you did lose a child.'

For a moment, Delphine was too overcome to speak, she covered her face with her hands, but they could both see that she was nodding.

'Yes,' she said finally.

Sasha and Adele looked at one another. Despite her suspicions, Sasha still felt overcome by surprise. Then, when their mother had recovered enough to be able to speak, she added, 'I lost my little Pierre when he was only eleven weeks old.'

'Oh, my goodness,' Adele said gently. 'I'm so sorry. I'm so sorry for you and for Dad.'

Sasha put her hands over her mother's and held them tightly.

'Was he the baby in the photo we found the other day?' she asked, gently.

Delphine nodded.

'He was born after Sasha?' Adele asked, looking even more surprised. No doubt, just like Sasha, she couldn't understand how she had no memory of their other brother and this whole family tragedy.

They were so focused on their mother that they hadn't noticed Beau coming quietly into the room.

'Hello, Mama,' he said. And as she looked up, a smile returned to her face in spite of the tears.

'Are you okay?' he asked, coming over.

'Yes, darling, I'm just telling your sisters about my baby Pierre.' Sasha understood straightaway that Beau already knew.

'She told me just last week when she came to see Dokus... she was so upset to see him because apparently he looks very like Pierre.'

'Oh, the spitting image, my darling. I was, how do you say? Bowled over.'

'Why didn't we know all about him?' Adele wanted to know.

'It was lovely Dr Parker, you know how much I trusted him. He told me it was best for you girls to let you forget, to not mention him, to let us all move on quickly and try for another baby boy. Least said, soonest mended, he told me. And I believed him. But I found it very hard. Very, very hard to just forget.' And Delphine began to cry again, breaking her children's hearts.

'Shhhhhh,' Beau soothed. 'I'll stay with you. We'll drink some tea and we'll go and play with Pica and Dokus. But we need to let Sasha get into a hot shower and Adele is probably going to think of a very clever way to get Sasha and Ben to the hospital.'

'Yes,' Adele agreed. 'Sasha definitely needs to warm up...'

'But when we're all back,' Sasha said, 'you'll tell us all about Pierre. We'll look at all the photos and maybe we'll remember.' She really hoped that she would. It seemed too awful to have completely forgotten all about a real little brother.

'He has a grave,' Beau said, which stopped Sasha in her tracks. There was a grave for this precious lost baby.

'We'll go and see it together,' Sasha said, 'just as soon as I'm back... just as soon as I know that LouLou is okay. I love you.' She was aiming this at her mother, but suddenly she felt it could spread out and encompass Beau and Adele too.

'Go shower,' Adele said, taking out her phone. 'We'll get you to LouLou.'

* * *

After her hot shower, which did a reasonable job of warming her up and bringing her a fresh burst of energy, there was only one thing Sasha wanted to do – phone the hospital and get an update on her daughter. After listening to the number ring out for a long minute, finally a voice answered.

'Oh, hello... I'm Sasha Greenhope, LouLou's mum. She came in by air ambulance. I wanted to find out how she was doing?'

'Hello, Mrs Greenhope, we've got her on the children's ward,' the brisk voice on the other end of the line told her. 'She's doing really well; she's been X-rayed and fully checked over by the paediatrician. There was some worry about the feet, and an ankle, but there are no broken bones, and it doesn't look as if there will be any lasting nerve damage. The doctor also suspects a concussion, so we'll certainly want to keep her in overnight. But she's doing really well. She's very cheery. Give me your number and we'll take in a phone and get her to give you a call.'

Sasha gave out her phone number on autopilot. No lasting nerve damage... concussion... these words were ringing in her ears. LouLou had been so lucky, so lucky.

* * *

Tony drove them to the roadblock with a small ladder and a rope. Ben got Adele and a very worn-out Sasha up and over the earth mound. A pre-ordered taxi met them at the other side and took them to a garage, where Adele had booked the hire car.

Then the journey to the hospital began and, at first, all Adele and Sasha could talk about was their mother's revelation about baby Pierre. But then Sasha had a question for her sister.

'Why do you think we both have only one child?' she asked.

'Well, I thought it would be too difficult to have a full-on career and more than one baby,' Adele said, but there was something a little automatic to that reply, as if she'd given it often – her stock response.

'Well, I have a different answer,' said Sasha. 'I hated the way our parents so obviously had favourites and I never wanted to put any child through not being the favourite.'

'But you never would,' Adele protested. 'You're a very kind and well-adjusted person; you would never play favourites.'

'That is exactly what I keep telling her,' Ben said, breaking the respectful silence he'd been keeping in the back seat.

For a moment, Sasha paused and took these kind words on board, but she still had to ask, 'But didn't our mother always say you couldn't help getting on with one child more than another? That it had so much to do with temperament, personality.'

Ben snorted at this and Adele added, 'Did she even try with us, though? I mean, Beau arrived and from that day onwards, we were second best.'

For the very first time, Sasha had an inkling that maybe this favouritism by Delphine had hurt Adele as much as it had hurt her. And also, knowing about the baby that had been lost in between might make Delphine's favouritism just a little more understand-able... even forgivable.

'But at least you had Dad,' Sasha reminded her, 'he gets on best with you.'

'It is a very nice relationship,' Adele agreed, 'but I did always feel bad for you and Beau about it.'

'Did you? You never mentioned... never said...'

'I thought that would make it worse.'

Quietly Sasha said the words as she realised them. 'I think it would have been nice to hear from you and Beau that you did notice and you did care. Because I was the one left out of the favourites game. I wasn't anyone's favourite.'

'You're my favourite sister,' Adele said.

That made Sasha smile, then with a grin, she added, 'And Beau's!'

'You are not!'

'I think I am!'

'You're my favourite wife,' Ben joked.

'Ha!'

'Oh dear...' Adele sighed, eyes fixed on the road ahead. 'What am I going to do about everything?'

'What everything?' Sasha asked. 'And why are you asking me? I'm the one with the business that's going down the tubes.'

'You know, that could all be much more fixable than you might think, but meanwhile, I've got all this muddy, murky emotional stuff to do... and I'm really not that good at it. I've got to "move forward" with Henry in a positive way; I've got to help Sylvie cope with it all and get through her exams. And let's not even get started on how they both feel about my new boyfriend... Plus, I've totalled my parents' nest egg... I mean that's a lot. That's a lot of things to fix right there.'

Sasha couldn't help smiling, but it was with kindness.

'Don't you think that sometimes we really do know what we have to do... but it's too hard and we don't want to? And that's why everyone needs a bit of help, or even a bit of a push?'

'It does all feel a bit hard sometimes,' Adele said.

'I can't believe I'm hearing this from you! You're the queen of doing hard things.'

'Couldn't it just sometimes be like in the movies, though? Wouldn't that be wonderful?'

'What do you mean?' said Sasha. 'Everything works out perfectly? You're a bit old to believe in happy-ever-after, aren't you?'

'No, what I meant was, in the movies, people have one big heart-felt conversation and reveal their real feelings and then, ta da, everything gets solved. But real life is much more tricky and messy. And you seem to have to have the same conversations over and over again.'

'Now that is completely true!' Ben chimed in from the back seat.

'Yes... but it's good to talk to you like this, you know... really talk to you, instead of... oh, I don't know... keeping up appearances.'

Adele laughed.

'I mean, I'm still so jealous of you. You live in Switzerland, you earn telephone number money; your daughter is amazing and she will probably become a corporate lawyer, or a Hollywood actress, or something incredible. Mum and Dad are so, so proud of you. They have a little humble brag about you to their friends whenever the opportunity arises. Even your divorce sounds like it's going really well,' Sasha said and realised how good it felt to get her little jealousies out there and off her chest.

'That's the showy surface,' Adele said. 'You've seen what's going on under the bonnet now. The job is stressful. Henry is so depressed and sad... and Sylvie... I just hope she will get through it all... but it's going to take some time.'

'Do you think Mum and Dad will have to sell up and leave Chadwell?' was Sasha's next question.

'It's the totally obvious thing to do, Pump... Sasha,' Adele corrected herself. 'It's far too big, none of us is going to ever move into it. It's madness they didn't do it years ago.'

'But we grew up there... and so did Dad.'

'Yes... I know. And it suits us all to have them here, to not have to think about it... to pretend that everything is the same and they're coping with it all. But I don't know if that is the truth right now and it certainly won't be in a few years' time.'

'It will just be so sad... for everyone, but especially them,' Sasha realised.

'Yes, it will be. But could it also maybe be something of a relief? And what other ending is there? Except leaving them to rattle around in there for the next ten years or so and then still having to do all the moving and packing and selling.'

'It will be a huge, huge job,' Sasha said with real dread.

'You can bring people in to help,' Ben reminded them. 'It doesn't have to be all down to you.'

They fell silent after this, Sasha thinking about Chadwell... her parents... her family. She had held onto the bad family memories. The ones that hurt her and made her think less of her family. Those times when Delphine hadn't paid attention, or Tony had said something insensitive, or Adele had dismissed her, or Beau had thrown an astonishing tantrum.

But there must have been many, many happy memories too,

otherwise, why would she still be coming here to be with them all? Why wouldn't she just have started to see much less of her family, like so many people did? It was time to let go of the past and build a relationship with her parents and her siblings that was based on the present and on understanding much more about them all. That was her goal now.

'Mummy! You are here!' There was LouLou's face on the pillow, her voice still husky and whispery.

'I know, darling. I told you I would get to the hospital. Daddy is here, too, and so is Adele. They've just dropped me at the front door and now she's gone to look for a parking space and he's buying some nice juice and yoghurts for you.'

'But how did you get through the landslide?'

'Well... that has been an adventure, I can tell you! Daddy got a ladder and some ropes from Grandpa's shed and then we sort of climbed up and over and scrambled down the other side. It wasn't very elegant.'

That was putting it mildly. Sasha's legs, already battered from getting down the pit to rescue LouLou, had suffered further bruises, scrapes and damage from scrambling over the mounds of earth. Then they'd had to direct the taxi driver over the phone to the road-block and pay him to take them all to the place where Adele had managed to arrange a hire car.

Adele had had to book the car, and drive it, because they were still in the throes of the credit-cards-not-working situation.

Sasha pushed her chair right up close to LouLou's bed and moved the hair out of her face tenderly.

'And what about you?' she asked. 'How are you doing? And you don't have to say much if it hurts your throat.'

'It doesn't hurt,' LouLou assured her, 'just sounds a bit crazy. So...' She smiled at her mum and began to explain her treatment. 'There are special bandages on my feet to help make them feel better. They got very cold at the bottom of the pit and then they got boiling hot and itchy and I know Dr Jo was worried that they wouldn't work properly any more. But I think they're going to be okay now. She said if I'd been there for another half an hour, she might have had to cut my toes off!' LouLou added, eyes wide and smiling at the drama of it all. 'She said it was quite like trench foot, which soldiers used to get in the war.' She followed this up with a giggle. 'And sometimes people get it when they go to music festivals.'

'I'm so glad you're going to be okay,' Sasha told her.

'Thank you very much for coming down to get me. That was quite brave of you,' LouLou added.

'Yeah!' Sasha agreed. 'Spiderman better look out. He may have a rival!'

This made LouLou laugh.

After a pause, Sasha put her hand over LouLou's and said, 'We don't need to talk about this now, if you don't want to... but I was kind of wondering—'

'What I was doing down there?' LouLou finished the question for her.

'Well, yes, I mean, you're so sensible, LouLou. I couldn't help thinking that for you to go down there, well, there must have been a very good reason.'

LouLou nodded solemnly. 'Yes, there was,' she said.

Sasha thought she should just wait quietly and let LouLou

speak in her own time. And after a long and thoughtful moment, LouLou did.

'Mummy, do you remember the last time I went to Grandma and Grandpa's? On my own?'

'Yes, it was near the end of the summer holidays.'

'Well... Grandma showed me her very special earrings and told me how expensive they were and showed me where she kept them to be safe.'

'Oh! I see...' This was all news to Sasha. LouLou hadn't told her anything about this.

'But I was reading this book about burglars...'

'Were you?'

'Yes. They were jewellery thieves in particular. And I didn't think the place Grandma was hiding the earrings in was very safe at all. Plus she is always forgetting things. So I told her she should keep them at the bank. But she laughed and said if there was one place where people would lose them, it was the bank. And then she told me about a friend whose bank had lost something very, very important – "The *dees* for a house, the *dees* for a house," she kept saying. Whatever that is.'

LouLou looked up and said in a confiding whisper, 'I think Grandma is *un peu folle quelquefois.*'

Sasha tried hard not to laugh and couldn't help adding, 'She's always been a bit like that, though... it's because she's *une Parisienne.*'

'*Naturellement!*' said LouLou.

'Anyway, sorry, I am interrupting,' Sasha said, 'and this is a very interesting story... so you thought the earrings should be somewhere safe.'

'Yes, and out of the house. Because in another book I read—'

'So many books!'

'Daddy thinks books and sports are the "most important things you'll need in life, young lady..."'

And again Sasha had to laugh at the expert mimicry on show here.

'So, in this book, a very old house, just like Chadwell, burst into fire because someone had left the candles on and, to be honest, Grandma is exactly the kind of person who might leave the candles on.'

'So, you thought the earrings might be stolen by a burglar, or burned in a fire... I'm sorry that you were so worried about them, LouLou.'

'I was worried,' LouLou agreed. 'Grandma said they cost more than some people's whole house, which is a lot. And it is kind of crazy to go around with a house dangling from your ear.'

'I agree,' Sasha sighed. Thinking, not for the first time, why the bloody hell hadn't Delphine sold the things years ago and done literally anything else with the money? Maybe they were some sort of security of last resort for Delphine. And a very special gift from her mother, of course.

'So...' LouLou paused, but it was all falling into place for Sasha now, who said, '*You* took the earrings, LouLou... but... how did you get into the drawer?'

'Grandma always takes her bracelet off and puts it on her dresser when she goes for her bath.'

'You took the key and opened the locked drawer when she was in her bath?'

LouLou nodded.

'And then you took the earrings out... in their box?'

LouLou nodded again.

'And then you...?'

'The next day, I walked to the clay pit, I climbed down ten

rungs, I counted them and then I dug a hole in the wall, right beside number ten and I put the box in there.'

Sasha put her hand over her mouth to hide the expression of utter astonishment that this news was causing.

'You climbed down into the clay pit... in the summer... and put the earrings into a *hole* in the mud wall? LouLou... that is... that was...'

'*Un peu folle?*' LouLou asked.

'Yes, it was... completely and utterly bonkers. I'm going to have to talk to Daddy about what books he's letting you read.'

'I think it was mainly Nancy Drew... he said you liked those books when you were my age.'

'I did,' Sasha remembered, 'but I never did anything as crazy as that because of them! So on Saturday when we spent all that time looking for the earrings, don't you think you could have just given me a hint, LouLou?'

LouLou did at least look apologetic. 'I'm sorry,' she said, 'but I thought I would get in so much trouble. I just wanted to get them back and not tell anyone what I'd done.'

'So this morning, you went back into the pit to get them for Grandma?'

'Yes... and it was so horrible and soggy and muddy and not like in the summer at all. I was digging the box out and it took ages because I couldn't remember exactly the place. I did put a stone on to mark it, but it must have fallen out. And just when I got my hand on the box, I must have given a little jump... and the rung broke and I fell into the water... not very far, but I couldn't reach back up. So then I was shouting and shouting and shouting because I suddenly thought what if no one finds me... because no one knew I was there. And just when I thought I might die because I was very cold and very wet and my voice was totally whispery, I heard you shouting my name and I threw the stones up. And that's when you came to pull me out... with your jeans!'

Sasha was trying very hard not to cry. She was squeezing her tears in her eyes and swallowing the ball in her throat.

'LouLou,' she whispered, 'this has been such a scary day. For you and for all of us.'

'Yeah...' LouLou agreed. 'But I did get the earrings.'

'Oh! You did actually get them?' With all her thoughts about clay pits and how LouLou could have had a really terrible accident down there, Sasha had forgotten about the earrings detail. That just seemed such a minor point, compared with everything else.

'They are in that drawer there,' LouLou said in her raspy whisper, pointing to the cabinet beside her bed. 'And I'm really glad you're here, because you can take them back to Grandma. I was worried I'd have to stay up all night guarding them.'

'Oh, LouLou... come here,' and Sasha pulled her daughter into her arms for as long as LouLou would let her.

LouLou finally wriggled out with the words, 'Shall we look in the box?'

'Yes... if you like.'

So Sasha opened the drawer in the bedside table and saw the familiar white mahogany wood box, but it was absolutely caked with dried mud.

'It's a bit of a mess,' she said, taking it out of the drawer.

'Yes, we better clean it up before we give it to Grandma, otherwise – *quelle horreur!*'

Sasha brushed off some of the mud, then carefully prised apart the edges of the box. Even in the dull fluorescent light of the hospital ward, the earrings, nestled against their pale velvet backdrop, looked stunning – pearls shimmering, multi-faceted emeralds winking in the light.

'Oh, my goodness,' Sasha gasped. 'I'd forgotten how absolutely beautiful they are.'

'Princessy,' LouLou agreed, her eyes fixed on the intricate jewels.

'Oh, LouLou... you took such a risk... imagine if this hadn't turned out so well... imagine if you'd lost the earrings, or really hurt yourself. Can you maybe check with me next time you think of such an adventurous plan?'

LouLou leaned back against her pillow. She suddenly looked very tired out by it all.

'I'm planning to stay here until you're fast asleep for the night and then Adele, Daddy and I are all going to stay in the hotel just five minutes away from the hospital, so if you need us, you just tell the nurse to phone us and we'll come. Is that okay?'

'Will you be here in the morning?' LouLou asked.

'Yes, of course. I think they're going to let you out then.'

'Can I hold the box?' she asked before giving a big yawn.

'Yes, of course.'

LouLou took the box and carefully brought out the earrings, laying them on the white hospital sheet over her lap. She admired them for several moments before turning her attention back to the box.

She put her deft fingertips onto the pale aqua velvet and pulled at it.

'What are you doing?' Sasha asked.

The velvet came out in a neat square and there behind it were several tightly folded pieces of paper, brown and aged, covered in faded handwriting that looked as if it had once been written in black ink.

'Well, well, well...' LouLou said, and it sounded so comical coming from her.

'LouLou... are you still planning to be a detective when you grow up?'

'Yes... definitely,' LouLou said.

'I think you'll be very good at it.'

Painstakingly, LouLou opened the delicate sheets of paper, and both she and Sasha studied the pages. In the middle of one was a pen and ink drawing, faded but recognisable as a regal-looking woman with her hair in an elegant bun, her head tilted slightly to the side and there, in her ears, were Delphine's heirloom earrings.

Underneath the drawing, Sasha could just make out the words:

Abigail MacGregor, 1865.

Before she married, Delphine's full name had been Delphine Anna MacGregor Carpen.

'MacGregor?' LouLou said in her croaky voice. 'Isn't that the same as Grandma?'

'Oh, my goodness... look at these beautiful drawings.'

'But this lady doesn't look like Grandma, does she?'

'No.'

'Well... this lady looks like she is African...' LouLou considered. 'I think her neck and her forehead look a lot like Grandma's. And definitely her earrings.'

'Oh, my goodness,' Sasha exclaimed, 'this is a sketch of Grandma's great-grandmother... I could never quite believe the story, but here is the proof.'

28

Much later, when Ben and Sasha were in their hotel room, Sasha took the earrings out of the box and showed them to him, along with the letters and the little pen and ink drawing of Abigail MacGregor. She tried to read the letters, but the handwriting was too faded, and they appeared to be in French.

'You've told me before that you had a great-great-grandmother who was African...'

'Yeah,' Sasha said, staring at the little sketch of this woman, 'born a slave, my mother used to tell us. She married a white man and together they ran grocery stores and became very wealthy.'

'How amazing,' Ben said.

'I can't tell you how incredible it feels to have the actual proof. Before, it was almost like a fairy tale that I just couldn't believe. There are no photographs of her. I didn't think there was any image of her at all... so it's really special to find this. Hopefully, Mama will be able to read the writing and tell us all about it,' Sasha said.

Lying down on the bed beside her husband, she asked him, 'How are you doing? Hanging in there?'

'Right now, the most important thing is that LouLou is going to be okay,' Ben told her. 'Everything else doesn't feel as if it matters so much...'

'Totally agree,' Sasha said.

'So that's kind of good... putting everything into perspective. And Sash? I love you,' he added. 'You're really strong and awesome, and you know what? I think the rest of your family is getting to see that too.'

She felt for his hand and gave it an appreciate squeeze. That was nice, she thought... very nice.

Then she sat bolt upright with an alarming thought. 'Ben! What should we do with the earrings... should we keep them in our room? Should we put them in the hotel safe? I mean, they're worth £150,000 – it's absolute madness.'

'Have you told your mother that you have them?'

'I know it's keeping her in the dark for another night, but I really want to see the look on her face when I hand her the box. Do you think that's okay?' Sasha admitted.

'Totally okay,' Ben said, then added, 'I think you should put them on.'

'Don't be crazy!'

'Yes, go on. Put them on,' he said, and Sasha felt the warmth of his gaze on her.

She sat on the side of the bed in the dim light and threaded the slim gold stalks into her earlobes.

She felt the rather shapeless vest top she was wearing didn't do the earrings justice, so she pulled it off over her head, and was now sitting topless in front of Ben.

He sat up beside her and touched the back of her neck, ran his fingers very gently across it.

'They look so beautiful,' he whispered. 'You look so beautiful.'

As he let his fingers slide across the nape of her neck again, making all the hairs stand up, she realised that she very much wanted the comfort and the thrill of being loved by Ben. She put her mouth on his and felt his hands move to her naked back.

But as soon as he kissed her back, all she could think about was Miss Scarlett Smith and the huge loan for the sustainable skis.

So she pulled back, breaking off from the kiss.

'Ben,' she began, 'we've not had a proper conversation about Scarlett Smith and her skis.'

'No,' he admitted, his eyes not leaving hers. 'Do we have to have it *now*?'

'Yes!' she said. 'Yes, we do have to have it right now. We have to have it whenever I say we have to have it. You have a lot of explaining to do.'

The earrings touched the side of her face as she spoke and, she had to admit, there was something a little power-enhancing about wearing jewellery like this.

Ben moved back from her and leaned against the bed's headboard.

'You and LouLou are the most important people in my life,' he said. 'Without you, I don't know what I would do or where I would be. And I really mean that. I'm really, incredibly sorry about the money stress, I think it puts everything that's really important to me at risk.'

'I didn't think it would,' Sasha said. 'I thought it could even bring us closer, working out how to get out of this situation... how to move on from it.'

'Marriages split up over money,' Ben insisted, 'it happens all the time. It's the number one cause of divorce. And that must be true because Google told me.' This came with a hint of a smile.

'I think infidelity is probably right up there as a major cause too,' Sasha countered.

'Oh... of course... but Sasha, honestly. That would be a huge word to use... and the wrong word,' Ben insisted. 'I met Scarlett several times, and I talked skiing and skis with her. We'd been on lots of the same ski runs, we'd even trained in some of the same places. We had a lot in common. Then I made a deal with her and borrowed money without telling you... which I should not have done.'

At this, Ben looked around the hotel room and gave a heartfelt sigh.

'And yes...' he added, 'I really enjoyed her company, more than I should have, and we definitely flirted, which I am unbelievably sorry about now,' he paused and held her gaze, 'but the only thing I need to come clean about is making the deal without telling you.'

'Borrowing money at an unbelievably stupid rate of interest, can I just remind you? Financial infidelity,' Sasha said sharply. 'It's a thing... you can look it up. And now, I see you as someone who could be persuaded by another woman; someone who could make a bad decision under stress; someone who doesn't necessarily want to make all the important decisions together with me.'

'I'm really, really sorry,' Ben said, 'if I could go back and undo this, I would. I'm going to talk to her again this week and see if we can come to some arrangement about the skis... something that's more beneficial...' Ben stopped in his tracks and read the look that Sasha was giving him.

'What am I saying?' he corrected himself. 'What about if *we* go and talk to Scarlett. Would you be okay with that?'

'Oh yes, *we* absolutely will go and talk to Scarlett. And not on Zoom either. I want to meet her in the flesh.'

For a moment, Sasha wondered if she could take the earrings to this meeting. She liked the idea of wearing the super-power earrings. But then walking around London with extremely valuable jewellery dangling from her ears struck her as pretty impractical. But then where was a practical place to ever wear these earrings? Inside your personal bank vault while your bodyguard looked on?

And wasn't it sort of ridiculous that just several little sparkling stones from this pair would probably solve her and Ben's problems completely?

Some people might have been sorely tempted, but not Sasha.

'Ben, we'll have to try to learn from all of this. Come out of it stronger and wiser.'

He nodded in agreement.

'Maybe we shouldn't do absolutely everything together,' she said. 'We're married, we have a daughter, we run our business together, maybe everyone needs some space... some areas that they are in charge of on their own. We need to think about that.'

'If you think it's a good idea,' he said, followed by, 'Please come here.'

He held out his arms to her and she knew that she was going to trust him. He wanted *them*. She could trust in that.

'What about the car?' she asked. 'Have we heard anything from the insurance company? It's the end of Monday... wasn't it supposed to be sorted out today?'

'Mmmmmm...' Ben kissed the side of her neck, 'please continue with your sexy talk,' he joked. 'Maybe you'd like to mention the overdue tax bill... and overdraft extensions...' he said in a husky, breathy voice as he kissed the top of her shoulder. 'What about those unpaid invoices... and bills in the red. Oh yeah... baby... bills in the red.'

She was kissing him back now, wrapping her arms around his shoulders, moving in on his neck and mouth, feeling his lean and sinewy body move against hers.

There was a muted buzz from the bedside table and both of them glanced over to Ben's upturned phone screen.

The name flashing beneath a photo of a chiselled pale face with a slick of black wavy hair was, of course – Sasha saw with a plummet of the heart – *Scarlett*.

29

Getting LouLou out of the hospital took some time. Final checks and sign-offs had to be made, medications ordered up from the pharmacy and everyone just had to be patient. But at last, LouLou – with her bandaged feet – was in the back of the car with Ben, and it was time to head back to Chadwell, where apparently the road had been cleared and Tony had finally been able to drive out and collect his copy of the *Telegraph* and bring supplies of non-party food to the house.

'Beau and Sura are staying on just to catch up with us all, which is very nice,' Adele had told them.

Ben had already plugged his phone into the car stereo and now hit the button on a playlist called 'Sunny Day Two' and a bouncy, happy song Sasha recognised filled the car.

When Adele's call was over, she reached into her handbag and brought out a beautiful pair of shades. 'Better than make-up,' she said as she put them on, 'and can I just say, it's nice to see you two so cheery.'

Sasha looked at her husband, who glanced at her, and they shared a knowing smile between them.

'Hotel rooms will do that,' Adele added.

Last night, that ringing phone with Scarlett's name had looked like a complete disaster to Sasha. She'd thought it was the end of everything. The end of trusting her husband and possibly the end of their marriage had flashed before her eyes as a real possibility.

But Ben had immediately answered the phone, putting it on speaker so he could let Sasha listen.

'Hello, Scarlett, how are you?' he'd asked in a perfectly business-like way.

'Hi, Ben... I really hope it's not too late to call you, but I've just had some very exciting news. And I couldn't wait to tell you.'

'Oh... what's that?'

'A company in France wants to take fifty pairs of skis. I've just received their email order and they're transferring the deposit tomorrow.'

Ben hadn't been able to help his smile at this. 'That is good news... that is really good news,' he told Scarlett. And he looked up to give Sasha a broad smile too.

'It's such a great opportunity,' Scarlett went on. 'Once they have the skis, I'm planning to go over there and take photos of people skiing with them and get some video reviews from other skiers. Some good marketing at this point could make all the difference. It could get the rest of the stock sold and maybe even pave the way for the manufacture of another lot.'

'That's great to hear,' Ben said, 'and are they buying them at the price we'd had in mind?'

'Yes, they are, so your share will be coming to you, which I'm sure you'll be relieved to hear. I thought it would be good to meet up,' she'd said next. 'I know it's been a bit of a complete disaster to date, and I've only cost you money. So it would be good to find out if you want to get in any further, or if you've maybe had second thoughts...'

Sasha was not so keen about this line of questioning. It had two obviously different meanings. Was this woman asking her husband if he wanted to be further involved with her business... or with her?

'My wife, Sasha, is my business partner,' Ben said, 'and I've been wrong not to involve her in this investment. To be honest, I'll need to talk it over with her. Then the three of us should meet up and we can talk about where we can go from here – what might work for us all. One thing I can tell you, Scarlett, is that Sasha has got a lot of marketing experience. She could work on that side and probably start a little bamboo ski revolution.'

At this, Ben had met Sasha's eyes and given her a wink.

'That sounds excellent, Ben. I'll send over some dates, and we'll see what could work for us all. And I'll look forward to meeting your wife.'

And shortly after that, the call had ended, and Sasha and Ben had fallen back into bed together, even closer than before.

* * *

The road to Chadwell was cleared; earth was piled up on both sides and the Tarmac was still red and muddy as they drove over it in the hire car. The slope at the side of the road had been covered with heavy-duty wire netting in an attempt to stabilise the ground.

'Don't you always love driving up to Chadwell?' Adele said. 'It always looks so elegant, and stirs all those memories of coming home and always the hope that this visit will be lovely and no one will get snarled up in the same old arguments and unhappy memories and it will all be a fresh start and a happy time.'

'I always thought it was just me who felt that,' Sasha said.

'No,' Adele said, 'not just you.'

Just then LouLou piped up from the back seat, 'Auntie Adele, did Mummy tell you about the earrings?'

'Yes, she did, and I'm just so relieved that everything has all turned out okay,' she said.

'And did she tell you about the letters and the drawing I found in the box?' was LouLou's next question.

'Yes, I've even seen them,' Adele said. 'It's wonderful... did Grandma know about the letters? We'll have to wait and find out.'

'Here you are! How wonderful!'

Delphine greeted them at the door with her hair in place, lipstick on, shiny gold jewellery, beautifully dressed. She had always told them, no matter the crisis, one must be put together. As Sasha saw her mother looking unruffled, standing on the threshold of her home, Sasha understood the need to look pulled together and capable. It gave everyone else confidence. It was as if Delphine was saying by her very appearance: *it's okay, everything is going to be all right.*

'Oh, my little darling,' Delphine fussed around her granddaughter, 'come into the house; come out of the cold. Beau has built a huge fire in the drawing room so you can have a sofa and be warm. And the big television has been set up in there and I've made scones and we'll have a giant pot of tea... and oh, my goodness, what an ordeal. What a relief that you are back now.'

LouLou was carried into the house and straight onto the sofa by Ben. He propped her feet up on sofa cushions, having made sure she had a good view of the TV.

'My rules are suspended for one week,' he told her, 'so go crazy... watch every single thing you want to watch and then it's back to sport and improving books.' He gave her a kiss, a big grin and smoothed down her hair. 'And maybe we'll calm down on the detective novels and thrillers just for a little bit.'

* * *

And then there was tea and the hubbub of everyone in the vast room, eating Delphine's delicately Parisian version of an English scone. That was when Sasha began to tell the story of what exactly had happened to the half of her family that didn't know yet.

'So, there is a reason that LouLou went down into that clay pit, but probably, a bit like me, you're going to find it quite hard to believe.'

'We are all ears,' Beau said, passing a scone to Pica, who was balanced on his knee.

'When LouLou was here in the summer, she went down into the pit for a very particular reason.'

'You went down there in the summer, LouLou?' Tony exclaimed. 'You mean this wasn't even your first time down in the clay pit? But what have we always told you?'

'I know, Grandpa,' LouLou said gravely, 'but I was doing something important.'

'LouLou was worried that something really special was going to get lost, or even stolen,' Sasha went on. 'So she hid it in the pit back in August and yesterday, she crawled down to bring it out again.'

'Oh, LouLou!' Delphine said. 'You could have asked us for help. We would all have wanted to help you get your treasure back.'

'Yes, I should have,' LouLou agreed. 'I shouted for a very long time, until my voice completely disappeared. And that's when Mummy found me and came down to get me.'

'And is your special treasure still down at the bottom of the pit?' Delphine asked. 'Because, if so, we will get someone with a ladder and a torch to bring it up. And then you will promise me never, ever to go near the place again. In fact, Tony, you will phone Mr Perkins today and arrange to have it filled in.'

'No, LouLou managed to get the treasure up,' Sasha replied for her daughter, and she opened her handbag and brought out the mahogany box, cleaned up to a rich polish now.

'Oh, *mon dieu*,' Delphine exclaimed, recognising the box immediately. She clasped her hands together and looked absolutely
astonished.

'Is that... *really*...?' Tony began. 'Good Lord!'

'The jewellery box,' Beau exclaimed.

'And are the earrings still inside?' Delphine asked.

By way of reply, Sasha opened up the box and handed it to her.

Delphine's reaction was a shriek of delighted surprise, but then
she looked as if she might cry. She stretched out her hand and took
a hold of Tony's arm.

'We could finally sell these and stay here... at least for some
more time,' she said. But this was not the breathless delight, the
high excitement and relief that Sasha had expected. Not at all.
There was questioning in her voice as she looked at her husband.

Tony looked back at her, as if he was trying to read her
expression.

'What would you like to do, my dear?' he asked and patted her
hand gently.

'What would you like to do, *mon cher*?' she asked in reply.

'We'll never get anywhere like this...' he smiled at her.

'Well...' She looked around the room at all her family members
in turn and then turned to look at her husband once again. 'To be
completely honest with you, I was just starting to like the idea of
living somewhere a little more... manageable.'

'Were you really?' Tony asked. 'Really? You? The *chatelaine* of
Chadwell?'

'I was just starting to think about how much money we would
have in the bank – a very comfortable, very secure amount. We
could pay for any care that we needed, but before all that starts – we
could travel to Paris every year... maybe even have a little apartment
there. I mean... we're not dead yet, Tony,' Delphine said with a
smile. 'There's still plenty of time left to have some fun!'

'I love the apartment idea,' Adele chimed in. 'We'll all come and visit you in Paris.'

But before everyone started discussing that, there was something Sasha wanted to ask first.

'Mama... do you know about the letters that are in the jewellery box? Do you know who Abigail is?'

'Oh yes, I know who Abigail MacGregor was,' Delphine said. 'She was my great-grandmother. The one I've often told you about – she was born a slave but died a free and wealthy woman. But I don't know anything about letters?'

Sasha could see the curiosity on all the other faces around the room.

'Behind the velvet in the box, there are some letters and a little pen and ink sketch that I think must be of her,' Sasha explained. 'She looks like a beautiful black woman and she's wearing these earrings.'

Sasha showed her mother how to lift out the velvet.

'Oh, my goodness!' Delphine exclaimed as she saw the faded pages.

'That must be her and look, those are the earrings.'

'So, it's honestly true?' Beau couldn't keep the surprise from his voice. 'One of our ancestors was a slave?'

'Yes,' Delphine confirmed. 'My mother told me the story many times. Abigail was born in Mauritius in 1825, the fifth child of a woman from Mozambique. They were all slaves and Abigail was not freed until the age of ten. She was given the surname MacGregor because that was the name of the landowner.'

This caused audible gasps around the room.

'It's an extraordinary story,' Delphine went on calmly. 'She married my hard-working, white great-grandfather, and his family never spoke to him again. But together, they started from scratch and built up a grocery business that made them very wealthy people. She died of an infection when my grandmother was a teenager. I've always felt so proud of her.' Delphine looked at the pages. 'I need to get my glasses and read what is written here. My mother was proud of the story too... but the rest of my family,' Delphine shrugged, 'I grew up in a very prejudiced family in a very prejudiced society. And it was something everyone else preferred to keep hushed up. That's why I'm not close to the rest of them any more... well, I haven't been for a very long time, as you all know.'

There was utter silence in the room as Delphine spoke; every member of her family was hanging on to every word.

'When I was a teenager, my plan was to go to Paris to study and take my mother with me. But, in the end, she didn't want the scandal of leaving my father, let alone a divorce, so she stayed on with him in Mauritius. And I had to leave her there... But she gave me the earrings when I left and she said that Abigail had thought they brought luck and good fortune, but they were also insurance, something you could slip into a handbag, steal out of a house, or out of a country even and start again.'

Delphine stood up and located her glasses on one of the little side tables. 'Let's take a look,' she said and, glasses in place, she began to scan the pages.

'Oh, you will like this, my girls. "*Sell them if you have to and know that you come from a line of women who are clever, strong, resourceful and determined.*"'

Adele, Beau and Sasha were all absolutely stunned. They stole looks at one another as if to see who was the most surprised.

'I feel like I'm on an episode of *Who Do You Think You Are?*' Beau said.

'In Paris, even in the 1960s, when I told some of my friends about my heritage, they were shocked and treated me differently,' Delphine said. 'You can't predict how people will react. I'm very proud of Abigail, and of my own mother, but that same pride in them makes me ashamed of my own father. These feelings are very strong... very mixed.'

'Well... you have to admit, it does explain a lot about the Griffon hair,' Beau said, obviously wanting to lighten the mood, and Sasha put a hand up to her unruly hair with a gasp of realisation. It had always been unusual to have an island in the Indian ocean as part of her history, but now she could really believe that she'd also had a black great-great-grandmother, who'd gone from slave to owner of fabulous jewels in one short lifetime. It was amazing – really amazing.

But there were some other items she wanted brought out of the family vault too.

'Mama... I don't know if now is a good time... but you said you would show us the photos you had of baby Pierre.'

30

'Oh dear.' Tony got up out of his chair. 'This is going to be quite difficult.'

'I'm going to go upstairs...' Delphine said. 'I will set some things out and I'll call you up when I... when we're ready. Come with me, Tony,' she said.

It was nearly half an hour later when Adele, Beau and Sasha were called to Tony's bedroom.

'What about us?' LouLou asked sulkily.

'I'm sure you'll be allowed to have a look very soon. But they probably don't want to be crowded,' Sasha explained.

Up in the bedroom, photographs – framed and unframed – a baby's blanket and a little hairbrush had all been laid out across the bedspread on her father's bed.

Sasha picked up the one in the frame that she'd seen with her mother to look at it more closely.

'You were right, Sasha,' Delphine began. 'In this picture you are only four years old. It's August and I'm bringing Pierre home from the hospital. It was quite a difficult birth, so they kept us in for a few days afterwards.'

'Oh, look at us,' Adele said, holding up another photo that showed the baby lying on the sofa with Adele on one side, very serious in her new school uniform, and Sasha smiling on the other.

'All three of you were so adorable,' Delphine said, 'and you two were lovely with him, so kind and so gentle. He was a beautiful baby,' she went on, 'very calm and easy to look after....'

There was a pause in which Sasha felt a cold shiver travel down her spine. How awful it was to think that he had died.

'One afternoon – and there was nothing, absolutely not one thing unusual about that afternoon, believe me, I've been over it so many times – I thought he had been asleep for a long time in his Moses basket, so I went to check on him. Well—' Their mother broke off with a sob. 'He—'

'I am so, so sorry,' Sasha said, not needing her mother to say any more if it was too upsetting for her.

But Delphine spoke through her tears. 'He was cold and blue... and I just knew that he had died.'

And with this revelation, confusing memories from Sasha's earliest childhood began to make sense. Before, there had been a jumbled kaleidoscope: her mother crying in the blue bedroom, and the lovely dinners that stopped, and Sasha and Adele staying with their auntie in Norwich for several weeks, but they didn't really understand why. And bear... the baby 'bear' that was taken away from her... something clicked into place for Sasha.

'Did I call him bear?' she asked.

Delphine looked up with a surprised smile. 'Yes, you did, Sasha, you did! You couldn't say Pierre, so you always called him bear.'

'Why can't I remember any of this?' Sasha asked, full of frustration.

'You girls were only little, and everyone told us we should let you forget him... that it would be best that way.'

For Sasha, her mother's endless joy at baby Beau also made so much more sense now. Her mother's insistence that Beau be with her all the time, that she must watch over Beau, touch him and check him every twenty minutes. Delphine must have found Beau quite the most wonderful and funny child in the world, because another beautiful boy baby had come into her sad and grieving world and made her so happy again.

Sasha felt as if the pieces were falling into place, and she was finally understanding the family dynamic now, in a way that she had never understood it before. Previously, she had even doubted her own memories and had thought that she must have made some of it up – feeling so alone and abandoned in that year before she went to school with Daddy at work, Adele at school, her mother crying in the blue room and the knowledge that someone had taken away her baby bear.

Maybe this was when Tony had forged his happy relationship with Adele, because he would pick her up from school and listen to all her jolly tales and cheerful chat and it was a lovely antidote to tearful Delphine and withdrawn little Sasha at home with nothing to tell.

Sasha felt as if she finally understood so much more about her parents. And to understand is, of course, to forgive.

And as she looked carefully through these treasured baby photos, Sasha's very happiest memories of Delphine came flooding back. It was when she had just had LouLou, of course. Delphine had packed a bag and come to stay with them for a full three weeks. Before this post-natal visit, Sasha had found it hard to stay in her mother's company for a full two hours, but Delphine had been amazing during that time. She kept house for them, cooked beautiful meals, bought vases for the flowers that arrived and washed all the new baby clothes. She did her Parisian thing of wandering round the local shops, chatting to the shopkeepers and finding out where to source the really good bread and the best ripe fruit and the speciality cheese, even in their unglamorous London neighbourhood.

And she had been so good with the baby. She seemed to instinctively understand everything that LouLou's brand-new, clueless parents did not. 'Now she's hungry, now you feed her. Now she is tired, so let's give her a little rock *comme ca* and there she is... already falling asleep.'

Sasha was so, so grateful for that time. When had she ever felt more mothered? Delphine had concentrated purely on her and her new little family and shone all her light and her love on it.

When the visit finally drew to its end, Ben had gone out and bought Delphine a beautiful silver photo frame to say thank you. Inside, they'd put a lovely photo of Delphine holding her brand-new granddaughter.

Before the arrival of LouLou, Sasha and Delphine had struggled to know what to talk about when they met one another or talked on the phone. After her arrival, it became easy. They talked about parenting and all the little achievements and stages of LouLou's development. The day LouLou managed to sit up, that merited a phone call. Baby food recipes were discussed at length – Delphine had a great belief in the power of carrot juice and thought this was something babies should be drinking from an early age.

Yes, her mother had made up for many of her missteps by becoming an absolutely wonderful grandmother. Maybe that was true of most mothers, though. All the many mistakes you made as a mother, you could try to undo them the next time round with your grandchildren.

'Why did we never talk about Pierre, or keep his memory alive and simply remember him?' Sasha asked her parents, but very gently.

'We talked about him between ourselves,' Tony said, 'we remembered.'

'You don't know how it was then... I felt ashamed,' Delphine began, 'as if I had done something wrong. People were embarrassed for me. They would meet me in the shops or at church and they didn't know what to say. And you, my darlings, you and Adele, you were both so sad. So we thought it was best not to talk... to take the photos down and pack the little blanket and basket away and then... if you asked, I changed the subject. I didn't want to talk about him. And you were small, so... very soon, I thought you had forgotten about him.'

'Are you okay, Dad?' Adele asked, because Tony was suddenly looking tired and had taken a seat in the small sofa in the room.

'Oh yes, I'm okay,' he said in as level a voice as he could manage. But he sounded a little shaky. 'Stiff upper lip. Keep calm and carry on... that's how we had to manage these sort of things back then.'

Delphine went to sit beside him.

'These sort of things?' Beau repeated. 'It was a very upsetting family tragedy and I'm really sorry that you didn't get the support you must have needed.'

'Oh, well...' Tony began but then he had to stop because suddenly his eyes were full of tears and he wasn't able to talk.

'I'm so sorry...' Sasha was at the back of the sofa with one arm around the shoulder of each parent. 'You must still feel so sad about it now and then... on his birthday and when you wonder what he would be doing now... maybe he'd be the one who'd be buying the house and making it home for a new generation of Griffons.'

Tony put his hands over his face and gave a deep and guttural sob. 'Forgive me...' he said, trying to clear his throat and get a grip on his emotions.

'It's okay, Dad,' Adele whispered.

'Tony, my darling, what is the matter?' Delphine asked tenderly.

'I don't want the Griffon era at Chadwell to end,' he said finally, his voice cracking with emotion. 'I just can't imagine it. I can't imagine packing, or leaving, or living anywhere else. I'm sorry if that makes no sense, or isn't practical... we'll have to find another way.'

'Well... maybe we will,' Delphine said, and gave her husband's arm a loving touch.

'I love this house,' he added. 'I've lived here my entire life... not many people can say that these days. And your mother loves it too. I was never really joking when I said that she married me for the house... well, let's say the house sealed the deal.' He turned to Delphine and almost managed a smile.

'But yes,' he went on, 'it is too big for us, of course it's too big for us – anyone with eyes can see that.'

'What do you want to happen?' Beau asked gently. 'In an ideal situation?'

'I would have loved one of my children to buy a big share and then take the house over. But it's a huge old house in the depths of the Norfolk countryside. Even with the internet – and our Wi-Fi is pretty patchy – I can't see that any of you would want to move here. Beau's business is in Birmingham, Adele's in Switzerland and you, Sasha, you seem happy in London.'

Sasha appreciated that her father said this, even though Adele was surely the only one who could realistically have bought a share of the house.

'So, we probably will have to let it go. But it will break your mother's heart... and mine,' he admitted, 'and maybe your hearts will all be broken too.'

Sasha, Beau and Adele exchanged looks. Sasha couldn't help

feeling that it was almost physically painful to see her parents so upset.

Adele took a breath and her face seemed to take on a very determined look. 'There is an awful lot of brain power and talent in this room,' she said. 'I think we need to brew up some coffee and start to come up with some really good ideas – together.'

31

In the village was the small, plain church, built by the Normans – or 'the first wave of French people who tried to civilise the English', as their mother liked to say. Way back when they were young, the church had been a regular feature of life. They'd gone with their parents, not every week, but at least once a month. Knelt on the tapestry kneelers, sung their way through favourite old hymns, watched bright English sunlight stream through the plain boiled glass of the leaded windows, and said hello to all the familiar faces in the congregation.

Behind the church was a small graveyard where graves from the past centuries were dotted, here and there, with the shiny stones of more modern times.

If their parents hadn't told them where to look for Pierre's grave, Sasha was sure they would have found it anyway, because in one corner of the graveyard there was a beautiful Guelder rose bush, one of their mother's favourite plants – white flowers in the summer and glossy berries in the winter – beside a perfectly plain beige headstone.

'Over there, I think,' she said to Adele and Beau, because it was just the three of them who had decided to make this visit together.

'I would take you,' their mother had said, 'but I think there has been quite enough emotional upset for one weekend.'

'Agreed,' Tony had added. 'I'm not up for it either, my dears. But you three don't mind going on your own, do you? We'll explain where to find it.'

Sure enough, when they got to the headstone, it was engraved with the name Pierre Anthony Griffon, the tragic dates of a life that spanned only from 28 July to 16 October, and words that made all three of them spill tears and hold on to one another: 'Love lives on'.

Beside the Guelder rose was a glossy green-leaved camellia bush, some five feet high now, with a thick trunk. *Camellia japonica*, Sasha guessed, another of her mother's absolute favourites, planted to drop big creamy flowers onto her baby's grave throughout the spring. The small plot was edged with beautiful smooth stones that had almost certainly come from one of the family's favourite beaches, some ten miles away. Sasha crouched down to touch the stones and push some of the leaves and moss from them.

As she put her hands onto the cool, smooth surfaces, all of a sudden, she remembered. She remembered an amazing, blue-skied, blue-sea day but chill, blustery, at the very end of autumn. She and Adele were out on the pebble beach with their mummy and daddy and they were all collecting these stones.

'Adele?' Sasha said, not able to take her hands from the stones. 'We were on the beach, the one with the prettiest stones, and Mum and Dad had two big buckets and we were only to collect the very nicest ones, the most beautiful ones, and they kept telling us—'

'—They were for the baby... oh my god, I remember it too,' Adele gasped. 'I remember it... because we never really did outdoorsy things like that... *the baby*,' she repeated. 'I remember being so confused about why the baby wasn't coming home again and why did he need—'

'—All these stones?' Sasha added quietly. She was angry with herself that she had forgotten so much. *What did Pierre look like? What was he like to hold? To touch?* For eleven weeks, she must have been with him almost all of the time, watching him being fed and held, changed and bathed. When they got back to Chadwell later, she would ask her mother to bring out all the photos that there were to see if any dormant memories were stirred.

'It's so sad,' Beau said. 'Incredibly sad... I'll pass Dokus around for extra cuddles when we get home.'

'Home...' Adele repeated. 'You still think of Chadwell as home, don't you?'

'Yes...' Beau replied. 'Yes... I do.'

Meanwhile, Sasha was imagining holding a plump, bundled baby in her arms and feeling a deep and unusual maternal pang.

After several long quiet minutes, taking in the lovely green stillness of the place, the peacefulness, Adele broke the thoughtful silence by announcing, 'I think we need tea... and cake, especially cake.'

'We need to go to Café Suze, don't we?' Sasha guessed.

'Oh yeah,' Beau agreed. 'Nowhere better.'

'I think you mean nowhere else,' said Adele.

* * *

Once they were settled into their seats at the café, Beau looked at the menu and then told his sisters in a stage whisper, 'I swear to god, nothing has changed... whenever I come in here with Mum, we look at the menu and it is exactly the same.'

'But are the cakes as good as they always were?' Adele asked.

'Oh yes, absolutely. Finest cakes in all of Norfolk,' Beau enthused.

'Coffee and walnut,' Sasha said after glancing for only a moment through the array of classic English treats. 'I cannot let it go. And you're going to have that weird chocolate mint slice thing, aren't you?' She looked at Adele.

'Well, this is the only place in the world I can get it... so most likely, yes.'

'And Beau will consider carrot cake... or maybe chocolate cake... but then he's going to for the classic scone with jam and cream.'

'So true, so true...' Beau said with the dimply smile that hadn't really changed that much from when he was eight.

It was odd to be just the three of them... with no spouses, or children, or parents attached. They never did this. But it was kind of thrilling too. It reminded them of nothing from the past. Beau was so much younger than his sisters that they'd hardly done anything together, just the three of them.

So, this was new... but somehow a reminder of their childhoods.

'The most important thing,' Adele began, once the orders for the coffee and walnut, mint slice and cream scone had been made, 'is to make absolutely sure that this is what you and Sura want, Beau. Your reason for doing this can't be because you feel guilty and no one else has stepped in. So you need to go home and really think it over before you make any moves.'

'We have done nothing but think about it and talk it over between us,' Beau said, face full of enthusiasm. 'We really, really want to do this.'

During the big brainstorm, Beau had revealed that he and Sura did, in fact, want to move out of Birmingham and, in Beau's case, back to Norfolk. Both had grown up in the countryside and wanted that kind of lifestyle for their young children. But they didn't know how to put this idea into motion. It was the family that helped them to flesh out the plan. So now, they were going to sell their two businesses in Birmingham, open one new one in Norwich and apply for planning permission to build a new house in the walled garden at Chadwell.

Delphine and Tony's faces, as the plan began to take shape, had been wonderful to see: the relief and the excitement.

'That way,' Adele had suggested, 'you can live close by and keep an eye on Mum and Dad... and in the future, if it makes sense, Mum and Dad can move into your all mod-cons modern house and you can move your family into Chadwell, paying a proper rent, of course.'

Then Beau, with his dimply smile, had added, 'And here's hoping that business will go well enough and I'll be the one buying up the Hall... maybe with the help of some investment from my successful sisters.'

Now, in the coffee shop, the siblings wanted to go over details a little further. 'Do you need an overview on the accounts?' Adele asked her baby brother.

'I love you, my darling big sis,' Beau replied, 'but that's why I pay an accountant. I've already had some good conversations with him and my bank. It really does look feasible.'

'And when do you think this is all going to happen?' Sasha wondered.

'We won't move over here until we've sold our existing businesses, got planning permission for the house and bought the new business Realistically, it might take about five or six months.'

It felt like a huge relief to Sasha. She had thought they were going to have to help her parents move out when they really didn't want to and now Beau was going to solve what had seemed like an impossible problem.

'Are you sure it's what you want?' she asked Beau, even though the question had already been asked.

'We really want to give it a go,' Beau replied. 'If there's a point in the future when we feel it isn't working out, then we'll just have to rethink. Is that so bad?'

'No,' Sasha smiled and shook her head. 'Can you imagine living at Chadwell?'

'Not on our own, to be honest... at some point in the future, maybe it would make a wonderful hotel or country club. I'd be interested in running that.'

'Yes...' Adele agreed. 'I'd love to see it getting a really glamorous makeover. But that would be the end of an era...'

'I guess eras do have to end,' Beau said gently. 'How else do new ones begin?'

'Spoken like a true youngest child – the disrupter!' Adele said.

'Mum is going to love this so much,' Sasha said. 'Having her favourite little boy living so close. I mean, are you prepared for that level of attention?'

'Does it help a little to know that she lost a baby before I was born?' he asked. 'I mean, does it explain why she's so overprotective, overattentive about me? It's not as if I didn't notice when we were growing up,' he added, 'and even now... yes, I do see that she always worries about me first before she thinks about the two of you.'

'Yes,' Sasha said. 'I think it helps to know. Poor Mama... I feel very sad for her. And it does explain a lot.'

'Life will get in the way for us too,' Adele said, 'throw all kinds of things at us that we never expected. Boy, I've got a lot to do when I get back home,' she added.

'But you do have a handsome young boyfriend to look after you,' Sasha reminded her.

'Oh... but Henry... it's a minefield. Some days... I don't know what I want.'

Adele looked Adele-ish, Sasha couldn't help thinking; her

strange mixture of relieved, moved, offended, affectionate and haughty.

'You're a funny old thing,' Sasha told her and moved her hand onto Adele's.

'What's that supposed to mean?' Adele said.

'I love you, that's all,' Sasha said. 'I miss you and we need to stay in touch more.'

'That's very nice... and all the same right back at you both.' She turned to include Beau.

'There is one other thing...' Adele began. 'Beau? Did you give Dokus a middle name?'

'Alexander, after Sura's father,' Beau replied.

'Oh!' was Sasha's response.

'Oooh!' said Adele.

'Yes... I know what you're thinking,' Beau said, leaning forward onto the table. He looked cute, Sasha saw, her kid brother – the baby of the family. In a denim shirt open at the neck with a fresh white T-shirt underneath, dark hair in those tight Griffon curls round his face. He still looked young and a touch studenty, like one of those cool French guys you date on your uni exchange term.

'We're only thinking of Dokus,' Adele explained, 'and his future years in the playground. Alexander is a lovely name.'

'And think how pleased Sura's dad will be,' Sasha added. 'And it's not so unusual to be called by your middle name. You still get to keep the Dokus part.'

'Or there might still be time to pop into the registrar's and say you've changed your mind,' Adele said.

'This comes from a place of love,' Sasha added quickly with a disarming smile.

'Love for Dokus,' Adele clarified.

'Okay... okay... I will talk to Sura... I will see what she wants to do,' Beau relented. 'I will grudgingly admit that "Dokus" is maybe just a tiny, little bit too out there.'

'So what about Abigail MacGregor... and her incredible story?' was the other important thing Sasha wanted to ask her siblings.

'What I love,' Beau began, 'is that we come from a long line of self-made men and women... who would sell their jewels if they had to.'

'I love the multi-national part,' Adele said. 'I've got Mauritius, France, England, now Switzerland in the mix. Maybe I need a really exotic posting next... maybe I can advise the fat cats of Cameroon how to run their investments.'

'We need to find out all about her... all about the family in Mauritius,' Sasha said.

'Is a family trip to Mauritius on the cards?' Adele asked. 'We could finally meet all those cousins and uncles and aunties and dig into the archives.'

'On the one hand, that would be amazing... on the other hand, it sounds very expensive... plus... we've only just survived a long weekend together,' Sasha said.

'Very good points,' added Beau. 'Maybe we need to start with some online research.'

'Oh...' he looked at his phone. 'Mama texting... in capitals, but then she always texts in capitals, so that she can see... COME HOME, VERY SURPRISING NEWS,' he read out.

'Oh, good grief...' was Sasha's response. 'What now?'

32

As Adele drove them through the oh-so familiar country lanes to get back to Chadwell, Sasha recognised the equally familiar feelings bubbling up in her mind. She loved her parents and siblings, but she could also feel quite stifled by them. Growing up, she had always known she would not be the person who could live within a ten-mile radius of home and be a daily, or even weekly part of her parents' lives. Adele had obviously felt the same, and now that Sasha thought about it, Beau was always the one who had liked life in Norfolk the best.

He still kept up with his old school friends and still went for occasional nights out on the town when he was home.

She loved her family, but even as a young teenager, she had wanted to get away from the stifling English and French properness of it all and from the constant stream of criticism and disapproval both parents seemed to rain down on her head when she was younger.

Her phone bleeped and bringing it out to look, she saw a message from Deepa... last seen at the till of embarrassment in Waitrose.

Hey Sasha, how was your visit to the folks? Want to get our girls together next weekend?

Hey, this weekend has been one adventure after the next: a landslide, an air ambulance, LouLou in hospital, Ben & I having to face up to fact our biz is in trouble. But we're all good. Really look forward to telling you about everything. Saturday afternoon? Big hug, S.

So sorry to hear all this... but glad you and LouLou OK. You guys are so amazing, you got this! See you Saturday. Our place? Dinner after play-time? Love you guys. XX

There... she felt relief flood through her system. That was going to be her new policy: that it was okay to be honest with good friends. It let them in, and it allowed them to be better friends. It was not Sasha and Ben's fault that the business was where it was. And they would do everything they could to get it out of this place, even if that did involve selling skis with sexy Miss Scarlett.

* * *

Back at Chadwell Hall, the news from Delphine took a good few moments to digest. 'We spoke to Finlay at the auction house... and he said he was in the area, so he would come round and take a look at the earrings... and...'

Sasha could feel the silence in the room as a physical thing, almost a vacuum, a slight popping of the ears and no one even taking a breath.

'They are beautiful imitations of the real thing,' Delphine said.

Whoooosh... breaths were let out and questions began.

'What?'

'Imitations?'

'And you didn't know?'

'When did this happen?'

'So aren't they worth *anything*?'

'They are so well done,' Delphine said in a voice that was shaking slightly, 'that they are probably worth about £1,000.'

'Oh. My. God.' Sasha sank back into the sofa. She thought about the risks LouLou had taken, all because of the myth of the value surrounding these earrings.

Tony sounded calm and philosophical when he said with a sigh, 'Well, I suppose that's life and that's often business too. Sometimes, you have to fake it till you make it; sometimes you have to sell the family jewels to get to the next level... in this case, it looks like they maybe had to do both.'

'I don't know who had the copies made,' Delphine added. 'My own mother thought they were real and that only the matching necklace had been sold to raise money for a property deal. Finlay thought this looked like quality work from the 1910s.'

Beau went and sat beside Delphine, so she had him on one side and Tony on the other. She instantly looked a little more comforted.

'So where does this leave you both?' was Sasha's next question. 'Will you still be able to stay here?'

'Yes,' Tony said, 'we have some money to live on, and we have some money to do the essential repairs.'

'Especially if Ben can come and help,' Delphine added with a smile. And Sasha couldn't help smiling, too, at her mother's new-found appreciation of Ben.

'So, we'll carry on here for a few years until Beau has built his new house, then hopefully, we can arrange a mutually beneficial swap. Money from the earrings would have been extra security... but there we go,' Tony said.

'And let that be a lesson to you, my dears,' he added, 'things aren't always as they seem and prepping for the later years is probably a very good idea.'

'Well, I've got an idea too,' said Beau, taking hold of Delphine's hand. 'This time next year, when my Norwich bar is up and running, and Sasha and Ben are back on their feet, Adele can find some time off, and Mama and Dad have sold some old candlesticks for pocket money...' this provoked some laughter, 'let's go do a long weekend in Paris! Let's have a forty-first wedding anniversary party over there to make up for the fiasco of this one.'

Everyone seemed to love this idea – Tony held out his coffee cup as if to toast it and Delphine beamed with delight.

'This time next year... that's a wonderful idea. The big Paris reunion!' Adele exclaimed.

'And if we survive that... then the year after, it's Mauritius,' was Sasha's suggestion, to general laughter and nods of approval.

Ben put his head round the door cautiously, wondering if it was okay to intrude on this Griffon family moment.

'Hello... I hope I'm not interrupting... the family... *fun*?' He sounded uncertain.

'Yeah,' Sasha said with a wink, 'fun it is. It's time for us to head, isn't it?'

'The car is all packed and LouLou is pretty keen to get back to school and show off her weird feet to her friends before they look completely normal again.'

'*Mais naturellement!*' said Delphine.

For Sasha, it felt bittersweet to say goodbye. She held every single member of her family close, Adele and Sylvie first, then Sura, Beau and little Pica, baby *Alexander* (Sura had agreed instantly), then finally her dad and her mother.

When she hugged her father, she realised he was a little smaller and slimmer than she remembered; and when it was time to hug and kiss her mother, Sasha couldn't stop the memory of finding her in that little blue room, crying alone, and felt her own tears well up.

It had helped to learn so much past family history. She saw her parents now as people who'd had some really difficult times and had done the very best that they could.

Feeling her mother's slim shoulders against her hands as she hugged her, never before had Sasha been so struck by the feeling that her time with them was slipping through her hands. The sand was moving through the hourglass and she didn't know when, but she did know that it would run out one day, and their time together would be over. Had she asked them everything she wanted to know? Had she told them all the things she wanted them to hear?

Not quite yet... but she did feel that big changes had been made over this bizarre weekend.

'*Je t'aime, Mama*,' she said, bestowing an extra hug and kiss on Delphine.

'*Je t'aime aussi, ma petite Sasha.*'

And it felt so warm and genuine and loving.

'This is for you... for good luck.' Delphine passed her a box wrapped in a plastic bag. And Sasha was so touched, thinking her mother had baked, or made them some sandwiches for the journey.

'Thank you, Mama.'

'See you really soon, Dad,' she told her father. 'Take care of yourself,' which was Dad-speak for 'I love you'.

'Take care of yourself too,' he replied.

She walked towards the snazzy red SUV that the insurance company had provided while negotiations around their own smashed car continued. Ben was already in the driver's seat and LouLou all set in the back. Sasha got in and buckled up as Ben turned on the ignition and they all waved to everyone standing at the front of the house.

He beeped the horn several times as he drove out of the

driveway and onto the first of the many roads that would take them out of the heart of Norfolk and back towards their lives in London.

Once they were out of sight of the house, Ben turned to his daughter in the back and said, 'Hit it, LouLou!'

And LouLou pressed play.

Loud music *blasted* into the car and Sasha began to laugh. She knew this song... from the gym, from nightclubs, from dancing and singing at the top of her voice... all about leaving home and never looking back.

All three of them shouted out the chorus together.

'You'll feel like this about us, one day!' Ben said to LouLou over the music.

'No, I will never, ever,' LouLou insisted.

'Yes, you will!' Sasha told her.

'Are we going to be okay?' Ben asked, turning to give Sasha a long and loving look.

'Of course we're going to be okay. You can't keep good people down, my darling. We need to tell ourselves that every morning.'

'I like it,' Ben said.

'And wait till you see my new marketing plans for Greenhope Gardening and Scarlett's Sustainable Skis. You're going to love them. Plus, Adele has made us a loan and our bank account works again – which fills me with joy!' she said and had to let out a laugh because that was really the biggest relief of all, to just have some breathing space to get back on their feet again.

* * *

There was a lovely surprise in store for Sasha as she peeked into the bag, expecting to find some homemade egg sandwiches or chocolate cookies. Instead, to her astonishment, there was a wooden box.

'Look what's in the bag Mama gave me!' she exclaimed and she held up the Mauritian white mahogany box for her husband and daughter to see.

'She's given them to me,' Sasha said, on the verge of tears now, 'given them to us, LouLou!'

Sasha opened the box and gazed at the intricate jewelled chandeliers. 'You know, now that I know they're worth £1,000, not £150,000, I like them so much more.' And that was the truth. They were so much more wearable now.

'That's so you,' Ben laughed, as Sasha threaded them through the lobes of her ears.

'I absolutely love them,' she declared, grinning at her reflection in the car mirror. 'How do I look?' She turned to Ben and craned round to LouLou.

'Gorgeous, Mummy,' said LouLou.

'I love you Sasha,' Ben said, 'onwards and upwards.'

'I love you too, Ben.' And that was when Sasha decided it was time to take a very first dip into the decision that was taking shape in her mind. 'Hey, LouLou,' she began, 'we've never asked you how you might feel about a little brother or a little sister joining the family? Not now... but maybe sometime in the future. Would that be nice? Would you like that?'

LouLou's reaction was instantaneous – she started to shriek with delight at this idea. 'Please, please, can we have a baby? Please? Or a puppy? Can we have a puppy? Or a puppy and a baby? But a baby would be better.'

This was such a positive reaction that Sasha felt tears well up in her eyes.

'Oh my god... so do *you* think this a good idea?' Ben asked, glancing at Sasha with as much of a delighted look on his face as LouLou.

'Yes, Ben, I think I do,' Sasha said. 'Maybe siblings aren't as bad as I thought.'

Ben's happiness was written right across his face and Sasha knew how much this meant to him.

'So I should probably cancel that ad...' he joked.

Sasha looked at him, momentarily baffled. Then she remembered their jokey conversation about trying to find her a more suitable family.

She began to laugh. 'Yes! You have to cancel the ad. Turns out no new family is required. We'll just have to try and make the very best of the one we have.'

ACKNOWLEDGMENTS

Huge love and thanks to my whole family for their love, support and at least a few of the anecdotes that may (or may not!) have made it onto these pages.

Thank you so much to team Boldwood, especially editor Emily Ruston, for so much good advice, encouragement, positive vibes and motivating deadlines!

Thank you also to my agent, Diana Beaumont, who I know I'm so lucky to have on my case. And I'm going to have to mention my darling wee Jack Russell, Jimmy, who we've just lost at the age of sixteen. He was my constant writing companion. After a busy time barking at everyone in the street, running us ragged in the park, refusing to come out from under the bushes, rolling in poo, and other adventures, he liked nothing better than to snuggle up on the sofa, or under the desk, in his blankie and keep me company while I typed. I miss him terribly and I'm so glad that I completely spoiled him in his old age. He was such a small dog, but the joy and the love he gave were boundless.

MORE FROM CARMEN REID

We hope you enjoyed reading *New Family Required*. If you did, please leave a review.

If you'd like to gift a copy, this book is also available as an ebook, digital audio download and audiobook CD.

Sign up to Carmen Reid's mailing list for news, competitions and updates on future books.

https://bit.ly/CarmenReidNewsletter

Worn Out Wife Seeks New Life, another brilliant laugh out loud emotional read from Carmen Reid, is available to order now.

ABOUT THE AUTHOR

Carmen Reid is the bestselling author of numerous woman's fiction titles including the Personal Shopper series starring Annie Valentine. After taking a break from writing she is back, introducing her hallmark feisty women characters to a new generation of readers. She lives in Glasgow with her husband and children

Follow Carmen on social media:

 instagram.com/carmenreidwrites
facebook.com/carmenreidwrites

Boldwood

Boldwood Books is an award-winning fiction publishing company seeking out the best stories from around the world.

Find out more at www.boldwoodbooks.com

Join our reader community for brilliant books, competitions and offers!

Follow us
@BoldwoodBooks
@BookandTonic

Sign up to our weekly deals newsletter

https://bit.ly/BoldwoodBNewsletter

Ingram Content Group UK Ltd.
Milton Keynes UK
UKHW041856070623
423066UK00004B/140